YO-ARH-876

No, this couldn't be happening . . .

Not here. Not in America. Not in Grunnell. Not in First Church.

It happened in Russia, in Eastern Europe, in the Germany of World War II. It happened to other men in other times, other places.

Their leader was speaking again. "What we're gonna do is march you up here one-by-one. You'll get down on your knees right here, in front of the pulpit. You'll be asked if you still believe in the false god, Jesus. You will answer, 'No.'

"Then you will be asked to swear your belief in the Father, Abba. Those who comply will be instructed in a new way of eternal life. Those who refuse will be shot . . ."

CULT SUNDAY

"The best novel to come out of the horror of Jonestown . . . read this and then hope a movie is made from it to keep others from living through another Jonestown horror."

West Coast Review of Books

CULT SUNDAY

CULT SUNDAY

WILLIAM D. RODGERS

3341

ACCENT BOOKS
A division of Accent-B/P Publications, Inc.
12100 W. Sixth Avenue
P.O. Box 15337
Denver, Colorado 80215

Copyright© 1979 Accent-B/P Publications, Inc.
Printed in United States of America

All rights reserved. No portion of this book may be reproduced in any form without the written permission of the publishers, with the exception of brief excerpts in magazine reviews.

Library of Congress Catalog Card Number: 79-54713

ISBN 0-89636-041-5

For
my father
and
business partner,
W. B. Rodgers
and for
my children,
David and Kara Lee

Christian Bk Club for Today's Woman 3-80 3.50
3341

12:00 midnight

There were three of them. College boys by appearance. Yet, clutching their uncollegiate M-16 automatic rifles, they were obviously far more than a trio of fraternity brothers out for a good time as they forced the lock of the downtown church and pushed their way inside.

They, the vanguard of the Chosen who would rise to join them in the hours after the sunrise, stood listening to the sounds of the dark old building. They heard nothing but the creaks and groans of a structure which had stood for the better part of a century.

Soundlessly, swiftly, well-drilled for their mission, they moved to the subterranean chamber to which they had been assigned, to wait for the dawning of the terrible day of him whom they served.

They bode their time in self-imposed silence, a silence broken only by the gnawing of the rats that shared their hiding place. And during the waiting moments, each reassured himself of the glory which would be theirs.

They remembered the oath of revenge sworn by their leadership and by themselves on the traitor to their Brotherhood. They clung to their rifles and dreamed of murder.

They dreamed also of their order establishing itself as

the world order, a promise which the Abba said would be written in holocaust. And they did not mind the darkness or the rats or the waiting.

Sometime during the night, one of their number left the others and stalked through the old building until he came to an office. There, in the dim glare of a streetlight that filtered through the windows from outside, he did a perverse thing.

He took a piece of soap from his pocket and on the edge of the shadows, traced a bizarre pattern on the flat surface of the heavy desk.

He knew it was beyond the scope of his orders, but he did it anyway. He did it for the same reason vandals scrawl graffiti on restroom walls—to fling an obscenity in the face of the establishment. He did it to scare them, to let them know he had penetrated their private, naive little world.

He admired his drawing with a smile, then carefully rearranged the papers scattered about the desk to cover his mark.

He did not tell the others what he had done. He rejoined them on the damp concrete floor and the secret of his action warmed him.

Upstairs, waiting to be discovered, was his proclamation of death—a crude Star of David overlayed with the Christian cross.

"Praise be to Abba," he whispered. The next time he made Abba's sign, it would be in blood.

5:03 a.m.

Malcolm Stansfield had been awake for hours before the phone call came. Not calmly. Expectation ran through the whole length of his long frame.

It was not easy for him to lie there quietly on his side of the bed, for if Malcolm Stansfield was anything, he was a man of action. On this particular Sunday, he longed for it, wanted desperately to be up and about the business of the day at hand. This day was such an important one, perhaps the most important of his career.

Yet, it was precisely because of that importance that he forced himself to stay still under the electric blanket and commanded his body to rest, even if his mind could not.

When he remembered, he kept his eyes closed, praying they would not appear too bleary, too dark, when he finally stood before his audience. He did not want his eyes to betray his sleepless night.

"The eyes are the windows of the soul," it had been said, and Malcolm Stansfield believed it to be true. A man who sought to lead should strive to show others the difference in his life. Others should be able to look at him and know that he was set apart.

That difference should not only be perceived in the way a man talked and the things he did, but in the way he took care of his own body. And, so, each morning Malcolm Stansfield observed a ritual of calisthenics that most fifty-three-year-old men would find more punishing than beneficial. Twice each week, he played handball at the YMCA. He always played with much younger men, because they usually set a much faster pace than would opponents in his own age group. His drive for fitness was as much in unity with his life as his ability to remain unperturbed at the daily problems of living.

But, in spite of himself, many times during the long hours of the night the excitement had gotten the best of him and his eyes had involuntarily snapped open to stare at the shadows.

And as those hours had ticked past, he had analyzed his emotions enough to give a name to the anticipation he felt: "Sweet Dread." Sweet in that if what he planned came to pass, the frustration of the past months would be finished. Dread, because there was a doubt—the slightest doubt, but doubt still—that the morning would not be all it and he promised it would be.

Yes, "Sweet Dread." That was the only name for it.

Earlier, when the doubt had become too acute and the shadows too oppressive, he had rolled to watch Miriam sleeping deeply by his side. He could not see her clearly in the dim light of the room, but in his heart, he saw her plainly.

Her face, once pretty in youth, was now beautiful in maturity, framed by the auburn hair that was slowly giving way to a lovely shade of gray. And the lines of age which so often marred others' faces only seemed to contribute to the loveliness of Miriam's features. How good God was, to give him a woman like her.

He fought the temptation to lean over and kiss her. She needed her sleep. The last eighteen months had been worse for her than for himself, he knew. It was not easy being the wife of a man such as he was, not even in the best of times, not for a woman of Miriam's spirit.

Yet, she had taken the pressured circumstances of their new existence in stride and had tried to make the best of them, and somehow endured as she had endured the years he had been on the road.

He had once asked her about that, and she had replied that she didn't want to bother him when so many people needed him so much more.

Malcolm found himself staring back at the shadows now receding in the eerie predawn light. It was at that moment he was jarred by the urgent ring of the nightstand telephone.

He jumped to grab the receiver before a second ring could awaken the household. While he was relieved for some excuse to be in action at last, he put the receiver to his ear with a certain uneasiness. At such an early hour, the phone rang at his house only for death or illness.

"Stansfield," he said in a low tone of practiced reassurance he hoped would give comfort for whatever the emergency. He spoke around the morning dryness in his mouth, quietly, to keep from disturbing Miriam any more than was absolutely necessary.

He was answered only by heavy breathing at the other end of the line.

"Who's calling, please?" he asked, louder, less reassuring in his surprise.

Just the breathing. From its texture, he guessed it might belong to a woman or a boy.

"Hello, this is Malcolm Stansfield," he said again. "Is there something I can do for you?"

The breathing stopped. Silence.

"What do you want?"

More silence, then an abrupt and heavy click.

"Please don't play games with me," he complained to the dead line, and was left only with the resumption of the dial tone buzzing in his ear.

"Malcolm, what is it?" Miriam asked sleepily. Her head was lifted slightly off the pillow as she tried to focus on him through her sleep-heavy eyelids.

"Nothing," he said, placing the receiver back on its cradle. Still, he felt a tiny chill at the base of his neck.

Miriam must have sensed it in him. "You never could tell a convincing lie," she said.

"It was nothing," he reiterated, not certain whether he was really trying to convince her or himself. "A wrong number. A prank call. It doesn't matter."

"Looks like they'd have more consideration than to call in the middle of the night," she yawned, seemingly satisfied by his explanation. She cuddled up to him, resting her head on his shoulder.

"It's just as well," he mumbled. "It's almost time to get up anyway." He groped for the alarm clock to shut it off before it buzzed.

"Oh," she groaned and then reached up to give him a good morning kiss. He kissed her back and held her close.

After a moment she asked, "Are you sure that's all it was?"

"What?"

"The phone. Are you sure it was just a wrong number?"

"Yes, I'm sure. Why?"

"Something's bothering you," she said, propping herself up on one elbow to stare down into his face.

"This is the day, the *big* day," he forced a smile for her benefit. "I'm just thinking about it, that's all."

But in truth, he had to admit to himself, the phone call had disturbed him. It left him a little unsettled.

"Oh, *the* day. Did you sleep any at all, Malcolm?"

"Some."

"Not very much, if I know you."

He let the observation go unanswered and stared at the ceiling. A phone call such as that on any other morning wasn't worth a second thought. But on this particular morning, was there any connection? It was possible, he supposed.

Suddenly, she bounced away from him and sat up on her side of the bed. "I guess I'd better put the coffee on."

"Why don't you sleep in this morning, honey?" he suggested. "You've been so tired lately, it would do you good."

"That's old age catching up with me, and I can't." At the dresser mirror, she ran a comb through her hair and tied the long strands back with a bright ribbon.

"How many times do I have to tell you," he asked, "that you don't have to get up so early on Sunday morning just because I do? You could sleep another hour."

"You've said that every Sunday morning for the last twenty-five years," Miriam grinned. "But no man should face his work without breakfast. And my man isn't going to—ever. I'm not about to start any bad habits I could enjoy."

"It wouldn't hurt one Sunday," he countered and then let it go. His mind wandered back to the breathing on the telephone, made so detached and, yes, even menacing by its anonymity. What did it mean?

"Well, not today. Not on this *important* occasion."

"Did you say something, Miriam?"

"I said—oh, never mind."

He threw back the covers and climbed from the bed.

"Do you want breakfast before you shower or after?" she asked.

"What?"

"Malcolm, what is wrong with you? You're so preoccupied this morning."

"Why wouldn't I be? There's so much to think about. So many things I have to do before I'm ready."

"Being cranky won't help," she smiled.

"Sorry, darling, I don't mean to take it out on you."

"I know. Now, do you want breakfast before or after?"

"Uh, after."

Shaking her head with amusement, she moved purposefully off toward the kitchen and he was alone.

It had to be a coincidence, he told himself. It was just too obvious to be anything else. Still . . .

Then, a sheepish smile broke through the stubble on his angular face, a face more distinguished than handsome, a face that belonged in his chosen profession.

He really *was* uptight, or such a silly little thing would not cause so much as a pause on his part. Well, nothing was going to spoil this day. It was too good for that, filled with too much sweet promise.

And, so, he deliberately pushed the strange telephone call out of his mind as he padded to the bathroom.

Later that day, Malcolm Stansfield would regret his decision.

5:22 a.m.

Shivering, the girl stood pressed in the dark alcove under the stairway, her fear-rounded eyes riveted on the Temple Guardian of the Watch, Brother Andrew. The light from the single naked bulb which dangled on its twisted cord from the high ceiling caught the blue barrel of the M-16 rifle that lay before him on what had once been the check-in desk of the old commercial hotel. Now, it served as the command post in the Court of the Gentiles.

That was the name which Abba, himself, had given to the lobby of the building which now served as the Temple of the Brotherhood. It was a narrow, long room. Its walls were covered with a peeling wallpaper from which the Sisters had scrubbed the grime of half a century.

Besides the desk of the command post, there was no real furniture. Only the worn Oriental rug gave the room any color, and even it was faded. A slightly brighter spot of color here and there across its length gave an indication where the overstuffed furnishing of its more transient days had been.

Oblivious to the cramps that were forming in her legs from standing frozen for so long in one position, the girl watched Brother Andrew and feared him. He was a tall and lanky twenty-five. His neatly combed close-cropped hair was a sandy blond and his eyes dark brown. She had known him for more than a year, but they had never spoken. It was forbidden for a Sister to speak to a Brother unless the Brother spoke first. Brother Andrew hardly ever spoke to anyone.

He worked mechanically, making entries in a large ledger opened on the countertop beside the rifle. His movements allowed for no wasted motion as the pen scratched its sentences on paper.

Suddenly, as she watched, he looked up in her direction. Her breath caught and she pushed tighter against the wall, as if the act would make her more invisible. And maybe it did, or maybe the darkness of the alcove beyond the circle of the single light, protected her.

She only knew that he stared for a long moment in her direction while his right hand adjusted the knot of the tie at his throat. Then he hunched his shoulders under his sports jacket as if relieving fatigue, yawned, and went back to the ledger.

Outside in the street, she heard a truck lumber past and then all was quiet again, except for the scratching of the pen on paper and her own breathing thundering in her ears.

There wasn't much time left before the Awakening began, before other people would be filtering down from the floors above. Somehow, someway, she had to get back up to the Court of the Women before the Maiden of the Chamber discovered her missing from her bed.

It had been such a foolish, stupid thing to attempt. She wondered at it, wondered why she had tried. What could she have been thinking? What had she hoped to accomplish?

At the time, it seemed the perfect way to serve the Abba. Oh, how she loved him, loved him beyond all else. The very thought of him filled her with such love and peace. Yes, even in her fear, there was love beyond knowing.

She had done it to serve him. Him. That's why she kept back the twenty cents from the money she had made selling the candy. All the money was supposed to go to the Brotherhood, but she had used the twenty cents for the Brotherhood in a very real way.

No, she had stolen it. That was the truth. And the Abba would know it. He knew everything, saw everything. He would know how she had waited for the Guardian Angels to pass through the Court of Women, waking each Sister sleeping there to learn their dreams. The good ones they wrote down, the bad ones they exorcised. The Guardian Angels came every night to every bed, for even the dreams of sleep must be pure.

And she had waited for them to pass, and then had sneaked down to use the pay phone in the Court of the Gentiles. It was the only one in the Temple, and guarded always, except in the few minutes when the Temple Guardian of the Watch made his predawn rounds.

She had dropped the two stolen coins into the slot so quietly, had dialed very slowly to keep the dial from any undue clicking which might give her away, and then waited for an answer.

But when she heard the voice of the enemy, she could not speak. Abba had kept her tongue still, she could see that now. And he had sent Brother Andrew back early from his rounds to keep her from speaking, although her intent had been to frighten the enemy into silence, to keep him from his evil doings.

And then, before she could speak, she had heard Brother Andrew's footsteps at the head of the stairway and had barely had time to hang up the phone and dart into the alcove before he came down.

If he discovered her, alone as she was, dressed only in her night robe without hose or fresh lipstick, she would be punished. The evil ones had tempted her, she understood that now. They had forced her to steal and to sneak about in the night. Despite her devotion and her time in the Temple, she was not yet clear. But she would make it up to the Abba, if only he in his mercy would forgive her. If only he would keep Brother Andrew from finding her and give her a means of escape.

Her thoughts were so guilty, she drove herself to think of other things. Behind Brother Andrew were the pigeon-holes which once held the keys to the rooms on the three floors above. The rows of little rectangular boxes were no longer used for that purpose, since no room in the Temple was permitted to be locked, except for the Pit of Infidels in the basement, and the Holy of Holies on the top floor.

The Holy of Holies was the private quarters of the Abba, where even now he abided—seeing everything, hearing her prayers. His twelve priests were the only ones ever allowed to enter there to minister to his needs. Only they were pure enough.

As for the Pit of the Infidels in the basement, it was better not even to think of such a place. She would be banished there if Abba did not forgive her sins. Not many ever came back from the Pit. The knowledge terrified her.

Blessed is Abba, she began to chant to herself, *who sees all, who knows all, who forgives those he loves.* Over and over she repeated it as she had been taught from the first day she had become his follower. As she chanted, she let her gaze move from Brother Andrew to the heavy drapes covering the plate glass windows at the front of the Court of the Gentiles. Already, the first rays of the new sun shined against them, turning them luminous at the top. So little time was left.

And, then, as if Abba heard her pleading, there was a subtle rattling at the front door. Brother Andrew's head snapped up. Another rattling, not loud, but loud enough. Brother Andrew picked up his weapon and came around the desk. He paused, then moved to investigate.

Opening the door a crack, he peeked out into the street.

The girl felt the draft of cold morning air.

"You can't sleep it off here," Brother Andrew addressed some unseen presence.

"Whaddayamean? ThishisAmerica, ain'tit?" It was one of the winos who frequented this part of town. The girl saw her chance. She darted from her hiding place and up the steps, afraid that Brother Andrew was right behind her.

She reached the top step and hugged the wall. She was alone. Down below, Brother Andrew was saying, "I said to move, old man."

"Isthatagun? Don'tshootmemisterpleasedon'tshoot—I'mgoing. See? I'mgoing!"

Seconds ticked by. All was quiet. The girl turned her head to search the hallway with her eyes. The Abba was with her. It was empty. The Guardian Angels must already be in the Women's Chapel, chanting the written dreams to Abba in prayer.

Allowing herself to take her first deep breath in more than fifteen minutes, the girl rested a moment, before she began to work her way down the hall toward her assigned sleeping place.

One by one, she tiptoed by the open doors of each of the women's chambers until at last she stood next to the door of her own.

So far, so good. No one had seen her. No one had cried out the alarm which would bring Brother Andrew plunging up the stairway.

Slowly, ever so slowly, the girl eased her body around the jamb, until she stood fully in the door. The five women she shared the cubicle with were all on their cots sleeping soundly.

She waited to make certain. Then, a step at a time, she started for her own cot. Four steps away. Three. Now, two.

The rough board under her bare feet gave. There was a creak that seemed to reverberate from the walls. Sister Charity stirred, mumbled something in her sleep and dozed on.

The girl quickly took the last two steps, knowing that if she hesitated, she would lose her courage. With one fast motion, she pulled the robe over her head and then hung it on a hanger in the wall above her bed.

Nude, she slipped between the covers and dropped her head to the pillow. She had been gone little more than twenty minutes, but her body ached as if she had been gone for hours. Abba was good. He had been with her. He forgave.

In the next instant, the Maiden of the Chamber was at the door. In a loud, clear voice, she said, "Abba has brought the morning. It is time to rise, Sisters. This is the morning of the great mission, for Abba has willed it."

The Maiden waited for each of the Sisters to reply, "Abba brought the morning. Abba loves me and I love Abba."

Satisfied that all in the cubicle were awake, the Maiden moved on to the door of the next chamber where she repeated the greeting again.

The girl lay in her cot, relief flooding through her. She was still lying there when Sister Charity stood over her and said, "Come, Sister Courage. You'll be late. We must hurry. This is *the* morning, you know. *The* morning."

5:57 a.m.

Wally Nichols returned to Master Control from the station's cafeteria in a foul mood. The cellophane-wrapped chocolate doughnuts had cost him thirty cents instead of the quarter they had been sold for in the vending machine only last Friday. The price had been raised without warning.

"Good old KBEX-TV gouges its advertisers, so why not its employees?" he told himself. "The rich get richer and the poor get poorer." His take-home as a technical director was little enough without being overcharged for breakfast.

Well, he'd fool them. He'd start bringing his own doughnuts from home, as he brought his own Thermos of coffee. He had begun that practice when the vending machine brew went from a dime to twenty cents.

Taking his seat in the armless swivel chair at the console, he glanced up at the red numerals of the flashing digital clock to the right of the bank of monitors. Two minutes and thirty seconds to sign-on.

He dropped the doughnuts on the wide ledge that ran in front of the console for its entire length, swung the chair so that he could reach and retrieve the steel vacuum bottle from the shelf behind him, and poured himself a steaming cup of its dark contents. He placed the cup beside the doughnuts and turned his attention to the day's master log.

The log had been prepared by the Traffic Department late Friday afternoon. It was a comprehensive list of the order of the broadcast day, showing each commercial, each promotion announcement, each program and the exact time at which they were to air.

The log was several pages thick, but for the time being, he concentrated only on the first page. It covered the period from 6 a.m. to 8 a.m. There were four half-hour paid religious programs and five station breaks—nothing out of the ordinary. But then, there never was during the Religious Ghetto, as Wally and his fellow engineers called the Sunday morning programming block.

Actually, Wally liked this shift better than any other during the week. For one thing, it was routine. For another, it was quiet. For the first three hours the building was occupied only by himself and George Peloubet who worked in the telecine and videotape room next door, loading the commercials and programs on the proper machines so they would be ready when Wally pushed the buttons. George valued peace and quiet almost as much as he did.

As far as Wally was concerned, the Sunday shift was so easy, it was almost like getting paid for loafing. It began at 5:15 a.m. At 5:30, he punched up the test pattern and then had almost a full half hour to get his doughnuts, pour his coffee and collect his thoughts.

The shift would end at 1:15 and Monday was one of his two days off during the week. That gave him plenty of time to pursue his hobby and his passion, model railroading.

The layout in his basement was his pride and joy. Built in the HO scale, it had more than three scale miles of mainline and eight locomotives, not counting the three switch engines for the two large yards. The only thing which would have made it better was if Grace could give him a son. But the doctor had said that was impossible, so there was no use in brooding over it.

One minute to air. Wally checked the air monitor—the test pattern looked good. He turned up his speaker to hear the high-pitched whine which accompanied the picture.

Almost immediately, George Peloubet's voice came cracking over the intercom. "For Pete sakes, Wally, have some mercy. Crank that thing down."

"What's the matter, George? Have a rough night?"

"Saturdays are always rough," George responded.

"That bad, huh? You should get yourself a hobby, George, then you wouldn't have so much time for raising Cain."

"That is my hobby, Wally."

Forty seconds to air. "You got the break loaded, George?"

"You're all set."

Confirming it for himself, Wally glanced at the monitor for the automatic videotape machine. Three code numbers appeared on the screen, indicating that three thirty-second announcements were ready to roll. Once he started that machine, the three spots would play in sequence one after the other without his having to do another thing. He checked the numbers against his log. They matched.

He reached over and took the voice cassette and placed it in the audiotape player. It cued itself and he was set.

Five . . . four . . . three . . . two . . . one. He punched the proper button on the complicated switcher before him and its ready light came on. He pulled two levers toward each other and the test pattern faded from the on-air monitor. The levers came together, then parted again in opposite directions and the air monitor was filled with the slide from Telecine One. It was a picture of the exterior of the KBEX studios. He hit the audio and there was soft music for two seconds, followed by the smooth, deep voice of the pre-recorded announcer. "Good morning. It's 6 a.m. and television station KBEX now begins its telecast day. . . ."

As the announcer droned on, Wally noted the time the sign-on had started on the proper column on the log and initialed it.

At the end of the announcer's spiel, the audiotape machine automatically shut itself off. Wally pushed another button and the first announcement of the break appeared. It was a public service message for the American Cancer Society. When it was over, the next announcement, an appeal for the United Fund, took its place on the screen.

When the third announcement of the break came up, Wally groaned. It was Malcolm Stansfield of the First Church of Grunnell.

The minister was looking directly into the camera and saying, "What would you do, if a loved one of yours suddenly renounced his ties with you and disappeared into a religious cult? This tragedy happens to hundreds and thousands of families just like yours across this nation every year.

"How can you keep it from happening to yours? On 'Cult Sunday' at First Church, we're going to expose one of these cults and tell you how you can prevent it from touching your life and the lives of those you hold most dear. We'll hear the shocking testimony of a former member of the Brotherhood, the most dangerous cult in America today. And, of course, I'll be bringing you the morning message about what the Bible says on false beliefs.

"Cult Sunday, 11 a.m. this Sunday at First Church. Be there, because the life of your child, your mother, your father is worth saving. I know you'll want to join us in person. But if you can't, watch this important service telecast live on this channel."

As Stansfield was speaking, Wally said to George over the intercom, "If I have to watch this spot once more, I'll freak out."

"Easy, boy," George said. "This is the morning of that big bash. You won't see it after that."

"That Stansfield must've spent a fortune just buying time for those announcements," Wally said.

"Yeah, well, there's big money in religion and cults these days."

"Yeah," Wally said cynically. It was a pleasure to push the button on Stansfield and start the program reel. "From beautiful Pasadena, California, it's 'The Back To God Hour,'" intoned the unseen voice. The camera began a long pan of a robed choir as they raised their voices in a so-so rendition of "Nearer My God To Thee."

Wally listened only long enough to make certain the sound was good, then turned down his speaker. He checked the oscilloscope for the program's color balance, finished his log entries and told George to load the next break.

His duties complete for the next twenty-seven minutes, he took his latest issue of *Model Railroad* magazine from the shelf, tore open the doughnuts and munched while he read an article on scratch-building a miniature boxcar.

It would be the last food he ate for seventeen of the worst hours of his life.

William D. Rodgers

6:12 a.m.

Malcolm Stansfield thought he must make quite a picture for the neighbors as he poked and searched through the hedge next to his front porch. Trying to keep his new dark blue suit clean as he looked for the morning paper among the dusty, winter-dead branches put him through some strange contortions.

Where had that boy thrown the paper this time? It wasn't in the middle of the yard, and it was not in the rose bed or on the roof. It had to be in the hedge somewhere.

The more he hunted, the more impatient he became. That was the trouble with youngsters these days—they just didn't care about doing a job properly. When he was a boy, he had been required to porch the papers he delivered every time. And during the stormy season, he had had to place each paper behind every subscriber's screen door.

Malcolm Stansfield was perturbed with himself, too. It was not his habit to read the Sunday paper until after the noon meal, in the few minutes he had before he began preparing for the evening service. Usually, he was too busy on Sunday mornings readying himself for the morning sermon. And that's what he should be doing now, but the temptation to purloin one quick glance at the announcement was just too great. So, he told himself, it was as right to check the paper this morning as it was to recheck his sermon outline. That is, if he could find the paper.

"Good morning, sir," the voice caught Malcolm off guard. He wheeled to find Lanny Blier standing next to his bicycle on the front walk. In the boy's hand was the missing paper. It hadn't been lost; it hadn't been delivered.

Feeling a self-conscious redness in his face, the minister accepted the paper from the newsboy. "Thank you, son."

"Something wrong with your hedge, sir?" Lanny questioned with sincere curiosity.

"No. I was just looking for . . . something."

The boy nodded and started to resume his route. Then he hesitated and turned back to Malcolm. "Can I ask you something, sir?"

Malcolm smiled.

"Is this 'Cult Sunday' all over town?"

"No, just at my church."

"Oh." Again, the boy started to go, then stopped. "Pastor Stansfield, what's a cult?"

"It's a religious group whose teachings differ from sound biblical doctrine—whose teachings are at odds with the accepted tenets of orthodox faith." Malcolm used the same definition he planned to give his congregation later. "Do you see, Lanny?"

The boy mulled it over. "I guess," he shrugged in a way that told Malcolm he really didn't grasp it. The pastor struggled to rephrase the explanation, but the twelve-year old had lost interest. Lanny remounted his bike and pedalled off down the sidewalk.

"Come to Sunday school," Malcolm called after him. "Maybe your teacher can do a better job of answering your question."

"I can't," the boy called back over his shoulder. "My dad is taking us to the football game."

That was another problem with children of this

generation and with their elders. There were too many weekend distractions that kept them out of the pews. It was tough for a church to compete, especially an old, downtown church like First.

And if people forewent sporting events, and television and all the other endless distractions to worship, they didn't want to go to large, central churches. They wanted to attend small, neighborhood churches that were close to home and didn't take much time out of the morning, and where everybody knew everybody else. That's what made his work so difficult.

He took the paper with him to the breakfast table. Miriam already had the bacon and eggs dished up and the coffee poured and places set for the children when she would get them up a half hour from now.

"Hurry up, Malcolm," she said, "it's getting cold."

"I just want to check something," he said, opening the newspaper. He thumbed through the first three or four pages before he found it.

"Since when have you started reading the Sunday morning paper on Sunday morning?" she gently chided.

"I'm checking our ad," he told her. "See?"

It covered an entire page. He held it up so she could view it.

The headline read:

> *The Inside Story of America's Most Dangerous Cult!*

Beneath it, in only slightly smaller type, appeared the subheading:

> *This morning at 11 a.m. the startling and shocking truth will be told for the first time — anywhere!*

On one side of the ad, there was a large picture of Malcolm, holding an open Bible and gesturing as if preaching. On the other side was a picture of the young man named Harold Thomas. He looked like a young Robert Redford. The way the artist had positioned the two pictures made it seem that he was sharing the platform with Malcolm, although the two had not yet met.

Boldfaced text went on to expound:

> *Less than a year ago, Harold Thomas was a member of the infamous Church of the Brotherhood. He will share some of his experiences as a high-ranking officer in America's most dangerous cult, and give his inspiring testimony of how Christ rescued him and changed his life.*
>
> *Reverend Malcolm Stansfield, pastor and world-renowned evangelist, will bring the dramatic morning message, "The Cults, Satan's Messengers."*

Most of the rest of the copy paralleled the television commercial. However, near the bottom of the page, again in large boldfaced type, a new twist had been added:

> *Cult Sunday—There's never been another Sunday like it!*

"Well, what do you think?" Malcolm asked of his wife. "Not bad, is it?"

"Too many adjectives," Miriam commented and took her place at the table.

"You don't care for it, Miriam, do you?" Malcolm was rather disappointed as he refolded the newspaper and sat down.

"It's just that it seems too overdone, too melodramatic. You've drawn some very large crowds as an evangelist and never stooped to something like that."

"I know," Malcolm said quietly, spreading the napkin over his lap. "But times have changed, sweetheart. To attract people today, you have to give them something exciting. And it has to be marketed and packaged and advertised, if you want to get results."

"It seems so wrong."

"To you and me, perhaps," he acknowledged, not wanting to admit how really put off he was by the new trend in church promotion, a trend of which he was not a part. "Still, we have to keep pace with the times."

"Advertising a church service as if it were a horror movie," she disdained.

"People go to movies in greater numbers than they go to church anymore," he defended, aware that she had hit a private nerve in him.

Quickly, he changed the subject. "Let's say grace."

They prayed over the food and ate in silence. Some of the edge had been taken off his morning by Miriam's unexpected reaction and his own contradiction of feelings which she had brought out of him. Cult Sunday had been his idea and he had thought Miriam approved—until now.

"It must have cost a lot of money."

"What?"

"That newspaper ad, the radio and television announcements. It's all very expensive, isn't it?"

"Joseph paid for it, bless his checkbook."

"Did he pressure you into it, Malcolm?"

"Joseph? No, it was mostly my idea. And, I still think it's right. This is the era of the media event. All of the most successful churches have learned that and practiced it. Besides, people need to be exposed to these cults, so they can see how bad they really are. How they brainwash kids and twist them."

But Miriam had gone off on her own tangent. "Is Joseph really as difficult as they say he is?"

Malcolm sipped his coffee. "No. At least, not for me. He's treated me well."

"Sometimes he acts like he owns the church," Miriam grumbled.

"I'm sure he's contributed enough money to buy it outright many times over," Malcolm said, attempting a mild humor to chase the doldrums which had descended over them. "He wants to see the church with five thousand members again, like it once had. Not the five hundred it has now."

"They say he eats ministers alive."

"Well, he hasn't eaten me. He hasn't even tried. He just wants the church to grow."

"And what Joseph Holmes wants, Joseph Holmes gets," Miriam appended sarcastically. It was uncharacteristic of her.

"Miriam, I believe God's hand is in this day. He supplied the inspiration for Cult Sunday. He brought Harold Thomas to us. He opened Joseph Holmes' checkbook. Don't you see, Miriam, this is truly the Lord's Day."

"Then why am I suddenly so frightened by it all? Why do I keep having this premonition that something evil is about to happen?"

Her eyes looked into his and he saw fright. "Honey," he said softly, taking her hand in his, "we're to put our trust in the Lord, not in silly intuition."

"It's not silly. It's that advertising. It suddenly occurred to me that if the Brotherhood is 'America's most dangerous cult,' you might be putting yourself in danger by exposing it."

"Hyperbole. That's all it is," Malcolm assured. "We got carried away, I guess. We should have explained that the danger is in what the Brotherhood does to young people's minds. That's all it is. Advertising hyperbole. It won't happen again."

"Are you sure, Malcolm?"

"You bet. I won't let any advertising writer—"

"No, I mean, are you sure there's no danger to you? To the church?"

"I thought about that, sweetheart. I won't fib to you. I considered calling the police in on this. Then, I thought, if we had to call the police in to guard the place, we shouldn't be doing it at all. Dick Whiting promised me that everything is okay."

"Who's this Dick Whiting?"

"Harold Thomas' booking agent."

"And you believed him?"

"Of course. He's an ex-preacher. Aren't we preachers *always* trustworthy?" He said it with a smile in his voice.

But Miriam didn't laugh at his gentle kidding of his own profession.

"Look, Harold Thomas has spoken in a lot of other churches before this. There were no police in any of those places, and nothing happened. Besides, if we had policemen standing around, think how many people their uniforms would frighten away?"

"Plainclothesmen. You could always ask for those," she suggested.

"Wouldn't that be dishonest? If a situation is dangerous enough for police, shouldn't the people attending be able to see that for themselves? No, Miriam, I told Dick Whiting if security was needed, then we didn't need Harold Thomas. It's as simple as that."

"Oh, Malcolm, why do you always have to be so naive when it comes to things like this?"

"A preacher's fault, I guess." He rose and gave her a tender kiss on the nape of her neck. "I have to be about the Lord's business," he said, and headed for the den.

The Sunday, "the like of which there had never been another," was now less than five hours away.

6:33 a.m.

Burch Zimmerman squinted at his watch and then sat sharply up on the edge of the bed. He had overslept again.

But he had come upright too quickly. His head throbbed as if it were being used as the dance floor at a Polish wedding and his lungs rebelled with hacking spasms that sent the sour phlegm rising in his throat.

He sucked frantically at the air, trying to fill his lungs, trying to force them to accept and hold it. They refused and he coughed until he thought his chest would turn inside out and the Polish dancers drummed his brain. He cursed them in Yiddish and he cursed himself for smoking and drinking too much.

Finally, his lungs began to quiet and the dancers left his head. He reached for a cigarette, lit it, climbed to his feet and stretched his overweight body. He felt awful.

"Zimmerman," he scolded himself, "you got to lose some weight or they'll kick you off the department. Wouldn't that be a fine fix, only three years short of your pension."

Scratching at the fringe of hair which surrounded his bald pate, he stumbled toward the kitchen. He didn't bother to throw a robe around himself. Who would see? Who would care if he lounged around this place all day in his shorts and undershirt? Nobody. It was one of the nice things about living alone again.

He found the coffee pot amid the clutter of the drainboard and added a handful of fresh grounds without bothering to empty the old ones from the basket.

The sink was too full of dirty dishes to get water there, so he went into the bathroom to fill the pot at the basin. He took the pot back to the kitchen drainboard to plug it in.

As it gurgled and boiled, he took a bottle of orange juice from the refrigerator and hunted for a clean glass. There was none, so he guzzled the juice out of the bottle until his thirst was quenched.

He set the bottle down by the coffee pot and regarded the sink. If he was going to fix his own breakfast, he'd have to wash some dishes.

"Where are you when I need you, Gerry?" he growled. His voice echoed through the empty apartment.

"Free of you, Burch Zimmerman," he mimicked his ex-wife's imagined reply in a shrill falsetto. The ash fell from his cigarette. He didn't notice.

Stepping in front of the sink, he pulled at one of the greasy plates, held it aloft disdainfully between a thumb and forefinger and made up his mind. He let the plate drop with a clatter upon the pile of dirty dishes and said, "You don't have time anyway, Zimmerman. You're running late already."

He showered, then looked for clean underwear and couldn't find it. All week he had walked around with the feeling he had forgotten something. Now, he knew what that something was. The laundry. It took a man time to get used to doing for himself after all these years of having someone else do for him.

Yet, he couldn't blame Gerry anymore than he could blame himself. It was the tension, the strain of a nightmare that wouldn't go away that had killed their marriage.

For two years they had searched the country. Two years

of jumping every time the phone rang. Two years of calling for favors from fellow officers all over the country. Two years of hopping planes every time someone, somewhere spotted a girl that even remotely matched Sandy's description. And for what? A stack of unpaid bills. The privilege of paying interest on five loans with five different loan companies, not to mention the second mortgage.

He knotted the tie and studied himself in the mirror. The underwear might be scrounged from the clothes hamper, but the shirt was clean.

"Zimmerman, you schlepp," he addressed the image in the mirror. "There you stand, forty years old and what have you got to show? Dirty underwear."

In the kitchen, the coffee was ready. He found a cup that was a little cleaner than the rest and filled it.

Sandy, why did you have to go away?

The coffee was awful, but at least it was hot. Why was he fooling himself? This apartment was awful. Being divorced was awful. Life was awful. But the silence was the worst of all.

The radio was broken. He turned on the TV. A religious program. He didn't bother to switch the channels, for it would only be more of the same. At least it was noise.

Maybe if I had been more religious, he thought, *maybe we would have made it through without this. Maybe if Gerry and I had been of the same faith . . . Maybe. And maybe if an elephant was smaller it would be a dog.*

And maybe if he could only stop remembering, but remember he did. He remembered Sandy at three when he had taken her to the zoo. He remembered her at fifteen in her first formal. He remembered how excited she was about going away to California to college. If they just hadn't let her go way out there, maybe . . .

He needed to talk to someone. Anyone. He needed to talk to Gerry. He went to the phone and dialed her number—*their* number. She still lived in the house they had shared since before Sandy was born. He had wanted her to have the house.

"Hello?" Gerry's voice sounded old.

"Hi, Gerry."

"Zim, it's nice of you to call."

"I was just thinking about . . . you. Wondered how you were getting along."

"I'm fine. How are you, Zim?"

They were talking to each other like strangers, like they hadn't been man and wife for more than twenty years.

"Fine. Everything okay?"

"Yes. How's it going down at the department?"

"All right."

"And are you getting along okay? By yourself, I mean. Do you remember to do your laundry?"

"Yeah, sure." The conversation was going nowhere, as their marriage had gone nowhere.

"Zim, I talked to a woman yesterday. Her son disappeared like Sandy. They looked for him for five years and they found him, Zim. They found him with one of those crazy religious cults. I thought maybe you could do some checking, ask around."

"Gerry, our daughter is dead."

"The identification was only tentative."

"She's dead. I saw the remains myself."

"I won't listen, Zim. You'd better not call again." She banged down the phone.

He stood studying the receiver in his hand. That was the problem. Gerry wouldn't face reality. He had been there in California. He had seen the shallow grave three miles from the university. He had forced himself to look at the decaying, decapitated skeleton and rusting locket which he and Gerry had given Sandy for her college going-away present.

The investigators theorized she had been kidnapped and raped before she was murdered. And he had seen the bones and the locket and had wept bitterly for Sandy. He wanted that to be the end of two years of not knowing. He wanted it to be finished.

Yes, he had grieved. Yes, he mourned that his daughter had died in such a tragic, maniacal way. But he had accepted it and wanted to go about the business of living. He wanted to forget the nightmare.

But Gerry did not. She would not accept the fact that their only child was dead, brutally murdered. She wanted to go on searching. She wanted to go on throwing their own lives away.

He couldn't take it. For Burch, two years was enough. One night, after they had fought about whether Sandy was alive or dead, he had moved out. Now they were divorced, and still Gerry would not give up her vain hope.

Sorry he had called his ex-wife, he hung up the phone, unplugged the coffee, turned off the TV, and strapped on the shoulder holster with the .357 Magnum.

Snatching up his jacket, he left the dishes and the apartment and the memories. At least at the station house, the work would keep him from thinking, he thought.

But Burch Zimmerman was wrong about that.

6:52 a.m.

There was nothing out of the ordinary about the way in which Malcolm Stansfield spent the hour immediately following his breakfast conversation with Miriam. At least, Malcolm tried to make himself believe that he was going about his Sunday morning ritual the way he always went about it.

In point of fact, he was more than slightly troubled and miffed by Miriam's unexpected reaction to the upcoming Sunday morning service and its promotion.

However, he had tried to put those feelings away from himself as he went into his den, and there among the shelves lined with more than five hundred beloved books—the majority on the subjects of theology and the Bible—he knelt in prayer.

His prayer started, as it always did, with a celebration of God's power and holiness. Through his praise of the Almighty, Malcolm tried to sense the magnitude of the universe and how much greater was the One who created it.

Sometimes, Malcolm could almost see the endless galaxies, the flaming suns and countless planets which had all been fashioned and set in motion by the Lord God. Sometimes. But not this time.

His prayer was overshadowed by the same Sweet Dread he had experienced in the early morning hours. The closest thing he had ever felt to it was the feeling he remembered the night before he preached his first sermon just out of seminary. He smiled at the aptness of the comparison.

How important that sermon had been. His entire future in the ministry had rested upon each word. He hadn't been able to sleep or to pray then, either, due to the jitters.

After all the years since, the thousands of times he had preached, he had thought himself done with pulpit fright. Stage fright, actors called it. Yet, it now haunted him anew. And for the same reason.

His entire future was once again at stake. When he weighed it in the balance, this morning's sermon was even more significant than the first had been.

Miriam knew it, too. Why did she have to bring up Joseph Holmes' reputation this morning, of all mornings? Perhaps it was her way of handling her own pulpit fright—a fright that must be worse than Malcolm's own, for while he could stand in the pulpit and work off his nervousness, she had to sit silent in a pew.

Miriam had a right to vent her nerves, he decided. Goodness knew, she had a right. Perhaps more right than he had.

She had stayed home raising the kids while he had gone off conducting those great crusades. He had enjoyed the spotlight of God's public work, while she had stayed in the background.

It didn't seem fair that just when he accepted his first permanent pastorate in years, just when they could live as a family without the threat of long separations, the bleak times had come.

Bleak, not in the sense of physical surroundings, for certainly the First Church of Grunnell had provided their new minister with a very fine parsonage. It was the kind of rambling New England style home he had always dreamed of occupying in the kind of posh neighborhood Miriam deserved.

No, it was a spiritual bleakness which surrounded them. The bleakness of a cavernous sanctuary less than a third full for Sunday services, of a church constituency which had seemingly lost the will to grow and multiply, no matter how Malcolm urged and beseeched. Never in his career had he failed so often to fill the pews.

And never in his career had he felt such pressure from the laymen he served. Despite Malcolm's denials to Miriam, Joseph Holmes was applying some intimidation. Not in a direct way, but by the very absence of any spoken demands. Joseph did it by looks and "harumphs," which Malcolm thought more effective than any overt threats.

If it had not been for Malcolm's abiding faith that he was going through these trials for some greater purpose in God's plan, and if it had not been for the support which Miriam supplied, he would have tendered his resignation long ago.

O, Lord, forgive my doubts, he prayed. *I thank You that by Your inspiration, I have been given a means to turn the bad to good. I know the plan for this great Sunday came from You.*

Ending with the benediction, *If it be Your will, in the name of Jesus Christ, Amen,* Malcolm rose and went to his desk, where he began to review the notes for his sermon.

Malcolm did not write out his complete sermon, as many other preachers did. Neither did he use an outline. Instead, he read all he could about the subject on which he wanted to speak, studying what God's Word had to say on the matter, reading as many reliable commentaries as he could find, filling himself with all the knowledge he could muster. In the pulpit, he would then rely on the inspiration of the Holy Spirit to reveal that which would do the hearts of men most good.

As he prepared, he would write down several thoughts

which he might wish to use in his message, four or five a sermon. These were his notes which he was reviewing now, the file cards on which they were inscribed spread across his desk.

The one which commanded his attention at the moment was on the definition of the word *cult*. Obviously, it was too involved for easy understanding. Lanny Blier had had trouble with it, and if a twelve-year-old newspaper boy could not understand it, it was wrong.

To Malcolm, it was particularly vital that the youngsters of the church knew what *cult* meant, for they were the ones who stood the best chance of encountering cults and falling prey to them.

Thus, he crossed out his first definition, ruminated for a time, and wrote:

> *A cult is a religious group that misapplies the Truth of God for its own gains.*

Reading it over several times, he decided it was better, but still not the best. He crossed out *gains* and wrote above it, *ends*.

> *A cult is a religious group that misapplies the Truth of God for its own ends.*

Ends was more appropriate than *gains*. *Gains* had the connotation of financial profit. And Malcolm knew that while some cults did exist solely for the monetary enrichment of their leaders, others practiced their beliefs through a misguided understanding of the Bible and a sincere desire to build a better kingdom on earth.

That barely settled, there was a knock on the door.

"Come in," he said, not taking his eyes from the notes.

It was Miriam. "I know you don't like your quiet hour interrupted," she apologized, "but there's a call for you. It's

Joseph Holmes."

"It's all right," he said. "I'm finished anyway."

He followed Miriam back to the phone in the kitchen, noticing that her hair was now festooned with electric curlers.

His ten-year-old daughter was at the table, picking finically at her breakfast. "Good morning, princess," he greeted. "Where's your brother?"

"In the bathroom, Daddy. Do boys always take so long combing their hair?"

"Only when they're fourteen and in love," he chuckled. He picked up the dangling receiver of the wall phone. "Hello, Joseph."

"Preacher, save some time for me before the service this morning."

"Anything I can do for you now, Joseph?"

"Nope. I just want to be certain you and your staff are prepared. There's a lot riding on this one. It cost a heap of money just to promote this idea of yours, and I want to be sure we aren't going to blow it."

But the cost of Cult Sunday would soon be counted in more than money.

7:00 a.m.

Later testimony would reveal that at about the same time Reverend Malcolm Stansfield received the telephone call from Joseph Holmes, the daily Assembly of the Temple of the Brotherhood was convening in the old hotel downtown. On this day, the Assembly would take on an importance of extraordinary measure for its participants.

The girl grasped immediately that the Assembly would not be the normal kind as she descended from the Court of Women and saw the Temple Guard posted in such force in the Court of the Gentiles. Her Yoke Maiden, Sister Charity, with whom she walked, stopped abruptly at the sight of the well-dressed young men standing rigidly with their legs slightly apart and their odd assortment of automatic weapons at the ready.

Usually, only two or three guards were on duty for Assembly. So many armed Brothers could only mean one thing, and the girl did not blame Charity for gawking so dumbly at the imposing squadron.

"Come on, Sister," she whispered, afraid that even the slightest pause would cause them to be noticed.

"Look at them, Sister Courage," Charity exclaimed, murmuring so loudly, the girl was sure one of the guards focused on them out of the corner of his eye.

"Yes, I know, Sister. Come on," the girl urged under her breath, grateful when they were caught in the anonymous press of the other members of the Sisterhood crowding toward the Court of Adoration. She had trouble making Charity keep pace so that they could enter the Court in the prescribed fashion, side-by-side.

The Court of Adoration had been the hotel's ballroom. As had the lobby, it had been stripped of all furnishings except for those on the roughly built platform at the far end. In the center of the platform was a large, old-fashioned wooden chair with arms. It had been painted a garish gold befitting the throne of Abba.

Above the throne hung a Star of David overlaid with the Christian cross, forming the sacred symbol of Abba, a thing above holiness. Flanking the golden chair on each side were six metal folding chairs which confirmed the girl's expectation. Routine Assemblies were conducted by only one of the Brotherhood's twelve priests who performed the ceremony on a rotating basis. The twelve chairs meant that all would be in attendance for this meeting and the girl's heart quickened with the knowledge of that.

For Assembly, the hall was always split by two long cloth partitions four feet high. Behind the partition on the right were the men, already in place and meditating on the teachings of Abba. The partition on the left formed the place of the women. Between the two, in the center of the room, was a pathway—the Holy Way—and only the Priests and other members of Abba's personal entourage were pure enough to pass over it.

The black partitions were actually bed sheets cut in strips and sewn together end-to-end before being dyed. The girl had helped with the sewing of them a few weeks after she joined the Brotherhood, singing praise to Abba with every stitch.

A small entry had been left on either side of the Court of

Adoration near the room's double doorway. As the respective pairs of Sisters passed through the women's entrance, they curtsied in the direction of the throne. The girl and Sister Charity did the same, then hurried to find their places among the more than two hundred other people assembling there.

They dropped with agility to their knees. Both were in their early twenties, and both attractive, although Charity lacked her Yoke Maiden's more fragile beauty. The girl was aware that she outshined her companion and was proud of it, although pride was supposed to be forgotten within these walls.

Dressed in the simple shirtwaists of the Sisterhood, their long hair pulled back in buns, they wore the same subtle shade of lipstick. Abba allowed the use of no other makeup, not even a light facial foundation. To be a candidate for membership in the Temple, one had to have a smooth, clear complexion. Women with blemishes of any kind were not recruited, nor were they admitted.

With the last row of Sisters filled, the girl saw the Keeper of the Horn mount the platform. He put the instrument to his lips, a highly polished bugle, and blew a single protracted note, imitating to the best of his ability the sound of an ancient ram's horn.

The Brothers and Sisters bent forward until their foreheads touched the floor in the Eastern tradition, and seven times chanted, "Praise be to Abba."

There was another sounding of the horn, and the worshipers returned to an upright posture, sitting on their heels. The Cantor took his position on the platform, saluted the Star, and in a clear tenor, without musical accompaniment, sang a sweet ballad of adoration.

It told of how Abba, when the world rejected his son, found it necessary to assume the form of a man himself, and came down from his heaven in a last attempt to save mankind. This time, instead of revealing himself to all the earth, he came to only a select few, the Chosen, the Brotherhood.

They were all familiar with the lyrics and joined in the refrain:

Abba is my father,
Abba is my father,
Abba is my father.
He has chosen me.

The girl thought she had never heard a hymn so sweet, not because of the melody or the words, but because it spoke of Abba. She closed her eyes to absorb the sublimeness of it.

The horn blew for a third time and was answered by another horn from the back of the room. The lights in the Court of Adoration suddenly lowered, and she heard the voice of the Chief Priest cry, "Prepare ye the Way. Abba comes. He comes!"

A drum began to beat a slow, muted cadence. Two of the Levites, the rank just beneath the office of Priest, came through the double doors, pulling behind them a long, white runner which symbolized the purity of the Holy Way. It was a runner purchased from a wedding supply house, but the Abba had consecrated it with the laying on of his hands. That made it pure.

As soon as the runner was spread, the Chief Priest and the High Priest came swaying down the pathway in time to the drum, bearing torches which flared to cast weird shadows over the congregation. One knew they were priests, because they wore skullcaps in the Jewish tradition.

Following them came the other ten of the Priesthood carrying candles, shielding their tiny flames with their fingers from the draft of movement.

The procession reached the platform, and the Chief

Priest, a short man with a blank expression, moved to the folding chair immediately to the right of the throne. The High Priest took his position on the left, and the other ten split to take up their stations as assigned.

Now came six of Abba's hand picked Guardian Angels, selected for their size and loyalty. A quarter of the way down the aisle, the last two dropped off; half way down, the second pair stopped. The lead pair continued to within a few feet of the platform before they too halted. The commander gave a sharp nod and as one, the Angels wheeled to face their respective sides of the path, their eyes sweeping the assemblage, machine guns up.

The beat of the drum grew louder, throbbing into the girl, pulsating through her as life itself. The supreme instant was almost at hand.

Even as she watched, the Cherubs were strewing crushed rose petals down the length of the runner. Cherubs were children taken from their mothers at a very early age, babies without spot or deformity, who were raised and trained in Abba's nursery removed from the Court of the Women by a sealed doorway. They were to be, Abba proclaimed, one hundred, forty-four thousand in number by the end of the Era.

The two who toddled down the aisle were almost hidden by the partition. Yet, the girl could see enough to know they were precious five-year-olds who performed their duty in a manful, disciplined fashion. And why shouldn't they? They served Abba.

Brothers were encouraged to mate with Sisters of their choosing, to breed such as these—to mate, but not to marry. Abba said that all in the Brotherhood were married to him, and thus, to permit marriage between men and women would be to permit harlotry.

Children born of the temporary unions who were deformed in the slightest way were removed from the Temple and not seen again. The others who were not ill-formed and still not worthy enough for Abba's use, were placed in the Slaves' Nursery. When they grew older, they would perform the daily chores of Temple life to free the Brothers and Sisters to devote more time to worship.

The girl saw nothing wrong in either of these occurrences. After all, Abba had ordained them. If anything, the girl regretted that she had not yet been taken aside by a Brother. To serve Abba in such a way would be a reward beyond imagining.

There was a pause. Then, imperceptibly, a whisper rippled through the room in time to the drumbeat. "Abba, Abba, Abba."

It grew in volume and force. "Abba, Abba, Abba!"

The girl took it up, screaming it, "Abba, Abba, Abba!"

All the people in the hall were yelling the name as a single voice and the girl could not tell where she began and the others left off. They were one in Abba.

"Abba, Abba, Abba!"

And he stood in the door! The brilliant white beam of a spotlight struck him and its circle followed his every move. Beside him were the two Holy Maidens.

He was of medium height, dressed as the other Brothers. If one passed him on the street, one would probably not recognize him as a god. His face was average. He had a dark, neatly trimmed beard and the gray streaks at his temples were styled to sweep back across the upper portions of his ears.

He had a deep chest that rumbled when he spoke and a build slightly inclined to middle-aged pudginess. It was his eyes which set him apart. There was a glint to them that changed their expression a hundred times a minute. At once they could be soft and angry and compelling and beseeching.

To look at Abba's eyes was to see the full meaning of holiness as the girl had come to understand it. Yet, the only concession which Abba made to that holiness in outward vestige was a white silk aviator's scarf which he wore draped around his throat, the fringed ends hanging over his shoulders and down his back.

In the same instant Abba appeared, a Moog Synthesizer gave forth a supernatural anthem and a bedlam of noise broke loose. People screamed and shouted, "Hosanna!" Some swooned. Some talked in tongues. Others, like the girl, cried for joy.

It reminded the girl of the Grateful Dead concert her biological parents had once let her attend when she was in her teens, except this was infinitely more consuming. The fact she compared them at all made her contrite. One was only a group of men, but Abba was supreme.

Never in her youth, never in her teens, never in her life had she ever dreamed she would stare on the very face of God, as she stared now at Abba.

For one brief instant, it seemed he beheld her, that his eyes searched her out from all the rest and his eyes were pleased. She dropped her own gaze, acutely aware of her own worthlessness. Yet, she vowed that someday she would prove herself clean, able to partake fully of the love he offered.

The praise continued as Abba made his way to the platform. In his wake came another six of the rifle-bearing Guardian Angels, walking backwards, facing away from Abba, protecting him from behind.

When he climbed to the dais, they took their positions across its width at floor level, facing the crowd in the same way the other Guardian Angels did. The Cherubs knelt at the foot of the throne, the Holy Maidens stood behind it.

Abba looked at his followers the way a father who is pleased by his children looks at them, and smiled and waved and blew kisses. He drank in the adulation. The girl knew he was doing it more out of thoughtfulness for them, than for himself. They needed to worship him. Out of kindness, he let them.

For ten full minutes, he stood patiently accepting their glorification. Then, he raised his arms and the Court of Adoration grew abruptly still. Abba sat on his throne.

Another hymn was sung by the Cantor, this one about Abba's goodness and mercy. Abba beamed while the Cantor sang, and led the applause at the finish.

The Cantor was so overcome, he threw himself prostrate before Abba and kissed the floor where Abba had walked until he had to be restrained and escorted from the platform by two of the priests.

The girl was cognizant of it only in the most peripheral way. Her gaze hungrily sought out Abba unashamedly. It was so rare that he appeared at an Assembly in person. He used to lead every one, but as his holiness had become more manifest, he had confined himself with greater frequency to the Holy of Holies. As he said, it was not good for mortals to look upon their god too often.

And now he spoke, saying, "Ye are the children of the Lord your God." His voice was rich, carrying easily to the uttermost parts of the Court.

In consonance, the response swelled from the Brothers and Sisters, "We are your children and ye are our true father."

"Ye are my people, Israel."

"We shall serve you with all our hearts, and all our minds and all our bodies, for ye are Abba, and we love you more than life."

"Ye are blessed above all people, thus saith Abba." He smiled and the girl basked in the radiance of his blessing.

Abba drew himself up on his throne and nodded to the Chief Priest who rose and gestured toward the back of the room.

There was a commotion and the girl could see a tight group of Temple Guards advancing toward the dais on the men's side of the Holy Way. Because of the cloth partitions, she could see only their heads and shoulders, until they were beyond the end of the obstructions and stood below the throne.

They had between them a well-built man of twenty. He was obviously not a member of the Brotherhood, for his hair was longer than Abba allowed. He struggled against the guards, who had tied his hands behind his back and were holding him firmly.

"Who is this debased creature that ye bring into the holy presence?" the High Priest demanded.

"A seeker of the Truth," the spokesman for the Guards answered. The prisoner could make no reply for himself. In addition to being bound, he was gagged.

"And how doth thou knowest he is worthy?" the High Priest posed. The girl caught herself mouthing the words with him, the ritual was so familiar. She had witnessed it many times.

"The Apostles have determined it," the guard explained. The Apostles were ordained members of the Brotherhood, who after many months of training, were sent out into the world. Their purpose was to find those who sought a deeper meaning for life.

The Apostles would then befriend these people, not revealing their real purpose, but measuring the potential of the prospective convert.

They measured the strength of his family ties. They measured his physical strength and material wealth. They measured his aptitude. If the subject met all the requirements, he was "Caught Up"—"kidnapped," she had heard it wrongly called. It was not kidnapping. It was salvation. Salvation which the young man sandwiched between the guards was about to be granted.

On his throne, Abba nodded, as if he knew the prisoner's heart. The girl had no doubt that Abba did.

Taking his cue from the movement of Abba's head, the High Priest rose and hovered over the truth seeker. "Truly, Abba has chosen to offer thee the gift of new life," he said.

The Chief Priest gestured and a guard removed the gag. The prisoner appeared surprised by the act, but just for a moment. Finding his tongue's freedom, he started to vocally and obscenely protest.

The effort brought a rifle butt smashing into his jaw. His head snapped back and he staggered, crying out at the impact.

The blow had been delivered with deftness, hard enough to draw blood at the corner of the prisoner's mouth, but not hard enough to render him unconscious. That would have terminated the ceremony and displeased Abba. The girl shuddered at the thought. She had seen it happen before. She did not care to see it happen again.

The young man shook his head as if to clear it. The Chief Priest waited impassively until he thought the truth seeker capable of continuing and then warned, "You will answer only when ye are asked to answer."

"Like he—" the prisoner started to scream. He was cut short by the rifle butt smashing home again. There was the unmistakable sound of a brittle breaking and the young man's jaw was pushed into an unnatural configuration. The blood flowed more freely from his gaping mouth. His body went slack and he slumped to his knees.

The guards on either side of him hauled the prisoner to his feet, supporting him to keep him erect. The Captain of the Guard stepped in to examine the captive. Satisfied, he grunted loud enough for all to hear, "He's still with us. We can continue."

"Praise Abba," several of the onlookers whispered. The girl was weak. She felt a kinship to the prisoner. She, too, had resisted once. She, too, had tasted her own blood; had almost choked on it before she gave in to the will of Abba. But Abba had forgiven. He had named her "Courage" for her bravery at her redemption.

"It is written," the Chief Priest took up the ritual, "'Can

a man be profitable unto God, as he that is wise may be profitable unto himself?'"

"Yea, verily," the Captain of the Guard said, taking a folded piece of paper from his coat pocket and handing it to the Priest.

The Chief Priest put the paper to his lips and kissed it. Then, bowing, passed it to Abba. Abba unfolded the sheet, studied it for several moments then gave it back to the Priest.

"Abba accepts these humble offerings," he said.

The Priest held the paper before the prisoner.

"And Abba's son hath said," the Priest recited, "'If thou wilt be perfect, go and sell that thou hast, and give to the poor, and thou shalt have treasure in heaven.'"

The Captain of the Guard took the paper from the Priest while one of the other guards untied the captive's hands.

A pen was handed to the Captain who, in turn, pressed it into the groggy young man's right hand. "Do you hear?" the Captain of the Guard asked. "Sign this and you shall receive the Kingdom."

"Sign for Abba. Sign for Abba. Sign for Abba," the audience chanted.

But the pen slid from the captive's hand and fell to the floor. The Captain of the Guard retrieved it and put it back into the prisoner's hand. This time, the guard on the prisoner's right clamped it there with his own strong fingers wrapped around the young man's wrist.

The Captain drew his automatic pistol and pointed it in the young man's face. Slowly, the Captain removed the weapon's safety and cocked its hammer.

"Sign it. Repent of your sins. Give to Abba and Abba will give you life and truth. If you do not sign the contract, your life will be taken from you."

The young man trembled. He gagged on the blood in his mouth. He looked frantically from one face to the other as an animal trapped in a snare. Then he moaned and tears came to his eyes.

The guard who held his hand forced it until the pen touched the paper and made a few crude, painful marks.

The Captain studied the signature, lowered his pistol and smiled. "It is done as Abba has commanded it."

The High Priest stepped forward and looked into the prisoner's face. "The Lord your God proveth you to know whether ye love the Lord your God with all your heart and with all your soul."

"Truly, ye have been found worthy."

"Take him to the Haven of Bliss," the Chief Priest ordered and both priests returned to their seats while the young man was dragged away.

The Haven of Bliss, the girl knew, was a windowless cell where a new convert was kept until cleansed of the world. It was kept lighted day and night while tapes of Abba's teachings were played continuously for the enlightenment of the subject.

It was a hard and cruel place. The convert was allowed only ten minutes' sleep in every twelve hours. There was no bed, no comfort. But when a person emerged from there, he possessed the Truth, the Truth of Abba's holiness and absolute rule, a truth few were privileged to share.

She was marveling that she was one of those few, when she felt a sharp poke in her ribs from Sister Charity. And she realized that the congregation was already singing the great hymn to Abba's beneficence which was always sung at the completion of every conversion. Redfaced at her lack of concentration, the girl joined in, raising her voice in gratitude.

As the prayers and hymns and chants continued, the gratitude gave way to love and peace within her soul. She felt the warmth of Abba, his great strength, his eternal mercy.

It was near the end of the service that the Chief Priest suddenly stood and announced, "Abba shall endure forever: he hath prepared his throne for judgment."

Abba came to his feet, the smile gone, his eyes sparking with anger. "Listen!" he barked, "and know that one among ye has sinned against Abba."

There was a recorded buzzing over the loudspeakers, then the soft ring of a telephone as one would hear it if they had placed a call. The ringing was interrupted by a man's voice. "Stansfield," the voice said.

And the girl knew she had been caught. The telephone in the Court of the Gentiles was bugged. There was no escaping this time. She was alone and guilty among the hundreds. Alone and waiting for the judgment of Abba.

8:16 a.m.

For there are certain men crept in unawares, who were before of old ordained to this condemnation, ungodly men, turning the grace of our God into lasciviousness, and denying the only Lord God, and our Lord Jesus Christ. . . . unto them! for they have gone in the way of Cain, and ran greedily after the error of Balaam for reward and perished in the gainsaying of Core.

Malcolm reread the fourth and eleventh verses of the Book of Jude again. They were his text for the morning's sermon, picked weeks past, and were just right for the subject of cults.

But as he arrived at the First Church of Grunnell only a few minutes ago, and walked alone through its empty halls, another passage of scripture had occurred to him, one which might fit his exposition even better. As soon as he reached his office, he had taken his Bible, opened it atop the stacks of paperwork on his untidy desk, and read both his first choice—Jude—and the other.

Still torn, he read Jude a second time, then marked the page with his index finger and flipped the well-worn pages back to Second Peter, chapter two, and started reading again at the first verse:

> *But there were false prophets also among the people, even as there shall be false teachers among you, who privily shall bring in damnable heresies, even denying the Lord that bought them, and bring upon themselves swift destruction. And many shall follow their pernicious ways; by reason of whom the way of truth shall be evil spoken of.*

Then, Malcolm skipped to verse fourteen:

> *Having eyes full of adultery, and that cannot cease from sin; beguiling unstable souls: an heart they have exercised with covetous practices; cursed children: Which have forsaken the right way, and are gone astray. . . .*

He finished with the eighteenth and nineteenth verses:

> *For when they speak great swelling words of vanity, they allure through the lusts of the flesh, through much wantonness, those that were clean escaped from them who live in error. While they promise them liberty, they themselves are the servants of corruption: for of whom a man is overcome, of the same is he brought in bondage.*

Yes, those verses described exactly the way modern cults enticed young people into their folds. *Beguiling unstable souls . . . great swelling words of vanity . . . allure through the lusts of the flesh . . . promise them liberty.*

But, so did the fourth verse of Jude. *Turning the grace of our God . . . denying the only Lord God.*

Which to choose? He laid the Bible open on his cluttered desk, ripped his half-moon reading glasses from his face, and paced to the window. There, he looked out onto the towering office buildings which surrounded the church. No matter the time of day, the buildings shielded the window of his office from the sun and kept the place in eternal shadow. Only the heartiest of plants could grow on his window ledge, only the plants which did not need direct sunlight. How he missed the direct rays of solar warmth at times like this. But, that was the price man paid for progress.

The street itself was Sunday-morning vacant. A tattered sheet of newspaper was lifted and stirred by the mild winter breeze. A single car roared by where on weekdays, hundreds crawled in the a.m. rush to the parking lots in the canyons at the foot of the aluminum- and-glass-fronted cliffs.

These images were melancholy, no help in solving his dilemma. By rights, he should stick with Jude. That selection was already printed in the bulletin to be distributed by the ushers to the morning throng. But the verses from Second Peter appealed to him.

Of course, he could use both, would use both, except for the time that would take. Time was something that was always in short supply on Sunday morning.

He calculated the timetable for this service. The testimony by former cult member Harold Thomas would take at least fifteen minutes. Add in the timing of the hymns and preliminaries and that left Malcolm with a maximum of twenty minutes for his own message. Television was the culprit. Since the church had started the live telecasts of its Sunday service, every second was a treasure. Malcolm did not want to fade from the home screens just as he made his most important point.

How he longed for the old days, when an extra five or ten minutes bothered no one but, perhaps, the ladies who had roasts in the oven. How he envied his great-grandfather, a country preacher, whose sermons never ran shorter than two hours and often longer than three without a word of complaint from the members of his congregation. Those old-fashioned churchgoers would have felt cheated by a thirty-minute pulpit dissertation.

Malcolm's train of thought was broken by a voice from the door. "May I come in, Malcolm?"

He turned to see Dick Whiting. The agent's bone-tinted trenchcoat was opened to reveal a smart blue blazer over a white turtleneck sweater and gray slacks. His shoes were patent leather with gold buckles. Whiting looked rich and he looked successful, because he was. Not bad, Malcolm thought, for a down-and-out preacher who hit Gospel Trail paydirt when he turned from preaching to representing the glittering names of the new evangelical explosion.

"Sure, Dick, come on in," Malcolm said. "I didn't expect Thomas to be so early."

"He isn't. I left him having breakfast in his room over at the hotel. This church certainly puts up its guests in first-class style."

"We do our best," Malcolm said, waving the agent to one of the red leather side chairs which fronted the desk. "So, what brings Dick Whiting over so early?"

"Just wanted to check a few last minute details," Whiting smiled. "This is my client's first big appearance, you know."

Malcolm sat down in his own swivel chair. "Yes, I know. Is he nervous?"

"Yes and no. By the way, thanks for the fee."

"Don't thank me. We were only complying with the terms of the contract." Malcolm clipped his words tighter than he meant to, but it galled him to pay a thousand dollars for a Christian testimony. The whole thing galled him, the theatrics of modern Christianity, the dealing with agents such as the one before him. Agents belonged in Hollywood or New York. They belonged in show business, not in church business. Yet, every major name in modern evangelical circles had an agent. Dick Whiting was, at least, less obnoxious than the lot. A minister had to deal with his kind, if that minister hoped to attract large crowds with big name Christian talent.

"Yeah, well, thanks anyway. You've bought yourself some headlines with Harold, I'll tell you," Whiting said. "And that's what it's all about, isn't it, Malcolm?"

"That's what it's all about," Malcolm sighed.

"I like the promotion you've given to this. And Harold is very pleased. Very pleased."

"We didn't do it to please him," Malcolm said.

"Those newspaper ads are knockouts. And the television? Dynamite. You'll have them hanging from the rafters today, Malcolm. And, boy, am I jealous. To think of preaching to a crowd like we'll have. The good you'll be able to do, the souls you'll be able to save. That's an opportunity any preacher would like to have."

"The good, the souls. They're the bottom line," Malcolm said.

"Right," Whiting said, leaning forward in his chair. "Say, Malcolm, Harold asked me to come over and find out about the security arrangements."

"Security?" Malcolm was surprised. As he had told Miriam, it had been previously discussed, and Whiting himself had convinced Malcolm there wasn't any need for security measures.

"Yeah, with all this promotion, Harold is kinda' frightened that some of his old associates from his Brotherhood days might turn up and cause trouble."

"But you said—"

"The Brotherhood is one of America's fastest growing and most dangerous cults," Whiting recited, sounding like one of the flyers he had mailed out promoting his client. It was just such a flyer which had piqued Malcolm's curiosity and led him to inquire into the possibility of obtaining young Thomas' services.

"You said there was no danger in bringing your client to our church, Dick. You *know* you said that. And, you said it because I told you if there was the slightest chance of anything harmful happening, I wanted no part of Thomas or you."

"Malcolm, I did warn you. I specifically remember telling you about Article Fourteen of the Brotherhood Creed. I even read it to you from the copy Harold brought with him when he left the group. Here . . ." Whiting fished in his pockets and withdrew a white card with black printing on it. ". . . I'll read it to you again to refresh your memory:

"'Whoever is not with us'—meaning the Brotherhood, Malcolm—'must be considered an enemy to our cause and may be eliminated by any fashion deemed necessary with any amount of force required by any member of the organization.'"

"You read me that," Malcolm agreed, his anger mounting, "but you also said that Article Fourteen didn't mean physical elimination. Murder, if you will. You said it meant nothing more than denouncements, boycotts, that sort of thing."

Whiting pasted a phony smile on his California-tanned face and started to say something, but Malcolm overrode him. "You said hundreds of former cult members speak out every week and nothing ever happens to them or the churches they appear in. If written creeds such as Article Fourteen meant anything, you said, and I'm quoting you directly, 'America would be awash in a sea of blood.'"

"Did I say that? That's pretty good," Whiting continued to smile, "but—"

"But now you come in here asking about our security precautions. We talked about that, and you said, 'no need.'"

"I was right, but, you can hardly blame the kid for being nervous, Malcolm. The Brotherhood plays rough."

"Then let's cancel the whole thing right now."

"You can't call it off on this short notice. You've got too much invested."

"I can call it off, and I will. And, I'll tell you what else I'm going to do. I'm going to see that the church sues your client for the return of his honorarium, and you for your ten percent. Plus, we're going to sue for damages. For misrepresentation."

"Now, Malcolm, we're brothers in Christ here," Whiting's tone was conciliatory. "There's been no misrepresentation. I promised you that Harold Thomas would reveal new information here, shocking information. I promised that if you gave Harold a forum, he would make headlines for your church and put it on the map. Did I tell you that I've contacted *Newstime* and they're going to have a correspondent here today?"

"Don't change the subject," Malcolm said coldly. "I only want to know one thing. Will the appearance by Harold Thomas at the First Church of Grunnell bring danger to this church and its membership and visitors?"

"Honestly, I don't think so," Whiting said it as if he meant it. "It's just that Harold Thomas is, well, nervous, as I said. And, not too nervous. He'd just feel better about the thing if I could report that you're going to have some kind of police protection for him. And you've only yourself to blame."

"Me?"

"It's those ads. Harold didn't expect such big ones, so many of them. To him, they're . . . I don't know how to tell you, Malcolm."

"Say it out, man."

"Well, he thinks they're inflammatory."

"They aren't meant to inflame anyone," Malcolm found himself on the defensive. "They're simply meant to bring out a lot of people."

"I told him that. I did," Whiting said quickly. "I told him that First needed to build its membership rolls. I told him that's why you were willing to meet our fee, but . . ."

"But, what?"

"Malcolm, this is the city where that faker, Abba, has his headquarters. Look at your promotion in that light, the way Harold Thomas sees it."

"I ask you again, Dick, is there really a danger?"

"From Abba? No, he's too smart to try anything stupid. But you gotta' remember, for two years Harold Thomas lived in that old hotel, held there largely by fear. That's the way these cults operate, you know, by groundless intimidation. This is the United States. People don't go around busting up churches. But, who can blame Harold Thomas for being a little nervous?"

Malcolm Stansfield could not. Dick Whiting's logic did make sense. This was the United States. Of course there was no physical danger or the idea of Cult Sunday would not have gotten this far.

Malcolm kept thinking it was the good old U.S.A., and the First Church of Grunnell was the inviolate House of the Lord. Then, Dick Whiting asked another question which Malcolm would have cause to ponder for a long time. "Tell me, Malcolm, even if there was a real threat, would you let that stop you?"

"What are you getting at, Dick?"

"I mean, did you hire Harold Thomas just to build safe numbers, or do you feel like I do? That it's our duty as Bible-believing Christians to expose as many of these satanic organizations as possible, regardless of the consequence?"

"Of course," Malcolm said. "That was the real reason behind Cult Sunday, wasn't it?"

"Good, because I was beginning to wonder, the way you came on so strong just now. But, I tell you, I look on getting exposure for ex-cultists like Harold Thomas as my most important mission. Sure, I handle clients like Tom Bryant and Buddy Smith and I make a lot of money out of their records and sacred concerts. And, it's easy.

"Building a kid like Harold Thomas isn't. Sure, if we're lucky and blessed, we might wind up getting him a shot on *Today* or *Good Morning America.* Sure, we might even get a book.

"But, I tell you, Malcolm, if I never made another dime, I'd count it gain to quit representing the Bryants and the Smiths as long as I could book a Harold Thomas into a small country church somewhere to tell the truth about these cults. That's my ministry, Malcolm, because the Good Lord has told me it's the cults that pose the most danger to Christ's earthly church."

"Amen," Malcolm said, thinking that perhaps he had misjudged the agent.

"And, I tell you, I want men like Malcolm Stansfield on that battle line with me." Whiting got up and headed toward the door. "Well, I guess I'd better get back to the hotel and make sure my client gets over here on time. The poor kid is so jittery this morning, he won't open his door for anyone but yours truly." He laughed nonchalantly.

"You will have him here by 9:30, won't you?" Malcolm reminded. "He is prepared to address our combined high school and college departments during the Sunday school hour?"

"It's part of the contract," Dick Whiting said over his shoulder. Then he stopped and turned. "Hey, Malcolm, what would it hurt to have a uniformed policeman on duty this morning? Or maybe a plainclothesman. You know, just one cop, so I could tell Harold police will be here to help protect him."

"I thought we had settled that," Malcolm said sharply.

"You're right. Forget it." Whiting smiled a genuine grin which exposed his even, white caps. "I tell you, Malcolm,

Harold Thomas is gonna' be a big name after today, and he's gonna' make First Church of Grunnell just as big. The Lord bless you, you hear?"

He was gone and Malcolm sat alone. Wondering.

8:34 a.m.

The agony of it. The two hundred and more on their knees, their heads bent forward to touch the floor. Muscles straining, bodies sweating, but all suffering in silence. And she suffering most of all, because she alone was guilty and yet, they were all suffering for that guilt.

The Chief Priest, hoarse with admonition, harangued, "I remind you, it is written by Abba's hand, 'Bring forth him that hath cursed without the camp; and let all that heard him lay their hands upon his head, and let all the congregation stone him.'

"Abba knows who made that telephone call to our enemy Stansfield. Abba knows and could strike you dead. Yet, he gives you a chance to confess, to seek his amnesty."

The girl wanted to confess. She did not want the others to suffer because of her. She had framed the words many times in the last twenty minutes.

"*Abba,*" she planned to say, "*I did not make the call to warn your enemy, only to stop him from hurting you. I could not bear to see your greatness ridiculed by evil persons. Have mercy upon me. I did it because I love you, not to save them.*"

She wanted to say it, could hear herself saying it, but something kept her from it. She did not understand what held her back. She only knew she did not have the courage to speak. She could not live up to her name.

"All right, there are two cowards present. The one who committed the sin and will not admit it," the Chief Priest paused for emphasis, "and the one who witnessed the sinner but will not testify. For I cannot believe someone left their cot last night and sneaked down to the Court of the Gentiles unseen and unnoticed. This is your last chance."

"*It was me!*" the girl wanted to blurt. "*Please, dear Abba, let me say it.*"

Her silent testimony was not enough. "Abba?" she heard the Priest say.

"Behold," Abba said, his voice angry, "all souls are mine; as the soul of the father and mother, so also the soul of the son and daughter is mine; the soul that sinneth, it shall die."

"Abba has spoken. Blessed is the name of Abba," the Chief Priest said. "Captain of the Guardians, you have heard. Carry out Abba's judgment."

"May Abba have mercy," the leader of the Guardian Angels replied, and then to his men, "Ready."

The girl could hear the rustle of movement, the metalic clatter of the weapons being cocked. It was fitting that her soul be destroyed, but the souls of all the others were pure. Their blood, their destruction would be on her head. She would be exiled from the presence of Abba in that other dimension.

Desperately, she strained to cry out. Her lips would not move. Her tongue had a will of its own.

"Aim!"

Sister Charity gave a small, frightened whimper. In another part of the room, someone else was weeping. But all held their prayerful positions. All were willing, all wanted to die if Abba willed it.

"Fire!"

There was a volley of flat reports which echoed in her ears and set them to ringing. They drowned out all else and for a solitary moment, her eardrums throbbed with pain. Then, nothing.

An acrid smoke bellowed through the Court and clogged her throat with the taste of spent powder. Another moment. Then slowly, her ears opened and she could hear. Others were choking and coughing, a few sobbed on the men's side of the partitions as well as on the women's. What did it mean? Was she dead or alive? If dead, why could she hear? Why could she feel her heart beating heavily beneath her breast?

"Blanks, my children," Abba said. "Ye are all alive. My hand has stayed its judgment. Arise, look up. Gaze upon my face and know that ye yet live."

The girl sat up, tears blurring her vision. She wept in gratitude for the miracle of Abba's kindness.

"Praise to Abba," others chanted, "Praise to Abba," glorying in the life he gave to them.

He raised his arms to silence them. "My heart is enlarged with the wonderment of your loyalty. I have put you to the test. I have used the clandestine phone call and the reality of its sin to measure your troth. I am pleased.

"As for the sinner, I know who ye are. I have heard your prayers. Ye are forgiven. But," and his countenance grew stern, "you must never try my patience in such a manner again. If you do, and do not pubicly confess it, you shall surely die. Amen."

The Horn sounded, and to the accompaniment of the synthetic anthem, Abba and his entourage swept from the Court of Adoration in magnificent holiness.

The girl wept until she could weep no more, staring at the vacant throne. Drained, her body shook with the alleviation of the strain, then calmed with the appreciation of Abba's eternal pardon.

Sister Charity reached over and groped for her hand.

The girl could see Charity was weeping, too. Her eyes were puffed, her cheeks stained. "The Assembly is over. We must go," Charity sniffled.

The girl got up off her knees. Her legs were weak. They felt as if they would give way at any moment. Her head spun. She felt giddy, unreal.

"Sister, could you help me?" Charity asked. "My legs have gone to sleep."

Reaching down, the girl pulled her Yoke Maiden up. Sister Charity groaned and stamped her feet to get the blood going again. Supporting each other, they joined the others moving toward the exit.

Some of the Sisters still cried while others giggled nervously. Most, however, made no noise. They simply moved as in a trance.

They had to stand and wait for the men to leave the Court first. Many of the Brothers appeared as empty of energy as the girl herself was. They walked, almost unseeing, in a swaying gait, their eyes staring ahead dully.

"Wasn't it cool?" Sister Charity leaned close and whispered. "Did you ever feel so alive?"

"Sister, you are not to speak in the language of the street," the girl scolded. "And, you're not to speak at all until we're back in our chamber."

Properly chastised, Sister Charity bit her lip and sulked. At last, the Brothers were out of the hall and the women were able to move forward again.

Just outside the door stood Brother Andrew. As they passed, he grabbed the girl's shoulder. "Sister Courage, you are summoned by Abba to the Council Chamber," he told her.

"What?" she stammered.

"You heard me. Come."

The two girls exchanged furtive glances. The fear showed in Sister Charity, and the girl wondered if it showed in her as well.

Together, they started after Brother Andrew. "Not you, Sister Charity," he snapped. "Wait over by the steps for the Maiden of the Chamber to take you back to the Court of Women."

Charity's eyes flared. She looked at the face of her Yoke Maiden, her worry and her grief now plain. Sisters were only summoned alone to the Council Chamber when they were to be punished.

"I'm coming, Brother Andrew," the girl said with all the poise she could muster.

Then, Charity did a brave thing which the girl would remember ever after. Charity kissed her gently on the cheek, a kiss of comfort, and turned quickly and walked away.

The girl was still watching after her Yoke Maiden when Brother Andrew grabbed her arm and led her in the opposite direction.

8:45 a.m.

Captain Burch Zimmerman entered the Communications Center, gingerly carrying the bagel and creamed cheese wrapped in a paper napkin. Fran Goldman was facing the console, her well-turned back to him, and didn't see him right away. But Hannah Wilcox, another of the compliant clerk-dispatchers did and gave him a knowing wink.

Burch winked back and leaned over the railing which separated the three female radio operators and their equipment from unauthorized personnel. As he watched Fran at work, he felt a little like a voyeur. Even from behind, she was a beautiful woman.

Some of the officers in the bullpen on the second floor had accused him of trying to make time with Fran. In truth, he had been dropping by the command center a lot lately. If he were a few years younger, or Fran a few years older, he might indeed have asked her out. But the fact was, she reminded him more than a little of his late daughter. The color and texture of Fran's hair was the same as Sandy's had been. And Fran, too, was part Jewish. No, he wasn't trying to make time with these visits; he merely wanted to talk with someone of the female gender from time to time. After he exchanged pleasantries with

Fran, the loneliness wouldn't seem quite so oppressive.

The speaker on the radio in front of Fran crackled with the transmission from one of the squad cars in the field. The young officer's voice faded in and out with static making whatever it was he was trying to relay, garbled and unintelligible.

Fran pushed her mike key and said, "Adam-3, 10-1."

She released the key and the officer's voice on the monitor said, "Subject . . . hearing . . . 10-10— . . ."

Fran pushed her key with ire and leaned into the microphone shouting, "I said I'm unable to copy. Change location, you turkey!"

The monitor gave forth only open air silence. Fran's message had gotten through and Burch had to laugh at her spirit.

Hearing him, she swiveled around, her eyes still spitting fire. "What kind of rookies are you putting on the street these days, Burch? They don't even know the Ten Code."

"Haven't you heard," he grinned, "the Ten Code is passé these days, honey. We must be the only department within a thousand miles that still uses it."

"Yeah, well, as long as it's good enough for the chief, it's good enough for me."

"The chief insists we still use it, only because he's too old to learn a new system," Burch soothed. "So, how's by you, anyway, kid?"

"Fine," her voice was husky and sexy. "And how's by you, Burch?"

"Aw, I'm makin' it. Here, I brought you something." He proffered the napkin-wrapped package.

She took it. "You shouldn't be bringing me presents, Burch. The station gossips are already wagging their tongues about us." She said it lightly, a private joke between friends.

"Let 'em," he said.

"A bagel," she exclaimed, unwrapping the napkin. "Oh,

and cream cheese. My favorite. Thanks."

"You're welcome, I'm sure. So, tell me, how you makin' out with that new boyfriend of yours?"

"None of your business, you dirty old man. Besides, what new boyfriend? Who do you think would want to date a half Jew, half goy?"

He rubbed the top of his balding head. "Don't put yourself down like that, Fran. I bet there are plenty of guys trying to get to first base with you."

"You sound like my mother," she parried. "You're the only man in my life, right now."

"Some man. More like your grandfather."

"Now who is putting who down?" She bit daintily into the bagel.

"Don't you want some coffee with that?" he asked.

"On duty," she said around the mouthful.

"I could get you some."

"No, I like to eat my bagels without. More crunchy that way."

He shrugged.

"So, how you gettin' on in that new captain's office of yours?"

"Too private, I miss the racket of the bullpen."

"Some big shot you are," she teased.

At that moment, a call came over her monitor and she turned to answer it. Burch waited.

"Adam-3 to Central."

"Central to Adam-3. Go ahead."

"Can you copy any better now? We've changed our location."

"Ten-4," Fran said, still chomping on the bagel.

"We have a citizen here who reports hearing gunshots."

A voice in the background spluttered, "Gunshots, sonny? Itwasawholedadgumwar!"

"Sounds like a real solid citizen," Burch observed to Fran.

"Yeah. Solid gin," she laughed, and then in the mike, "What's your 10-20, Adam-3?"

"We're at the corner of Seventeenth and Welsh."

"In the heart of the wino district," Burch remarked.

"We've investigated and found negative," the officer reported.

"Well, give 'em a gold star," Burch grumbled, pushing through the gate in the railing and hovering over Fran's shoulder. "Ask 'em for more information, honey."

"Ten-43." Fran said cryptically.

"Subject reported hearing shots in the seventeen hundred block of Welsh," the monitor said. "He stopped our squad to make the report. The buildings on that block are mostly empty except for an old hotel that's now a temple for some strange religious outfit."

"Ask them if they contacted anyone at the temple," Burch told Fran, who relayed the message.

"That's a 10-4," was the report. "We contacted a man there. He said he had heard nothing. Please advise."

In the background over the officer's last words came the witness's voice. "It'sthemwhatdonetheshooting. They gotawholearsenalthatchurchhas!"

"Did you copy?" the officer asked.

"Ten-4. Stand by."

"What do you think, Burch?" Fran inquired.

Burch rubbed his head. "Shots? A church with guns? I'd say it beats pink elephants by a mile."

"Advise, Central," the officer repeated urgently.

"Tell 'em to use their own field discretion," Burch said, then as an afterthought, "What am I getting involved in this for? I only came down to bring you a bagel."

Fran giggled and advised the officer.

"It's my opinion," the officer said, "we have a 10-56. Could you dispatch the wagon to this 10-20?"

"Well, he finally realized he has an intoxicated pedestrian on his hands. Maybe there's hope for this department yet," Burch said.

Fran paid him no heed. "Ten-4, Adam-3."

"Could you give us an ETA on the paddy?" the officer wanted to know.

"Ten-12," Fran said and then went through the motions of calling the paddy wagon and relaying its estimated time of arrival to the squad car on the scene.

"Now, where were we?" Burch asked when Fran had completed her duty.

"We were talking about dirty old men, I think," Fran said.

"Oh, yes. As I was saying—"

"Captain," Hannah interrupted, "you have a phone call on two."

"Oyvey," Burch said in his best Yiddish and Fran laughed. He punched the flashing button on her telephone and took the call.

"Captain Zimmerman."

"Captain, this is Malcolm Stansfield. I'm the pastor over at First Church."

"What can I do for you, Pastor?"

"I have what may sound like a rather silly request."

"Try me, Pastor."

"We're having a special service today. We're calling it 'Cult Sunday.'"

"Yeah. I've seen the ads."

"Anyway, one of our speakers is fearful that someone might attempt to stop his speaking out. He thinks he might be in physical danger. I was wondering if we could arrange some sort of police protection for him?"

Burch shook his head in consternation. Citizens had no concept of what it took to arrange a police detail, the shuffling of schedules, extra-duty pay, a drain on both the resources of the department and the taxpayer. He'd like to tell this citizen what he could do with his request, but department policy demanded an officer use tact in all

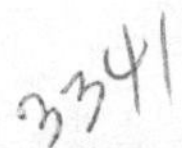

situations. Instead, he asked, "What do you think Pastor? Is this guy really in danger?"

"If I thought that," Stansfield said, "I'd cancel the service."

"Yeah. Well, it's just too late to supply a protective detail. But, I'll tell you what, what time does this Cult Sunday of yours start?"

"The main service is at 11:00."

"Eleven, huh? I'll have a squad car cruising in the area a little before that. It's the best I can do on such short notice."

"That will be fine, Captain. I appreciate your cooperation."

Putting down the phone, Burch turned to Fran. "Can you believe that?" he said. "First guns in one church, and now another church wants police protection. What have we got going, a holy war?"

8:56 a.m.

The girl had always thought of the Holy of Holies as being one large golden room with, perhaps, a small bedchamber to one side where Abba might lie to rest his body. Everyone knew that Abba's consciousness never slept, of course, but she imagined his arms and legs must sometimes get tired.

It had been such a relief to find that God did have a body, after hearing all the college discussion about God being a spirit, an entity without form or substance, a pure mass of energy. She had always thought of God as being a person—a man with white hair and beard who was up there somewhere on a cloud looking down on the people he made, dispatching his angels to answer the prayers of all the billions of people who inhabited the earth. After all, the Bible said that man was made in his image.

But, as she grew older, her teachers had confused her. They had made God an abstraction. They talked of Theism and Deism and a hundred other "isms," when all she really ever wanted to learn was the great Truth of life and how she, individually, was a part of it all.

And when all the theories and abstractions did not—could not—satisfy that thirst, she began a search of her own. And that search had brought her to Abba's Temple.

She had learned so much. Some of it had been painful, such as the fact that the two people she had called her "parents" were really nothing but carnal creatures who had been lied to so often, and had lied themselves so much, that they had become the dupes of the Evil One. She had been forced to break her ties with them, as well as to give up all the beautiful things she had held so dear.

Yet, for every painful experience, the blessings of Abba made up tenfold. And she discovered that her idea of God had been correct all along. Abba did have a body. He did watch over her.

When you belonged to the Brotherhood, there were new and exciting experiences every day. It was exciting to learn, for example, that the Holy of Holies was not one big room as she had always imagined, but a floor just like the Court of the Women and the Court of the Men below. There were many rooms, chambers, some for sleeping, and others that were offices with desks and file cabinets and adding machines and telephones. It was amazing and thrilling, despite her fear of the punishment which would certainly be meted out to her. She wished Brother Andrew would walk more slowly so she could truly absorb all the sights.

She had not been privileged to see much of the Temple in the two years she had dwelled within its walls. Most of her time was divided between the Court of Women, the kitchen and the Court of Adoration. Of course, she had been through the Court of Gentiles many times, and a few times had even seen the Court of Men when she was assigned to the cleaning detail.

The Holy of Holies, though, was marvelous. The decor was so beautiful, the furnishings so plush. It was like another world compared to the rest of the building.

Suddenly, Brother Andrew stopped before a closed door. He rapped on it three times. There was a shuffling behind it and then a voice which the girl recognized as that of the High Priest. "Who goes there?"

"Brother Andrew. I have brought Sister Courage as I was bid."

That was another thing the girl loved about the Brotherhood. No one ever spoke in a common manner. They spoke in lofty, lyrical style, as the chosen people of Abba should. It was one of the specific disciplines taught and practiced.

The door opened just wide enough to admit them and the girl found herself in the Council Chamber. It was a conference room, really, with a large dark wood table and thirteen matched chairs with black upholstery. These were occupied by the twelve priests, with the chair at the head of the table vacant.

What surprised the girl most were the more than twenty other Brothers and Sisters standing around the room. She recognized some of them as Guardian Angels, but the majority were common members of the Brotherhood like herself. They couldn't all be here to bear witness against her, could they?

Seeing her, the Chief Priest rose and went through another door at the back of the room. The rest said nothing. But the girl could feel the urgent sense of purpose that sparked around the table.

Presently, the Chief Priest came back and stood at attention to one side of the back door. "Abba is coming," he announced.

The priests leaped to their feet as Abba entered. They bowed from the waist, low. The ordinary Brothers and Sisters fell to their knees, prostrating themselves.

Abba took his place at the head of the table. "Rise, my children," he said. "We have little time for formalities."

To the girl, Abba did not look quite as formidable as he did in the Court of Adoration with the spotlight upon him. But those eyes, those holy eyes, were even more arresting at close range.

He turned directly to her, as if she were his sole purpose for being there. "Sister Courage, welcome."

His smile was absolutely dazzling. She was so benumbed by it, all she could manage was a bow of gratitude for his acknowledgment.

He turned to the Chief Priest. "Has she been briefed on her purpose here?"

The Priest seemed to shrink before the question. "No, holy father," he stammered. "There wasn't time."

"No matter," Abba said, dismissing the concern with a wave of his ringed hand. The Chief Priest fairly melted with relief.

"Sister Courage," Abba said, "you have been brought here due to a rather unfortunate circumstance. Sister Ability, who was to serve in a wonderful mission this morning, has fallen ill." Then, quickly, he added, "I, even I, caused the curse to come upon her. She has become too prideful lately. And I, even I, could heal her, if I so chose. Rather, I have selected you to take her place."

"You're . . . you're not going to punish me, Father?" It escaped her before she could stop it.

The others gasped at her brazen inquiry. Abba, however, laughed—a deep, genuine laugh. "Punish you, Sister Courage? No, I am going to make of you another Deborah, a woman of power, a woman who will judge my people."

She was puzzled, but she dared not ask any more.

Abba stood, so swiftly that the priests had a difficult time rising fast enough to bow in homage. "My Chief Priest will brief you. Remember, Abba will be with you in all ways."

He exited as he had come. What had he chosen her for? The girl wondered if it was to bear a child? The idea warmed her.

It soon faded as the High Priest said, "I don't like it."

"Abba has ordained it," the Chief Priest told him.

"She could jeopardize everything," the High Priest refused to be put down.

"Are you to be Abba's Judas, Brother?" the Chief Priest hissed. "Are you the one who made the call to Stansfield?"

The High Priest glared, but said no more.

The Chief Priest pressed a button on a little box in front of him on the table. A screen lowered from the ceiling. Another button, and the drapes on the windows whirred shut.

"Now, Sister Courage, watch closely. There isn't much time. You must remember everything you see. Everything. If you do not, the wrath of Abba will rest upon you."

Slides began to flash on the screen, the High Priest explaining each and how the girl fit in.

The more she understood, the more she praised Abba. It was Revelation come to life. The seals were about to be broken. It was the beginning of the End of the Age. And she was to be part of it all. How wonderful! It was even better than bearing a child for Abba. She was truly chosen above all other women.

9:06 a.m.

Harold Thomas was shorter, less robust than Malcolm had guessed he was from the publicity photographs. The boyish good looks were there in his features, all right, but Harold Thomas seemed almost fragile as Malcolm shook his hand in greeting.

The young man was stooped as a thin old man might be. His handshake was limp, the palm moist as the palms of the terribly ill often are, and his skin had an almost transparent quality. It was pale and wan. Harold Thomas reminded Malcolm a great deal of some of the returning prisoners of war he had counseled after Korea.

"Well, we finally meet," Malcolm said, while making these assessments.

"Yes, sir," Harold Thomas said uncomfortably.

Dick Whiting, who stood to one side remarked, "I hope we're not too late, Malcolm."

"No, no. You're just about right on the button. My staff will be gathering for a little prayer time in a few minutes. You're both welcome to join us."

"I'd like that, sir," Harold Thomas said.

"Good. Come on in and sit down. Both of you." Malcolm showed them to the leather couch on the south side of his office. There was a coffee table there and a leather host chair facing toward the couch, forming what was popularly called "a conversation area."

Malcolm used it for his counseling duties. It had been carefully designed for that purpose. The coffee table was less a barrier than was the desk on the other side of the room, but enough of a barrier to set folks at ease and not make them feel that he was sitting right on top of them. It helped encourage people to talk.

Before Malcolm could settle in the chair, Thomas asked, "Sir, could I trouble you for a glass of water?"

"No problem," Malcolm said and went to his desk to pour a glass from his carafe. When he handed Thomas the glass, he couldn't help but notice the tremor in the young man's hand.

"Thank you, sir." Thomas drained it thirstily.

"Would you care for more?" Malcolm offered.

"No thank you, sir."

Malcolm sat down.

"It's funny how speech making can make a person so thirsty before the fact," Dick Whiting said, making small talk. "I used to have that same trouble when I was a preacher. Took me years to dry out. Used to slosh when I walked." He laughed loudly at his own joke.

Malcolm grinned politely. Harold Thomas showed no reaction. He sat, staring at the empty tumbler in his hand.

"Mr. Whiting says . . ." he faltered, "he says he thought you were going to arrange some police protection."

"I talked with the police about a half hour ago," Malcolm nodded. "They promised to keep an eye on things for us."

He saw no need to tell the boy that they had only pledged to have a squad car drive by.

"That makes us feel better, doesn't it, Hal?" Whiting gave his client a thump on the back. "With the police around, nobody's going to try anything, you hear?"

"Mmmmm," Thomas grunted, not taking his eyes from

the glass.

"Are you that frightened, Brother Thomas?" Malcolm posed kindly.

The boy placed the glass deliberately on the coffee table as if he was afraid he might drop and break it. He cleared his throat. "That's what *they* used to call me—Brother Thomas. All the men are given names from the Bible. They call the women after qualities. Love, Charity, Patience, names like that."

"That doesn't sound very dangerous," Malcolm said, and was sorry for it. It was a stupid thing to say.

The boy looked up, meeting Malcolm's eyes straight on. "That Abba is an animal, sir. Abba, that's what the head man calls himself. Do you know that comes from the Bible? Mark 14:36. Jesus addresses God that way when He's praying in the garden."

"Yes, I know," Malcolm said.

"That's the way they pervert the Scriptures all the time, sir."

"I see."

"Abba claims to be God. He's very clever about it. If something happens to someone, he says he caused it to either punish or reward them. And, if they're sick or hurt, he says he could heal them, if he wanted. And, if they get well, he says he did it. He's very, very clever, sir."

"And you're still afraid of him?" Malcolm shook his head.

"Yes, sir, because he's afraid of me. He's afraid of the truth being told."

"We're sure gonna' tell them the truth this morning, aren't we, Hal?" Whiting broke in.

Malcolm ignored him. "But I understand you've spoken out before, in other churches."

"Oh, yes, sir," Thomas said. "In smaller churches. In churches a long way from here. In churches that didn't play it up like you have, sir."

"I guess we have gotten a little carried away." Malcolm stroked his chin thoughtfully. "I'm sorry."

"Don't be, sir. I want to talk about it. I need to talk about it. I wish I didn't have to, but by the grace of Jesus Christ, I was brought out. People need to know about the Brotherhood. They need to know and maybe it will keep it from happening to them."

"Amen," Malcolm said.

"Hal pretty much has his testimony in mind for the service, Malcolm," Dick Whiting butted in again. "But what do you want him to say to your Sunday school?"

"Whatever the Spirit leads him to say."

"I thought I'd tell them how I got involved with the Brotherhood. What happened," Thomas suggested. "Then let them ask me questions, if that's all right, sir."

"That would be fine," Malcolm agreed. "How *did* you get so deeply into it?"

The boy shrugged. "It was easy. Too easy. I was in my second year at State and things weren't going too well."

The words flowed easily, almost compulsively from Hal Thomas as he sat on the couch. They were made the more engrossing because the boy spoke in a plain, unemotional tone.

"I came from a Christian home," Thomas was saying. "I won't say, 'a *good* Christian home,' because it wasn't. It wasn't my parents' fault, not really. They took me to Sunday school and all. But, they were too busy with their own lives, just making a living, enough to keep the family going. Enough to keep up with the Joneses. But I never saw a manifestation of real Christian love. Do you know what I mean, sir?"

"Yes."

"Anyway, by the time I left for college, I thought I knew a lot about Jesus and God and all. I didn't worry about it. But then, in my second year, I had to take this basic philosophy course. The prof talked a lot about alternative religions and how valid they were for the people who practiced them. And, for mid-term, he asked us to write down our own religious philosophy. That's when I really began to run into trouble.

"My philosophy only filled half a page, typed and double-spaced. I realized that something was missing. It bothered me, and I did a lot of talking about it to other students. You know, in the Union, in buzz groups, that kind of thing."

"That's common," Malcolm remarked, folding his hands under his jaw in an interested listening posture.

"Yes, sir. I started to notice these two guys hanging around. I knew they weren't students and they didn't say much. But they listened well. And then, one day when I was lying on the grass in front of Old Main studying for an exam, they came up to me and we got to talking. We talked a lot after that.

"They knew a lot of Bible verses and got me to agreeing with them. They made sense.

"They called each other 'Brother' all the time, like I had heard the people in my home church call each other when I was a kid. Like you called me now. It kinda' put me off, but I got used to it and after awhile I even got to calling them my brothers, too.

"Well, one day, I came back to my dorm early. I skipped Chem I. They were in my room, going through my things, taking an inventory. That should have warned me, but by that time we were friends and they said they just wanted to see what I had, in case they ever needed something and wanted to borrow it. I believed them—that's what I'll never understand."

He crossed his leg and picked at an imaginary piece of lint on his trousers before continuing.

"They asked me if I could meet them that night, out in the parking lot. That's when they 'Caught Me Up,' kidnapped me and took me to this old house. The Brotherhood didn't own the hotel down on Welsh street in those days. They tied me up and kept me in this dark room without food or water for a long time. They said it was for my own good. They said I had to learn about suffering because I had been 'Chosen.' Called out.

"Could I have some more water, sir?"

As Malcolm fetched the pitcher from his desk, Thomas went on with his story.

"They said they served Abba, who was God in flesh. Not Christ come to earth again, but above Christ. They quoted from the Bible to prove it.

"They wanted me to sign over all I owned to Abba. When I wouldn't, they . . . they beat me, and worse." He was overcome by the memory. It took him several moments to collect himself again.

"After how long, I don't know—it seemed like days—they took me before all the Brotherhood. Abba was there. In spite of all I had been through, I still didn't think he was God.

"And I wouldn't say it. They beat me some more, then put a Luger in my face and made me sign the contract giving up all I had."

"And nobody did anything to stop it?" Malcolm was incredulous.

"No, sir. They were conditioned. They had all been through it themselves. It's the way the Brotherhood gets new converts.

"Once I had signed the contract, that made me a convert, too. They put me in another room, one they kept lighted day and night. And there was an audiotape going constantly. A tape of Abba and his teachings. They only let you sleep a few minutes at a time and then they beat you awake.

"I was really bloody and bleeding. The sores were beginning to fester. I was hallucinating. I thought I was going to die. Some have in that room. But this guy, one of the Brothers, came around and dressed my wounds and gave me food and water. He told me how much he loved me. How much Abba loved me and wanted me to live for him.

"I was in no condition to argue. I bought it. I became a member of the Brotherhood in good standing. I thought Abba was God. I thought only what he wanted me to think, did only what he wanted me to do. I thought he knew everything I did and said and thought."

"But your parents," Malcolm said. "What did you tell them?"

"Nothing. The Brotherhood told me they were evil and I was to have nothing more to do with them. And I didn't."

"Surely they must have tried to find you."

"Yes. They hired a detective. They searched for me for years. Whenever they got too close, Abba would have me sent someplace else. Once, they even staged a false death for me. They used another body. One of the converts that didn't make it through the conversion. But my folks didn't take the bait."

"And even after that, you still followed this Abba?" It was more than Malcolm could fathom.

"Yes. He was to me then all that Jesus is to me now. Listen, he was God. He acted like God. Once, I remember, he wanted an orange. I was a priest by then. We waited on Abba's every need. Anyway, this other priest and I went out and bought a whole crate of oranges. We went through it and picked the most perfect one. We threw the rest of the crate away, because it was cursed. Anything or anyone not fit for Abba was useless.

"We took the perfect orange in to him and he peeled it. All at once, he looked at me and said something like, 'I really want this orange, but I'm giving it to you, Brother Thomas, because I love you.'

"I kept that peeled orange for months. It was all dried up and shriveled, but to me it was beautiful. Abba had given it to me. It was a sign of his love for me."

"My word!" Malcolm exclaimed.

"I still had that orange when my folks' detective kidnapped me back. It took two weeks of deprogramming before I began to think for myself again."

"What did I tell you?" Dick Whiting raved. "Isn't my client everything I promised?"

"I'm sorry sir," Thomas apologized. "Sometimes when I talk about the Brotherhood, I get to rambling."

"Don't apologize," Malcolm said.

Gil Anderson, the assistant pastor, and John Swallow and Allen Lloyd, the ministers of youth and music respectively, entered the office. Malcolm made the introductions. They went over the order of service and prayed.

At Malcolm's urging, Harold Thomas shared a portion of what he had already told Malcolm with the others. Although he had heard it before, Malcolm found it all as terrifying as it had been the first time.

Yet, the thing which Malcolm found the most terrifying of all was in the statement Harold Thomas made just prior to the meeting's end.

"It was the love that I thought held me," he said. "Until I really came to know Jesus, I have never experienced anything that approached the love the members of the Brotherhood say they have for each other.

"But now I know it's not really love. It's fear. Jesus helped me see that. And the higher you go in the Brotherhood, the more fear you see; the more fear you have.

"The leadership are all just jockeying for position. They are afraid Abba will show more favor to someone else. You've never seen such backbiting as goes on behind the closed doors in the Holy of Holies.

"When you have the love of Jesus, you have love. They have only fear, but they pretend it's love and believe that it is. They'd kill for it. It's that fear called love that scares me. I'm glad you arranged for police protection, sir."

And Malcolm felt that prickly feeling at the back of his neck, the same feeling he had had after the early morning telephone call.

9:19 a.m.

If they had used professional movers as Stan had wanted to do, Peggy Brown knew she wouldn't be in this mess now. It must be the German blood from her father's side which made her so practical.

But movers cost money, friends didn't. Stan and she would need every penny they could squeeze out since at last they owned a home of their own. They had scrimped and saved five years for the down payment. They'd just barely had enough. The monthly payments were huge, because the interest rate was higher than they had figured it would be. The old family budget was going to be stretched mighty tight, but with the Lord's help and her practical side, they would make it.

It would have been nice to use professional movers, though. They would have put all the boxes in all the right rooms. The friends had dropped them wherever they found an empty spot. That's why she was searching so frantically now through the endless mountains of boxes in the living room. She had thought she had marked them all, but in the last minute rush she must have missed a few. She had already been through three unmarked boxes and still hadn't found what she was looking for.

"Why can't I be as efficient a wife and mother as I was an

R.N.?" she scolded herself.

"Babe, if we're going to make that Sunday school, we're going to have to step on it." Stan's rough voice from the entry was followed by Stan himself, picking his way through the mass confusion of yesterday's move. He looked impatient and uncomfortable in his Sunday suit which had always been tight across his bricklayer's shoulders.

"I'm hurrying," she said. "I know that box has to be here someplace."

Stan made a great show of checking his watch. "Did you try those boxes in the kitchen?"

It was his way of trying to be helpful, she supposed. "Wait a minute."

"We haven't got a minute," he groused.

"Here, hold these." She shoved an armload of cartons into his unsuspecting hands and tore open the carton that had been under them on the floor. Tea towels and linen.

"Come on, Babe. Forget it. We'll just have to go on without them."

"Your son may be a chip off the old block," she said, putting her hands on her hips, "but he can't go to church in his old tennies. Now, help me hunt."

"I don't see why we have to drive all the way down to First Church anyway," Stan said, stacking the boxes he held on top of other boxes. "I mean, it seems to me that moving would be a good excuse to look for another church a little closer to where we live."

"If that's what you want," she said. "You're the head of the house. But, wouldn't you feel guilty leaving First? It needs us. It never has recovered from the split."

"You're right, Babe. But if this Cult Sunday business works like the pastor and the deacons say it's going to, maybe they'll turn it around. And First Church will go back to being what it was, and they won't miss us."

"We'd miss them, then," Peggy said. "Where could that

box have gotten to?"

"What's it look like?" Stan was shifting boxes rapidly now, moving them from one pile to another.

"Medium size. It has 'Kid's Shoes' written on the side in magic marker."

"Nuts. I didn't know we had so much stuff."

"Wait a minute, Stan. That box you have in your hand."

"It's not marked."

"Shake it."

He joggled it and there was a loose thumping.

"That's it," she announced.

"But it isn't marked."

"So, your wife isn't perfect." He gave it to her and she tore it open. Sorting through the miscellaneous jumble inside, she found the two small brown oxfords and held them aloft proudly.

"See? I knew they were here all the time," she said.

Impulsively, he pulled her close. She felt the hard muscles under his jacket. "I married a smart woman," he said playfully. "Not organized, but smart."

"I thought you were the one in a hurry," she cooed. "Better let me go, so I can go shoe the kid."

"Aw, why don't we stay home this one Sunday, and hang pictures . . . or something?" He gave an exaggerated leer caricaturing a matinee idol.

"Not today," she said smugly. "This is one Sunday I want to go to church more than anything in the world."

"You'd rather go and hear about an ol' cult, when you could spend a quiet Sunday with me?" he feigned hurt.

"No, I just want to thank the Lord for giving me a fine husband, and a wonderful little boy and a house all our own."

"If you'd married a doctor like the rest of your nurse buddies instead of a laborer like me, you'd have a much bigger house to be thankful for," he teased.

"But I've got more man," she brushed his lips with hers.

"Oh, Stan, we've just got to worship Him. He's given us so much. So very much."

"He really has," Stan said quietly, releasing her. "Get Bobby and let's head 'er out."

She lingered a moment longer, feeling secure in his huge arms. God's world was such a beautiful place. She felt so at peace.

Less than two hours later, Peggy Brown's peace would be shattered.

9:36 a.m.

"There you are, Brother Stansfield. I want a word with you!" Joseph Holmes bellowed the length of the second floor hallway.

Malcolm was guiding Harold Thomas and Dick Whiting toward the Youth Department in company with Allen Lloyd, the minister of youth. He turned at the summons to see Joseph Holmes navigating his way through the people on the way to their respective classes and around the little knots of friends who had stopped to visit before the 9:45 bell called them to their own rooms. The bustle and buzz abated for a moment as people turned to stare at the industrialist.

It was hard not to stare at Joseph Holmes under any circumstances. He was a big man, well advanced in years, whose ruddy face was topped by a thatch of milk white hair. His suit was expensive and rumpled, with one pant leg caught up mischievously in the black kangaroo leather cowboy boots the old man always wore. When Joseph Holmes was not at his factory, he liked to play cowboy on his estate on the outskirts of town where he raised quarter horses. The silver head on the cane he used was formed in the shape of a horse's head.

"Hello, Joseph," Malcolm said warmly. "I'd like you to

meet our guest speaker, Harold Thomas. And his agent, Dick Whiting."

"Howdy," Joseph Holmes grunted.

Dick Whiting extended his hand, but Holmes, much to Whiting's chagrin, did not take it. Joseph Holmes never shook hands with anyone. It had something to do with his fear of diseases, another of his growing list of eccentricities.

The old man stared at Whiting's hand until the latter resorted to hiding his friendly intention by tugging his tie straight with the errant appendage.

"I thought I told you to save me some time this morning, preacher," Holmes snorted.

"I thought you meant a little later," Malcolm alibied. Then to Lloyd, "Show our guests to the room. If you'll excuse me, I'll catch up with you in a few minutes."

Holmes waited until the others were out of earshot before he said, "That boy don't look like a 'cultist' to me."

"He's an *ex*-cultist, Joseph," Malcolm reminded, slightly amused by the industrialist's reaction. "He's come to know Jesus as his Lord."

"Good for him," Joseph said. "But I thought he'd be wearing a robe or something."

"They don't wear robes in the cult he used to belong to, Joseph."

"You sure that boy's a good speaker, Malcolm? We got a lot riding on this one."

"I've heard some of his testimony, checked his references," Malcolm assured. "I don't think you'll soon forget what he has to say."

"He'd better be a good speaker. A thousand dollars is a lot of money." Holmes stuck out his lower lip in a sour expression. "We can't talk here, Malcolm. Let's go someplace more private."

"My office—"

"Fuss and feathers. Your office is too far away for these

old legs. And I don't want to be late for Sunday school. I haven't been late for Sunday school since I wore short pants."

They settled on the balcony of the sanctuary. It was empty as was the main floor of the auditorium, save for Mrs. Bruce practicing the organ.

Television cameras were located against the lower rail on either side of the balcony. They seemed forlornly expectant, waiting to be "fired up" by the cameramen who would soon be there to run them.

Holmes led their way past them to the center of the wide gallery. "We don't want to be overheard by just anybody who might take a notion to stick his nose in the door," he explained. He settled in one of the balcony's front pews, and Malcolm followed suit.

"Preacher," Holmes sighed, "some of us is worried."

"About what?" Malcolm asked. "If you think there's any danger—"

"Not about that. About the whole idea of Cult Sunday. I don't know much about these here cults, and I don't care. You tell me they're newsworthy, that people are interested in 'em more than ever 'cause of Jonestown and the congressional investigations. You say you think they'll bring out the folks and fill this old sanctuary again. I pray you're right."

"We'll soon know, won't we, Joseph?"

"That we will, that we will. Can't say I'm overly impressed with the advertising campaign that's been waged."

"It was prepared by your advertising agency, Joseph."

Holmes shook his shaggy head. "Not my advertising agency, Malcolm. They work for my company. I don't own 'em. And, I don't always agree with what they do, either. I learned a long time ago that you have to keep a tight rein on 'em. I don't think you've learned that, yet."

"There are a lot of things I haven't learned yet,"

Malcolm admitted. "But the Lord has given me His help."

"That was a good answer, preacher, a good one. But the point I'm trying to make is, I hope you've got a better handle on the service."

Malcolm outlined the order of worship. Holmes made no comment until Malcolm had finished.

"Malcolm, I don't care what you do down there this morning. I got me this vision, see? A vision of many people, many families coming down that center aisle when you give the pulpit call. That's what I care about."

"Me, too," Malcolm said. "I want this church to grow in service and spirit as badly as you do, Joseph."

The old man suddenly spun in his seat and gestured with his cane toward the big stained-glass window at the top of the balcony. It was circular, fifteen feet across, made up of pale hues of pink and deep shades of lavender in a lovely geometric pattern. In the center was a single pane of brilliant red, representing the blood of Christ.

"Take a look-see at that window yonder," Holmes said. "That glass means as much to me as anything in this church. My daddy gave it when this place was built. Said it would be there until Jesus came again. I promised him it would be, too.

"In the summertime, the sun streams through that window every Sunday morning. Not even the high buildings they've built these last few years can keep it out. It's an inspiring sight, preacher, I tell you."

"I know. I saw it last summer."

"I hope you're still here to see it next summer," Holmes said.

"Is that a threat, Joseph?" Malcolm found himself on edge. He didn't like threats.

"I don't make threats," Joseph Holmes said, his voice syrupy. "I act. I was making an observation, that's all."

He pulled a heavy gold watch from his vest pocket and pressed the stem. The engraved lid flipped open with the tiny sound of "Sweet Hour of Prayer."

"Time I was getting to class," he said. "Haven't been late in more than fifty years. The Lord be with you, preacher."

He rose and limped away on his silver headed cane. *So that's how it feels to be eaten alive by Joseph Holmes,* Malcolm thought. *Help me to love him, Lord, in spite of it.*

Mrs. Bruce saw him standing there. "Good morning, Pastor," she called, her hands still on the organ keys. "It's a lovely morning, isn't it?"

"That it is, Mrs. Bruce," Malcolm returned the greeting, his eyes straying back to the window.

"I'll be here to see the sun," he whispered to himself. "You can count on that, Brother Holmes."

9:39 a.m.

It had been less than an hour since the girl first entered the Holy of Holies. The intensity of the experience had been mind-numbing. The slides and the diagrams which she had been shown danced in her brain, almost too much for one person to absorb in so short a time. But absorb them she had. Abba had given her the power to do so.

It was beyond belief that she had been chosen to participate in the mission at all. Along with the others of the Brotherhood, she had known there was to be a mission this morning, of course. They had known it ever since word first came that Harold Thomas would betray the love of Abba by telling lies to outsiders at the abomination called First Church.

She drew his image in her mind. Brother Thomas, the priest who desecrated the priesthood. The traitor who dared to proclaim Abba a false god. Brother Thomas—how she despised him. What could possibly have blinded him and turned him against his God?

Abba had warned them all of what would happen should they ever violate the blood covenant of the Brotherhood. "Thou shalt surely die," he had said.

Brother Thomas was the first to mock that commandment. He was so filled with wickedness, that he would defiantly stand before the multitudes and spew from his mouth vile pronouncements, "exchanging good for evil," as one of Abba's earlier prophets had put it.

On the second day of this week, the girl remembered Abba standing before the morning Assembly, his face fiery with rage. "I, even I," he had thundered, "will strike down Brother Thomas and turn him to stone, as I, even I, once transformed Lot's wife to salt. Mighty is Abba's wrath and mighty shall be his vengeance."

He had spoken of the need for a mission, and in her ignorance, the girl mistakenly thought that Abba meant he personally would go to First Church on Sunday and strike down Brother Thomas by supernatural means.

Abba had talked of the mission with such agitation, that obviously he found it degrading to do such a thing. To protect him, to keep him from having to do that, was why the girl had attempted the warning call to Malcolm Stansfield.

She would never have done it, if she had only realized how much more perfect was Abba's plan than her imagining of it. He had assembled a secret force of twenty-seven. Segregated from the rest of the Temple body, they had been carefully trained. Hours of work had gone into the gathering of intelligence.

Step by step, minute by minute, the operation had been charted and organized in secret. The security had been so absolute, that even as the general membership prayed for the mission's success, they had no idea what they were praying about.

It was by Abba's grace that she was privileged to know the mystery still hidden from so many others. More than that, by Abba's wish, she was to be an elite tool of Abba's justice.

That was the wonder of it, the real mystery of it. As her understanding broadened, she realized how right the mission was, how appropriate it was that Abba himself would not need to be bodily present. Rather, Abba's spirit would accompany the twenty-seven chosen minions whose task would be to strike down Brother Thomas and those polluted by his falsehoods.

"One more time, Sister Courage," the Chief Priest was drilling her. "Tell me again what you are to do."

"I enter the church with Brother Andrew. It is to appear that we are married, a couple attending church together."

"Yes, and then what?"

"We are to sit as close to Position 7 as circumstances will allow."

"And, if those seats are occupied?"

"They won't be. Brother Bartholomew will be there ahead of us."

"Why will he be there ahead of you? What if he gets delayed?"

"He won't, because he's there already."

"In the pew?"

"No, in the church."

"Be specific, Sister. Precision is vital in this matter." The Chief Priest glared sternly at her. "Now, where is Brother Bartholomew?"

"He's now in Position 1."

"Is he alone?"

"No, Brother Philip and Brother Nathanael are with him."

"And, where is Position 1 located precisely, Sister. Precisely."

"Uh . . . the basement."

"Just the basement, Sister?"

The girl strained to recall the charts. Position 1 eluded her.

"Come on, Sister, we haven't much time. Where is Position 1?"

"It is down, I know that, sir," the girl said. "It's the basement."

"Where? Of the Temple here?"

The girl gave a nervous giggle. "Of course not. It's in the basement of the church."

"What church, Sister?"

"The First Church, sir."

The High Priest blew through his lips. "It's no use. She'll never get it."

The Chief Priest regarded him disdainfully. "She will get it," he said, banging his fist on the conference table for emphasis. "Abba has said she will."

"Never in time," the High Priest bit back. "She'll ruin any chance of success."

"She *will* get it," the Chief Priest reiterated. "Won't you, Sister Courage?"

"Praise be to Abba," the girl said.

To the High Priest, the Chief Priest gave a bitter smile. "See? She has enough faith."

He turned his head slightly to address another Sister who stood behind his leather chair. "Sister Clever. Tell Sister Courage where Position 1 is exactly."

"Position 1 is in the sub-basement of the First Church," Sister Clever sang out.

"Do you understand, Sister Courage?"

"Yes," the girl said. Why couldn't she remember something so simple? "In the sub-basement of the First Church, sir."

"Once more from the top," the Chief Priest said. "Tell me again, what are you to do?"

"I enter the church with Brother Andrew. It is to appear that we are married . . ."

This time, she repeated everything as she was supposed to, exactly in order, every detail.

"Excellent," the Chief Priest smiled, a smile of victory in the direction of the High Priest, who returned it with a scowl. "Now, show us how you will assemble the weapon."

The girl had been provided with a large oversized

handbag. She balanced it on her lap and reached in as if fumbling for a compact or a tube of lipstick. Her hands came out holding an eighteen-inch M1 carbine of the Universal Enforcer make. The weapon was so compact because it did not have a traditional rifle butt. Instead, it had a pistol-type grip behind the trigger.

"No, no, Sister Courage," the Chief Priest coached. "You must remember to insert the ammunition magazine just as you remove it from your purse."

The High Priest gave a cruel laugh. "This girl is conspicuously not acquainted with weapons handling."

"She has had the training," the High Priest replied. All members of the Brotherhood were instructed in the use of automatic weapons. Abba said that someday, the Infidels might attempt to storm the Temple. He wanted his followers prepared to defend it.

"Could I make a suggestion, your holiness?" the girl asked in a small voice.

"About guns?" the High Priest howled.

"My parents had guns around all the time," the girl said.

"You mean your carnal parents?" the High Priest was quick to point out. "Abba is your true father."

"Yes, that's what I meant. It's just that . . . wouldn't it be easier if I left the clip on the carbine all the time?"

"Give it a try," the Chief Priest said. But the curved, thirty-shot magazine protruding from its underside kept the weapon from fitting out of sight in the bottom of the bag.

"You must learn to insert the magazine the instant you pull the carbine out," the Chief Priest said, when it was obvious her suggestion wasn't going to work. "In one smooth, fluid motion. You must do it very quickly and then hand the carbine to Brother Andrew sitting beside you. That way, if anyone notices, they won't have time to give alarm."

"And she says she knows guns," the High Priest gloated.

The girl sighed and put the clipless M1 back in the handbag with the magazine beside it. Wiping the sweat from her icy palms, she tried again.

The clip glanced off the bottom of the stock the first time she went to jam it home, but clicked into place in the next thrust.

"Much better," the Chief Priest said. "And again."

"We're running out of time, Brother," the High Priest pointed toward the clock on the wall. "Why don't you admit this girl is stupid and will never do?"

"I've had my fill of you, Brother," the Chief Priest sputtered. "It's difficult enough to train a replacement at the last moment without your jibes."

"Why replace Sister Ability at all? We have enough manpower. We don't need this exercise in futility."

"Because Abba has determined we need ten armed men at the moment of attack," the Chief Priest said. "Isn't that good enough for you, Brother?"

The High Priest said no more, but the girl felt his stare as she replaced the weapon for yet a third try.

Hot tears bubbled at her eyes in frustration and spilled down her cheeks. She had to do it the way they wanted. She had to.

Her fingers slid into the bag, closing around the hard stock and cold blue barrel. Out came the carbine in her left hand, the magazine in her right. The two met above the bag. Click. She thrust the gun at Brother Andrew, who took it and pretended to pump the first cartridge into readiness.

"Very good," the Chief Priest applauded. "And now, yet again."

"The time, Brother, the time," the High Priest reminded. "The Brothers are in position, out of contact. They will start their phase of the operation at precisely 11:15, whether Sister Courage is there and ready or not."

"One more time," the Chief Priest insisted, "just to make

certain you have the moves down, Sister Courage."

"Stupidity!" the High Priest exploded and stormed from the conference room.

As she rehearsed with the weapon, the girl prayed to Abba for assistance. She could picture the Brothers Bartholomew, Nathanael and Philip waiting, waiting for her, depending upon her, in the shadows of the sub-basement in a church a few blocks away.

She vowed she would not fail them.

9:43 a.m.

It was George Washington Isaiah Perkins' bad luck to encounter Joseph Holmes as the old man came charging out of the second floor entrance to the balcony. George had been down the hall in the Dorcas classroom changing a fluorescent tube which had picked Sunday morning, of all times, to start flickering. It had been bad enough to endure Mrs. Effie Randolph's nagging about his inability to keep the lights up to snuff. Now, here was that pesky old Joseph Holmes.

George tried to swerve and take a path as far away from Joseph Holmes as he could get. He knew what was coming, if Joseph Holmes should spy him.

"George!" Too late. He had been seen. That old Mr. Holmes had the eyes of a hawk.

"George!"

"Yes, Mr. Holmes. Good morning, sir." He waited for Holmes to approach. Here it came.

"George, have you been down to check the pipes and the boiler yet?"

"Oh, Mr. Holmes, you ask me that every time you come into the church. Would I forget something that important?" George evaded a direct answer.

"Don't kid a kidder, George. Have you done it or

haven't you?"

"Well, I . . . ahem . . . No, Mr. Holmes."

"What's the matter with you, George? Haven't I told you often enough that's one of your most important duties as janitor here? Those pipes, that boiler, is old."

"Yes, sir, old."

"It just wouldn't do to have a burst pipe or no heat on Sunday morning."

"I know that, Mr. Holmes."

"Then, go down there right now and check them out."

"But, Mr. Holmes, there's heat coming up the radiators. Just put your hand on one of 'em. You can feel it, certain."

"Now, George. I'm gonna' ask you again after Sunday school, and I want you to be able to look me in the eye and say you've done as I said."

"Yes, sir, Mr. Holmes. I'll do it this minute."

Satisfied, Mr. Holmes limped away.

"Mr. High-And-Mighty Trustee," George said after him under his breath.

Humor the old man, the pastor said. He's done enough for this church to deserve respect, even if he seems eccentric at times. That's what Pastor Stansfield said.

And every single time that Mr. Joseph Holmes got within ten feet of First Church, the pipes and boiler had to be attended to. What was that old man afraid of? They were old, but they weren't going to blow up. George Washington Isaiah Perkins kept everything about First Church in tip-top running shape.

George sighed. It was a long way down to the sub-basement. A long way. And a man never could tell what he would find down in that dark hole—rats, mice or some bum who had come in off the street looking for a warm place to sleep off his whiskey. The sub-basement was not a pleasant place to go.

But humor the old man, the pastor had said, so humor him, George would. He started down the stairway, bemoaning the fact that the church had no elevator. Five stories and no elevator—but then, elevators probably hadn't been invented yet when Mr. Holmes' daddy bought and paid for the building.

Some of the young people passed him, heading up, late for their classes. "Good morning, George," they shouted.

"Hey, George, you're headed the wrong way," one pimply teenaged boy bantered.

"Not if I'm going down, which I am, Curt." George knew most of the children and young people by their first names. He had known most of them since they were in cribs in the nursery. He liked them, and they liked him. They brought him candy and cookies at Christmas by the bucketfuls, and on Valentine's Day he received more mail than the postman.

Passing the first floor landing, George looked out at the narthex. It was empty, the floor still shiny with the fresh coat of wax he had given it. It would still be another hour before the gloss was ruined by two thousand pairs of heels. Monday, he'd have to drag out the heavy old polisher and start all over again.

This job wasn't easy. Dragging floor polishers and vacuum cleaners from one floor to the next. Without an elevator. Cleaning toilets and picking up after people. No, it wasn't easy.

But it beat sharecropping in Alabama, and the pay was better than any man with only a third grade education could expect. He even had a pension and a small savings account. The savings account was for his son. That boy was going to go to college. He wasn't going to wind up a janitor like his daddy.

The stairs ended in the basement social hall. The room was immediately below the sanctuary and was almost as long. At one end was a stage, its red velvet curtain closed. In front of the stage, Mr. Harvey was teaching a class of young marrieds. George tiptoed diagonally across one corner of the hall to the kitchen.

They said the church membership was smaller than it should be. But George didn't believe it was in as much trouble as some folks claimed. There were new people every Sunday, and more mess every Monday. That new Pastor Stansfield was a good man. He was getting the job done, if that old Mr. Holmes and his cronies would just leave well enough alone.

The kitchen was empty. There was no potluck scheduled for this noon, for a change. George was glad about that. At least, he wouldn't have to clean it this week.

It could be worse. There were worse janitorial positions. Why, this church didn't have any big stained-glass windows that needed washing, except for the big round one above the balcony. There weren't even any small windows in that auditorium to fuss with. That was one good thing about the job.

George stood before the door which led from the kitchen to the sub-basement steps. He hesitated. "A fool's errand," he complained aloud, since there was no one around to hear him.

He could turn around right now. He could tell that old man that he had "been to the sub-basement." He wouldn't have to say he had only been to the sub-basement door.

But that would be a fib. And Mr. Holmes would recognize it for what it was. That old man didn't miss much.

Besides, George might be poor and uneducated, but he did not lie. His mama had raised him to be honest. He couldn't go against that, no matter how much he hated to go down to the boiler room.

As soon as he pushed open the door, he could hear the roar of the furnace. He grabbed the iron railing and made his way down the naked concrete steps.

Flipping the light switch, he turned on the forty watt bulb that dangled over the boiler gauges. It was a spooky place, a lonely place, away from everything and everybody.

Well, the gauges looked all right and there was no water on the floor and the contraption was purring right along. He turned to go.

It was then he heard the noise. It seemed to come from the alcove to one side of the boiler where he stored some of his cleaning supplies.

"Who's there?" he demanded timidly.

To make himself feel better, he grabbed a mop which leaned against the wall near the light switch.

"Is anybody there?" He took a step forward and listened.

Aw, it was likely only a rat or a big mouse. It was getting so the rat poison he set out didn't do any good any more. The rodents were becoming immune. He was going to ask the pastor for a cat.

"A cat will take care of you, Mr. Rat," he said.

He leaned the mop back against the wall and started to go when he caught a movement out of the corner of his eye. It looked like the shadow of a man!

"Who are you?" he demanded once more. "Come on out of there."

Nothing.

"Look, if you're just lookin' for a place to stay, man, George will help you. I'll take you up to the kitchen and give you something to eat. Wouldn't that be good?"

Still nothing.

"All right. All right, play your way. Old George will just go up and call the police, that's what I'll do."

No answer. No movement. He had just imagined he had seen something. It was no wonder—this place gave him the creeps.

He turned toward the steps, glad to be getting out of there. Suddenly, he heard footsteps rushing at him from behind. He wanted to wheel, to see who it was, but a powerful arm seized him from behind. There was the flash of a knife blade streaking down, and he saw it plunge into his own stomach.

Oh, Lord, help me! he thought. Strangely, he felt no pain. Only the unrelenting grasp of the arm. Only the hand clamped tightly over his mouth, cutting his wind.

He struggled to breathe. The hand wouldn't let him. The room grew darker around him. Darker and darker.

"Praise be to Abba," a voice whispered. It was the last thing George Washington Isaiah Perkins heard.

9:51 a.m.

Again and again and again. The knife rose and fell, and he was provoked by it, stimulated by it, spiritualized by it. The very act of killing was an act of praying, an act of power, a catharsis of the soul.

At first, the body convulsed, strained against his grasp. It had a life and a will of its own. A will he conquered, a life he claimed for his own ends. Then the body no longer moved and acted on its own. He had transformed it into a mass of dead weight and pulp.

"Praise be to Abba. Praise be to Abba. Praise be to Abba!" A cry penetrated the spell, and the prayer was his own.

"Stop it!" another voice said harshly. "Stop it, Brother Bartholomew! He's dead. Can't you see? He's dead."

Bartholomew came back to himself, back to the boiler room, back from the trance of the knife and the blood. He was weak, drenched in sweat.

It was Brother Nathanael who stood next to him, who pried loose the arm lock. The body collapsed on the floor.

"Get hold of yourself, Brother. Someone might hear."

Bartholomew nodded, his senses still stunned, still drunk with the act.

"Brother Philip," Nathanael expelled a loud whisper

toward the alcove behind the furnace. "Brother Philip, get out here."

Slowly, Philip emerged from the shadows. He moved fearfully, clutching the AR-15 automatic rifle in front of him as if to shield himself. Seeing him, the rage was born anew in Bartholomew. "You," he muttered. "You gave us away."

He lunged, his anger spilling out, the knife raised. Philip shrank from him, his face white, his eyes ballooning with panic.

Brother Nathanael stepped between them, ducking under the thrust of Bartholomew's knife. There was a pain in Bartholomew's wrist as Nathanael grabbed it and twisted. The knife fell free, its blade breaking on the concrete floor.

In the next instant, Bartholomew was staggered by a smashing blow of Nathanael's fist that sent him sprawling backward. He grabbed wildly to keep from going down, caught one of the pipes, and clung to it desperately while fighting to keep at bay the blackness which threatened to consume him.

"I couldn't . . . couldn't help it!" Brother Philip was pleading, his lower lip trembling.

Vision clearing, the wave of dizziness abating, Bartholomew choked, "If you hadn't moved, he wouldn't have seen you."

"Stop it, both of you!" Nathanael's dictate echoed harshly. "Philip, guard the stairs. I said, guard the stairs! If anyone heard us, they'll be down on top of us any minute."

Brother Philip hesitated. He eyed the dead body and the pool of red forming beneath it.

"Move!" Nathanael hammered.

Brother Philip gave a sharp sob, then sidled around the victim and took up a position at the bottom of the steps. Glowering at him, Bartholomew saw his shoulders shudder and heave with weeping.

"A fine Guardian he is," he spat, tasting now the salt of his own blood. Nathanael's blow had opened a cut inside his mouth.

"He'll do, you'll see," Nathanael said.

Bartholomew released his hold on the pipe and took an unsteady step. He nudged the body with his toe.

"Foolish man," he cursed. "Stupid Infidel."

"You did the right thing," Nathanael said, laying a comforting hand on Bartholomew's shoulder. "He'd have called the police."

At that moment, Brother Bartholomew saw the corpse clearly for the first time. He saw the blood spattered everywhere—on the walls, the floor, the pipes, his own hands. His nostrils filled with the smell of death. He retched.

When the vomiting had spent itself he wiped his mouth with the back of his hand. "I never killed a man before. Not this way. Not this way."

"Abba will be pleased with you," Nathanael said quietly.

"But what if someone else comes down here? What if they come looking for him?"

"Then they will die, too."

"Shouldn't we . . . shouldn't we do something with him?"

"Let him lie. There's nothing more to do but wait." Nathanael picked up his own rifle from where it had fallen in the fray. He gave Bartholomew another pat on the shoulder and took a place beside Philip, watching up the stairway.

Wait. They had been waiting since early last night in this dungeon when they had broken into the church. It had been a sleepless night with the spiders and the mice. Now, the wait was almost ended.

In just a little while, a very little while, the flower truck would arrive. That would be the next big step. And, if someone else came in the meantime, he, Bartholomew, would kill him, too. Nothing could interfere with their assignment. Nothing. At 11:20, they must begin their sweep of the building to secure it for Abba and his squadron.

If Brother Philip wasn't up to the task, then he, Brother Bartholomew, would have to make up for it. For the love of Abba, he would.

10:04 a.m.

Malcolm Stansfield slid as quietly as he could into a chair at the very back of the room and watched Harold Thomas over the heads of the very pleasing crowd of young people. Their rapt attention was upon Thomas, who stood at the lectern.

"After my deprogrammers got me to start thinking for myself again, they gave me a Bible," Thomas was telling the youth. "And I began to read it like I'd never read it before. I began to understand that God loved me and had a plan for my life. But I realized that the Bible also said I was separated from that love by my own sin. I was sinful by nature. And that kept me from the true holiness of God. But the cross of Christ had torn down that wall. All I had to do was accept Christ as the Saviour He was and is and I would be set free from the consequences of my past sins, and more than that, my future sins. I was set free once and for all from the terrible influence of the Brotherhood."

Thomas paused. The audience was silent. No one moved. Their united enthrallment was upon the young man and the words he had spoken. It was a holy moment, a moment none could presume to break.

Malcolm was pleased and deeply touched all at once. If the rest of Cult Sunday was a failure, this one experience would make it a success.

Even when Thomas began speaking again, the power of the instant hung on. "Are there any questions? . . . I hope."

His smile and delivery brought a titter of sympathetic laughter.

Several hands went up. Thomas pointed toward a studious young man in brass-rimmed glasses who rose to his feet. Since Malcolm did not recognize him, he assumed he was a visitor, one of the many in the room.

"Your personal story is very moving, Mr. Thomas," the young man said, his manner modulated. "However, if I may play devil's advocate for a moment, when you accepted Jesus Christ, didn't you just exchange one cult for another?"

"Not at all," Thomas said evenly. "First John, 5:20 says, 'This is the true God, and eternal life.' That is said of Jesus. Over and over again, the Bible confirms that statement. It says, 'Christ is Lord of all.' Thus, if I am a true follower, a true believer in Him, I follow the true God. A cult deviates from that in some way or other."

"But hasn't it also been said, 'all roads which lead to God are good roads'?" the young man debated.

"Not in the Bible," Thomas said. "In John 14:6, Christ Himself proclaimed, 'I am the way, the truth and the life: no man cometh unto the Father, but by me.'"

Malcolm led the applause, but the young man with the brass-rimmed glasses shouted over it, "That seems very narrow, very exclusive."

As the applause died, Thomas quoted, "'Narrow is the way—'"

"Yes, I've heard that," the young man cut him off. "I'll even grant it's in the Bible. But it seems to me to obviate all the good in all the other great religions of the world. Jesus made an exclusive claim for himself. How is that any different than the claim this Abba you once followed made for himself?"

"Christ gave Himself," Thomas said, "Abba takes for himself. Which is the most Biblical view? Christ's. The entire Bible talks of one Messiah. If you read it carefully, completely, Jesus is the only one who fits all the requirements of that Messiah."

"That's if you take the Bible as the *literal* Word of God," the young man retorted impudently.

"Yes," Thomas agreed. "And, I challenge you to read it from cover to cover, keeping an open mind. I think you'll come to see why Jesus is no mere cult leader."

"You're asking me to deny my own intellect," the young man was on the defensive.

"On the contrary. I'm challenging you to use your intellect, the brains God gave you, to seek the truth from the only valid source."

The applause was wild and spontaneous. Malcolm found himself whispering, "Amen."

The young man's face reddened. He sat down. *May God use this to reach you,* Malcolm prayed.

Other hands shot up. But before Thomas could recognize anyone, Malcolm saw Ruth Evans, his secretary, standing in the door and motioning for him.

He slid from his seat as a young girl was asking Harold Thomas, "Do you really believe the Brotherhood brainwashed you?"

"You could call it that," Thomas nodded. "But in reality, they utilized my thirst for the truth of life, coupled with my complete lack of knowledge about Christian doctrine and my desire for love and . . ."

Harold Thomas' answer faded from hearing, as Malcolm closed the classroom door and joined Ruth Evans in the hall.

Ruth was young, vivacious and lovely. Too lovely, some said, to be a pastor's secretary. But Malcolm disregarded the gossip. He knew Ruth to be intelligent, firm in the Lord, and very good with detail and people. All the qualities that any good pastor's secretary must possess.

"Why didn't you tell me that you'd scheduled a wedding for this afternoon?" she chided with a smile.

"A wedding?" Malcolm searched his memory. "I didn't schedule any wedding."

"But you must have. Don't tell me you forgot?"

Malcolm fished his pocket calendar from inside his suit coat and flipped it open to the date. "There's no wedding on my calendar," he said, showing her the page.

"But there must be. The florist is downstairs right now."

"Did you check the church calendar?"

Ruth looked hurt at Malcolm's question. "Of course."

"And?"

"If there was a wedding on it, do you think I'd be up here troubling you?"

"Then the florist has made a mistake, Ruth. That's the only logical explanation."

"They insist they haven't."

"*They*?"

"Actually, they're the florist's delivery men. And they act like I'm the one who has made the error. Could you talk with them?"

"Get George. He'll handle it for you."

"I can't find him. I hunted all over the building before I came for you. I knew he'd know whether or not there was a wedding. George always knows those things. But I couldn't seem to locate him."

"Okay. Okay, you win," Malcolm said. "Where are they?"

"At the east alley entrance," Ruth said. "Oh, and when you're finished with them, there's a reporter from *Newstime* waiting to see you in your office."

"Tell him I'll be right there," Malcolm said. Dick Whiting really *had* gotten the news magazine to cover the event. Malcolm whistled to himself. This thing was getting bigger and better all the time.

The florist's white panel truck was backed up to the entrance in the alley, as Ruth had said it would be. The two clean-cut young delivery men had already unloaded several long, sealed boxes of cut flowers and had put them in a storage room just off the back of the sanctuary.

"There must be some mistake," Malcolm told them.

"That's what the lady said," the chunky delivery boy said. "But there's no mistake. See?"

He waved an order form at Malcolm. The form had plainly written in large block letters, "Deliver flowers to First Church for 3 p.m. wedding."

"We do what the order says," the delivery boy stated.

"I'm afraid the order is incorrect," Malcolm contended. "You'll have to take these flowers back."

"Can't do that," the delivery boy said. "Don't have the authority."

"Well, who does have the authority?" Malcolm demanded. He didn't like the young man's attitude.

"The boss. You'll have to talk to the boss."

"How do I do that? Does he have a name? A telephone number where he can be reached? I'll call him right now."

"Can't," the delivery boy shook his head. "He's out of town for the weekend."

"There are a lot of flowers here," Malcolm tried a different approach. "How will your boss like it if they wilt and go to waste, because you delivered them to the wrong church? He could wind up losing a lot of money."

The delivery man mulled it over. His partner said, "We could be in a lot of trouble, Jack."

The first delivery man rubbed his jaw. "The designer is supposed to be here at 1:00. Maybe he would have the authority."

"I imagine he does," Malcolm said. "So, why don't you just take these flowers back until then?"

"Can't," the delivery boy said, beginning to sound as if he was a broken record. "We'll have to leave 'em here, like we were ordered to do. But we'll come back at 1:00."

"If that's what you want to do," Malcolm said. "But the church can't be responsible."

"Right," the delivery boy said as he pulled another carton from the truck.

Malcolm left them and headed toward his office and the reporter from *Newstime*. He couldn't know the boxes contained something other than flowers, and that the white panel truck would later be found abandoned on Washington Street.

10:16 a.m.

The reporter from *Newstime* was waiting in one of the chairs in the outer office by Ruth's desk. He was not what Malcolm had anticipated.

The man was thin and nervous. His head seemed oversized for his neck, the scrawniness of which was accentuated by the thick turtleneck that hugged his throat. The features of his face were dwarfed by the bulbous nose which did not, itself, appear compatible with the thinning hair combed carefully down in bangs over the high forehead.

His clothing was as mismatched as his physical countenance. The Harris Tweed jacket with leather patches at the elbow and the brands of several cigarette burns, clashed with the brown checkered slacks. Over his shoulder, the man carried a tote bag of the type which always reminded Malcolm of a woman's purse.

With glasses perched on the end of that massive proboscis, the man was intently studying notes scrawled on a small yellow pad as Malcolm entered.

"Hello, I'm Malcolm Stansfield." Malcolm extended his hand.

The reporter pushed his glasses up and settled them on top of his head as a movie starlet might do. He looked at

Malcolm's hand with disinterest, then took it and gave it a limp shake without rising from the chair in which he slouched.

"Hi." His vocal quality was nasal. "Warren. *Newstime.*"

"Well, come in, Mr. Warren." Malcolm's gesture marshaled Warren from his chair into Malcolm's private chamber.

"Sit down," Malcolm offered.

"Prefer to stand," Warren said pacing, idly glancing around the room. "Nice. Very nice. Do you mind if I smoke?"

"I'm sorry, but smoking isn't allowed anywhere on the church premises."

"Against your religion, huh? Some churches aren't so strict. They're more modern, if you know what I mean. Once even saw a minister smoking his pipe in the sanctuary before a service."

"I don't think we're old-fashioned," Malcolm said. "I prefer to believe we're enlightened in principle."

"No offense," Warren shrugged. He took a stick of gum from his pocket, unwrapped it and stuffed it between his lips. Chewing in tight noisy chomps, he wadded the wrapper in a hard little ball and rolled it absently between his thumb and forefinger.

"May I dispose of that for you?" Malcolm asked, forcing himself to be polite toward a man he had already decided he did not particularly care for.

"What?"

"The wrapper."

"Oh, no. Save it." Warren rammed the wrapper into his jacket pocket, and there, out of sight of Malcolm's gaze, he continued to roll the ball in his fingers.

"We're glad you could be with us today, Mr. Warren," Malcolm said as cordially as he could. "Did you have a nice flight?"

"What makes you think I flew in?"

"The bag," Malcolm said.

"Oh, my tote. Guess it is misleading. Fact is, I'm local. A stringer. I'm with *Newstime,* not from *Newstime.*"

"I see," Malcolm said.

"No, you don't," Warren said brusquely. "It's okay, most people don't understand. I'm a free-lancer. Write for the confession mags mostly. But *Newstime* pays me a few bucks a month—a retainer—to send them a short squib from time to time. They hardly ever use my stuff, but it helps pay the rent."

"In any event, we're glad to have you." Malcolm was beginning to wonder just what it was that Warren wanted.

"Frankly, I came to do this story, 'cause I haven't sent 'em a single word this month. Figured if I didn't send 'em something, they might decide they can get along without me. Besides, I owed Dick Whiting a favor."

Malcolm perched himself on the edge of the cluttered desk. "I think you'll find it interesting."

"Sure," Warren was unimpressed. "Editors are always interested in cults and the 'born again' stuff. I mean, I figure it's at least worth a try. Right?"

Malcolm didn't know what to say. Warren cracked his gum and the sound grated on Malcolm's nerves. He had a lot to do and a very short time to do it in. He wished Warren would come to the point and get it over with, whatever it was he was after.

"Tell me, Stansfield," Warren smacked his lips. "What brand are you?"

"Brand?"

"Denomination. You know, brand? Baptist, Methodist, Holy Roller, what?"

"This church is non-denominational."

Warren made a note on his pad. "A little something for everyone, huh, Stansfield?"

"No. We teach the whole Word of God here. We are believers in Christ as our personal Saviour. We practice baptism by immersion. We—"

"I get the picture," Warren stopped him. "How would you characterize yourself, Stansfield?"

"I beg your pardon?"

"You know, are you conservative? Flamboyant?"

"Well, I—"

"Flamboyant. I think that's what you are. Flamboyant and born again kinda' go together. Make good copy."

Malcolm looked down at his dark, three-piece suit and somber tie. Flamboyant? He had to smile to himself.

"Just put me down as a fundamental, Bible-believing Christian, Mr. Warren. That's enough label for me."

"Huh? No, I think flamboyant is better." Warren wrote again on his pad.

"Now, see here, Mr. Warren," Malcolm's dander began to rise, "I'd want you to write a fair and objective story about this church and about me. I don't wish to appear rude, but I don't want to be something just because it's good copy either."

"No problem. The story isn't about you, anyway. You're just background," Warren said, unfazed. "The story is the kid Thomas. Tell me, is there a press section, Stansfield?"

"No, no press section. You're free to sit anywhere, go anywhere you choose."

"Too bad. Most big churches have a special section set aside on days like this, just for pros like me. Got any handouts?"

"You've got me again, Mr. Warren."

"You know, a canned release, a fact sheet, a press kit. Anything like that?"

"Only the material Dick Whiting sent me when we first invited Mr. Thomas to speak. Oh, and copies of the advertisements we've been running this week. I could have my secretary run a copy of those for you."

"Whiting has already given me enough of that stuff to keep me in tissue paper for a year. Thanks for the interview."

Interview? Malcolm didn't feel he had given an interview. What kind of reporter was this?

"A piece of advice, Stansfield," Warren offered from the door. "Get a professional P.R. man. You need it."

Ruth squeezed by him on her way in as Warren was on the way out.

"You look like you just ate a lemon," she said to Malcolm.

"Ruth, you've worked for me long enough to know I sincerely try to find something good in everyone. But I'm having a hard time doing it with that man."

Ruth grinned, "And I thought it was just me."

"Maybe I'm getting too old," he grew reflective, "but I don't know if I can ever get used to dealing with agents and reporters. Sometimes, I think we're making Christianity a circus, and church a pale imitation of television in our great quest to be relevant."

"He really got to you, didn't he?" Ruth said.

"He's that kind of fellow, Ruth. That kind of fellow." He hesitated. "Would you . . . would you consider me to be 'flamboyant'?"

"Is that what he said?" she couldn't hide her amusement.

"An exact quote, except when he said it, he made it sound as if I was some flimflam artist."

"Don't let it worry you, boss. He was off base."

"If I'm not flamboyant, what am I, then? How do you see me, Ruth?"

"Behind schedule," she quipped, then changed the subject by holding up the manila file folder she carried. "Want to see the preliminary attendance report on Sunday school?"

"You tell me," Malcolm said, crossing to the window and peering out at the street. He was looking for the squad car the police had promised.

"We're substantially ahead of the year's record,

especially in the youth and college departments."

"Praise God." He smiled, still watching the street. The traffic was heavier now. People were looking for parking places. That was a good sign.

"Put the report on my desk, would you, please, Ruth?"

"Sure. What did you do about the flowers, boss?"

"The flowers? Nothing. They insisted on leaving them. We'll have to ask George to wait after the service is over until the designer shows up. The designer seems to be the only one with the authority to recognize a mistake in delivery."

He turned away from the street. Ruth was straightening the papers on his desk.

"Did Miriam and the kids get here all right?" he asked. "I've been too busy to notice."

"Yes. They came while you were taking Mr. Thomas up to the college department. Miriam said they'd see you after—" She froze.

"Ruth? What is it?"

"Look . . . look there," she stammered.

Malcolm followed her gaze. There, on the desk top which had been hidden by the scattered papers, was chalked a Star of David with a cross drawn through it.

10:24 a.m.

"Religious Ghetto calling Television Land. Come in, Base."

At the summons of the squawk box from the shortwave radio, Wally Nichols put down his *Model Railroad* magazine and scowled. When would Roger Uttenmeyer ever learn to use the appropriate call number designations as required by FCC rules? The boys at the Federal Communications Commission frowned on clowning over the two-ways. And, if Roger was ever caught doing so, the station would be reported. Wally didn't even like to think of the ramifications that might bring.

But, who was Wally to tell Roger that? Roger was the chief engineer of KBEX-TV and Wally's superior. Roger should know better than anyone about FCC rules. The trouble with Roger was, he was an easygoing, fun-loving individualist who somehow seemed to Wally to be a misfit in the relatively cut-and-dried technical world of television electronics.

This morning, however, Roger was in his element, acting not so much as an engineer, but as the director for the remote telecast from First Church. That irked Wally, too. Here was Roger, virtually a member of management, picking up the overtime and extra pay which more properly should belong to one of Wally's fellow technical engineers.

Wally also knew why Roger always gave himself the assignment. Roger had eight kids to support, and he wasn't even Catholic. A man should have a greater sense of responsibility toward a world faced with the prospect of overpopulation.

Thus it was with a sense of irritation that Wally picked up the microphone, depressed the talk button, and clearly and distinctly identified both the receiving and sending radio call letters.

"Good morning, Wally," Roger sounded bright and sunny. "For a minute there, I thought you weren't going to answer me. How are things in Master Control?"

"All right," Wally answered with a begrudging civility. "How are you, Roger?"

"Cramped, how else?"

Roger's reply made Wally chuckle in spite of himself. Once, out of curiosity, he had stopped by First Church to see the setup for the telecasts. He had found oversized Roger stuffed in an undersized cubbyhole off the church's balcony along with two camera monitors and a field switcher.

On that occasion, Roger had complained jokingly that there wasn't enough room for him to put on the headset of the intercom by which he could give directions to the two cameramen.

"I bruise my tongue every time I talk," Roger had cackled.

Now, over the shortwave he said, "We have the cameras fired up. Would it be too much to ask, Wally, for you to check the signal we're sending your way?"

That was another thing about Roger which got to Wally. The man could never ask a simple question without stretching it out with words that didn't belong. Why couldn't he say, "Check the signal"? Why did he always have to talk as if he were speaking to a novice?

Wally pushed a button on his master switcher and looked up at the remote monitor in the battery of television screens before him.

He studied it a second, then said to the shortwave microphone, "Signal looks A-OK."

That's how a television technician should talk, Wally thought. The picture was being beamed to the station via microwave. A large "dish" had been installed on the roof of the church, aimed at a similar antenna on the roof of the station. Once in a while, the dishes were knocked out of line by wind or vibration, but this morning, everything was in order.

"That's Camera One," Roger informed him. "Now, here's Camera Two."

The picture on the remote monitor went from one view of the empty sanctuary to another. The second picture lacked definition.

"Who's on Two?" Wally inquired.

"Dave."

"Mighta' known. Have him put on the color bars and we'll see if we can't make that camera better."

There was a pause while Roger relayed the instructions to his cameraman, then a set of vertical color stripes appeared on Wally's screen.

Wally got up from his chair and went over to a rack of instruments. He tweaked a few knobs and asked for Dave to do the same with controls on the camera.

It took a few more adjustments before Wally was satisfied. He had Roger ask Camera Two to return to taking a picture of the sanctuary. It looked much better.

Just to be certain, Wally had Roger switch rapidly back and forth between the two cameras while they zoomed in and out with their lenses. The levels matched reasonably well.

"Great," Roger said. "I'm having Dave lock his camera

down and go check the mikes on the podium. It'll take a few minutes for him to get there from the balcony. We'll send you a sound check after your station break at the half hour."

"Right," Wally sighed and signed off with his shortwave call letters.

Roger failed to give his, but Wally had no time to worry about it. The red digital clock told him that the 10:30 station break was only five seconds away.

Quickly checking his log against the preview monitor's computer readout, he was relieved to see that Peloubet in the tape room had the four announcements loaded in the correct order. At least, some people at KBEX knew proper procedures.

The air monitor faded to black as the program material ended and Wally dissolved to the first spot. It was the commercial for Stansfield's Cult Sunday.

Wally gritted his teeth. That commercial had run nine times this morning alone. It was enough to drive a man to distraction.

"Your sins shall not go unpunished," he said to the television screen. He meant it to be a derisive comment. Instead, it would turn out to be the closest thing to prophecy Wally Nichols had ever uttered.

10:41 a.m.

Malcolm watched as Ruth Evans applied the pungent-smelling cleaner to his desk top and began to rub at the strange composite symbol soaped there. He had the feeling he should somehow know what that symbol meant.

"That George Perkins is never around when you need him most," Ruth complained, smarting at the fact she had had to fetch the cleaner and the rag from the first floor janitor's closet. More than that, Malcolm guessed, she was upset that he overruled her on calling the police.

"Oh, now, Ruth," Malcolm clucked, "George is a good man and a very good janitor, and you know it."

"Just the same, he's never around when you need him," she grumbled.

"Here, I don't mind doing that," Malcolm volunteered reaching for the cloth in Ruth's hand.

"It wouldn't be proper," Ruth said stubbornly.

"What? For a minister to get his hands dirty? A little dirt on the hands never harmed the soul," he jested.

Ruth didn't laugh. She continued to rub vigorously at one point of the Jewish star. "Well, one good thing," she announced, "I don't think it scratched the desk. I think it's soap instead of chalk. Who do you suppose would do such a crazy, wicked thing, anyway?"

"Kids, I suppose," Malcolm ventured. He knew he should be angry that someone had violated the sanctity of his private office, and, perhaps, that they should call the police. But he had already done that once this day. They had patronized him then—what would they think of him now?

Nothing had been taken, as far as he could determine. No real damage had been done. There were no broken windows, no forced locks. The matter was really inconsequential; trivial, when stacked against the other problems of the day.

"Vandals!" Ruth's sudden outburst broke in on his thoughts, almost as if she had been reading them. "That's what they are. I still think you should have let me call the police."

"Over what? A harmless prank?" Malcolm's internal contentions became verbal. "And what could they do, Ruth? Search every youngster in Sunday school until they found one with a piece of chalk or a chunk of soap squirreled away?"

"You're right," Ruth said, "but if we let them get away with drawing on your desk, no telling what they'll do next time."

"I don't like the idea of having a juvenile delinquent on the loose any more than you do," Malcolm admitted. "But, I was young once, myself. I did some pretty dumb things. God dealt with my conscience. He'll deal with the kid or kids who did this."

Ruth stopped rubbing and looked up at him. "You aren't going to do anything, then?"

"I'm going to start keeping my office door locked and my eyes open. We'll catch them eventually."

"I should hope so," Ruth said. "Such a weird thing to draw on a person's desk, anyway. What's it supposed to mean?"

Malcolm frowned. He had seen something like that

symbol before. In recent years, some Jews who had accepted Christ as Messiah had sported the symbol to designate that they were "saved Jews." But who would use it in this vandalistic manner? To Ruth he said, "I don't know. I guess we should just be thankful that whoever did it has at least been to Sunday school enough to use religious marks for their graffiti."

"There," Ruth gave a deep breath, "it's off."

"Thank you," Malcolm said. "Let's get on with the morning's business."

"I'll have George put a coat of polish on it tomorrow." Ruth closed the cap on the liquid cleaner.

The sound of a bell echoed through the building, proclaiming the end of the Sunday school hour.

"My word, is it that time already?" Ruth scooped up the rag and flew from the office.

For a moment, Malcolm fingered the spot on the desk where the Star of David and its Christian cross had been. What else was his memory trying to tell him about that mark?

The class bell rang a second time and he lost the thought in the new excitement that beat through him. It was almost time. After all the planning, all the praying, all the effort, the big service was at hand.

Rushing himself now, Malcolm moved to the office closet and opened the door. He glanced at himself in the small mirror he kept there, took a comb from his inside breast pocket and ran it through his graying hair, patting a few unruly strands in their place with his free hand.

In a few moments, Harold Thomas, Dick Whiting and the assistant pastors would be returning for another prayer before they went together to the sanctuary. This was Malcolm's favorite time of any Sunday morning, the moment of anticipation when hope was the greatest.

He put the comb away, shut the closet door and strode to his desk. He extracted his sermon notes from his coat pocket and put them in his Bible at the book of Jude.

He was just closing the Bible when Joseph Holmes came boiling in without so much as a knock on the door.

"Where is that fellow?" Holmes demanded.

"What fellow do you mean, Joseph?"

"You know perfectly well, preacher. That fellow George." The old man banged his cane on the carpet as he said the name.

"He's around somewhere," Malcolm said. "What's the problem, Joseph? Something I can help you with?"

"Find me that janitor. I sent him down to check on the furnace. Told him to report to me after Sunday school. He knew where to find me, and he didn't have the common courtesy to show up."

"I'm sorry, Joseph," Malcolm placated. "He's probably gotten tied up on another emergency."

"Like thunder!" Holmes boomed. "He didn't do what I told him to do, and now he's afraid to face me."

"Oh, I don't think so, Joseph. He's not like that."

"Fuss and feathers, he isn't. I always have to get after him to check the furnace. He'd even forget to oil the darned old thing, if I didn't remind him. He's got all the sense and dependability of a hammer-headed mule. You're gonna' have to have a talk with that ol' boy, Malcolm. If you're too soft to do it, I will."

"I'll look into it, Joseph, first chance I get," Malcolm pledged. He hoped it would assuage the trustee's anger, calm him down before the others arrived.

But there was never any calming a riled Joseph Holmes. "You do that, preacher," he ranted. "In the meantime, I'm gonna' do what I shoulda' done in the first darn place. I'm gonna' hike down there and have a look-see in that sub-basement myself."

10:54 a.m.

Joseph Holmes charged from the pastor's office in a blind rage. He hit the hallway, his cane tapping a furious warning on the tile floor with each lunging step to those who might foolishly hazard getting in his way.

The cheek of that George! To disobey a direct order from Joseph Pardee Holmes was the epitome of insolence. It just wasn't done. Ever! Joseph Holmes did not brook insubordination from underlings or horses.

Even if he weren't a man of power, the old man reasoned, even if this church hadn't been built by Holmes money, even if he didn't practically own this building—if not actually—even if he wasn't a close friend of senators and congressmen, even if he hadn't been invited to the White House many times by personal invitation of the President, he would think George Perkins would have the courtesy to do what he had asked out of deference to his obviously superior age and station.

Joseph Holmes wished George Perkins were a horse. He'd jam a spade bit in his mouth and plow-rein him until he learned his place and some manners.

Why, that janitor had ruined Sunday. How could he ever sit in his favorite pew and know the security of being Joseph Holmes and the peace of worshiping Joseph

Holmes' God, after the scurrilous behavior of that janitor?

Fuss and feathers, it wasn't fair. It wasn't fair at all for a man of his advanced position in life—a Holmes—to have to traipse down to the basement to check the darn boiler as if he were some plain ol' field hand. To have to go way down there, with his bad knees, was unthinkable. But it had to be done.

George Perkins didn't understand. Nobody understood. That boiler was old and worn out. Sure, he could have purchased the church a new one with his pocket change. Sure, he could do that and folks would love him for it. But it was time these good people learned to do for themselves. He was getting to be an old man. They weren't gonna' have Joseph Pardee Holmes to look after them—to think for them—much longer.

Why, they should get a fund drive going. That old boiler was liable to blow anytime. Didn't they care about that? Hadn't they read what could happen when a boiler exploded with fire and destruction almost as bad as the preacher spoke about?

Sure they had, but they didn't care. They didn't believe it could happen to them. And it wouldn't, because Joseph Holmes cared. He'd look after them. He'd play the part of the clown for their sakes.

Well, he told himself, there would be stars in his crown when he got to heaven, bought and paid for by Holmes' money and Holmes' sweat and Holmes' caring. Stars in his crown. That was one consola—

He bumped into a big young man with wide shoulders, a man who hadn't gotten out of his way in time as he came barreling into the narthex.

"Excuse me, Mr. Holmes."

Who was this? The face seemed familiar. Brown? Yes, Brown, that was it.

"I don't know if you remember me, Mr. Holmes," the face said. "I'm Stan Brown."

"Sure, I remember you," Joseph Holmes said. "You laid some brick when I built that new tack house last spring."

"Yes, sir, that's me." Brown was pleased. "And this is my wife, Peggy."

The woman was pretty enough, Holmes supposed. But she looked tired and worn.

"So, how are you, Mr. Holmes?"

"Sorry, Brown. I haven't got time to talk now. I gotta' go down and check on the boiler."

"You, Mr. Holmes? The boiler?"

"Can't get anyone else to do it."

"I'd be glad to do it," Stan Brown said eagerly.

"You know about boilers, do you?" Holmes searched the young, suntanned face.

"A little," Brown said.

"I know a lot," Holmes spit. "Thanks anyway, I'd better do it myself. Nice to meet you, Mrs. Brown."

Fuss and feathers. People annoyed Joseph Holmes. They were always fawning over him, trying to please him. And he knew why. They wanted a favor, some of his money. That young bricklayer Brown was no different.

Sure, he could let the young man go down and check the furnace. But what good would that do? How could he be certain the bricklayer would know trouble if he saw it?

Besides, Joseph Holmes had an ulterior motive. He suspected that no-good janitor was hiding down there. He could hardly wait to give George Perkins a piece of the famous Holmes mind.

He was only two steps down on the way to the basement when Kate Holmes caught up with him.

"Joseph? Joseph, where are you going?"

He looked at his wife, still tall and willowy, her hair swept up as the Gibson girls of an earlier age used to wear their hair, and he melted.

"I'm going down to check the boiler," he said softly.

"Don't be silly, Joseph, you're not going to do any such

thing. All those stairs. Why, land, you wouldn't be able to walk for a week. Your knees just can't take it."

"Aw, Kate," he moaned. "Somebody has got to take a look-see at that old pile of metal. It might blow or something."

"Now, Joseph, you're being silly. Let the janitor do it."

"But, Kate, I—"

"Come along, Joseph. We don't want to be late for the service. And smile. These folks will think you're nothing but an old grouch."

And so, Joseph Holmes, the scion of the church's oldest family, the man of wealth and power, the friend of senators and congressmen, the man whom the President called "Joe," was led through the narthex by his wife as if he were a gentle colt broke to the lead rope.

Charlie Elliott, the middle-aged sales manager of Holmes & Pardee Manufacturing, was the usher who greeted them by the door to the middle aisle. He smiled and led them to their pew seven rows from the front.

There was a young couple sitting there on the aisle. Charlie bent down, smiling, and whispered to them.

The girl shook her head and Charlie came up looking sheepish. "They won't move, Mr. Holmes," he said timidly. "I told them this pew was always reserved for you, but they won't scoot over."

"It's all right, Charlie," Kate cooed, "we'll sit a pew ahead this morning."

"We will not," Joseph hissed. "I'll handle this."

"Oh, for pity's sake, Joseph," Kate protested. But on this point, not even her charm could stop him.

He leaned down slightly. "Folks, my name is Joseph Pardee Holmes. You must be visitors, 'cause all the regular members know this pew is mine. My daddy bought it and paid for it way back yonder. And from that day to this, come Sunday morning, there's been a Holmes sitting in it here on the aisle."

"We were here first," the girl said coldly.

"Wrong, Miss. The Holmeses have been here since the very beginning. Now, you're welcome to slide over and stay, if you want. But the two seats you're sitting in now, are mine."

The girl glowered at him and started to say something, but the young man stopped her.

"Let's not cause a scene, Sandra," he said.

The girl looked over at him, surprised, but she moved and so did he. Joseph, feeling victory, stepped aside and gestured for Kate to sit.

"I'm so embarrassed, Joseph," Kate scolded as she went past him and took her seat. She said it loud enough for the young couple to hear.

"This is our place, Kate," he defended, plopping down beside her on the aisle where he belonged.

Kate turned and whispered to the young man, "I'm Kate Holmes, and I do apologize for my husband. Sometimes, he thinks he owns this church. But don't hold that against us. We're really very friendly people here at First."

The young man gave her a quick smile, but the girl continued to stare straight ahead, snubbing her.

Joseph was glad that the organist began the prelude at that moment, making further conversation between his wife and himself impossible. Kate would forget all about it by the end of the service. As far as being sorry about anything, Joseph Holmes was not.

Suddenly, the bright lights for the television cameras came on. He shaded his eyes from the glare. He tolerated those lights, because they were necessary, but that didn't mean he had to like them. Against the starkness of the marble walls, their brightness was uncomfortable. And, even in the wintertime, they made the sanctuary so hot the air conditioner had to be run.

Fuss and feathers. He had forgotten to have the air conditioning checked this morning. But when he considered it, what difference did it make? The unchecked boiler would probably blow anyway.

The choir entered the loft and the preacher and the guest speaker and the two assistant ministers trooped out on the platform looking to Joseph as if they were a bunch of trained gorillas. He'd have to speak to Malcolm Stansfield about that.

Gil Anderson approached the microphone on the podium. "Good morning," he smiled, "I'm Gil Anderson, the assistant pastor of First Church. Welcome to all of you, our members and guests, whether you're here with us in the sanctuary or viewing at home over KBEX Television.

"As you know, this is a very special Sunday for us. We're glad you can be a part of it. Now, let's turn in our hymnals to number 302, 'Amazing Grace.' Let's join our hearts in song as we praise God with His music."

Joseph took a hymnal from the rack in front of him and fumbled through it until he found the right page.

Gil Anderson made a motion and the congregation stood. Joseph Holmes pulled himself to his feet by hanging onto the back of the pew ahead, then extended the hymnal to Kate so they could read the words together.

But Kate pulled the hymnal from his hand and gave it to the young man on her right. If that didn't beat all!

With a sigh of complaint in his wife's direction, Joseph dug another hymnal out of the rack. By the time he found 302 again, the rest of the congregation was already singing—everyone except the young man to whom Kate had given the hymnal, and the young lady with him. Joseph had always had an eye for the ladies, and this girl, while not obviously pretty, did have a kind of fragile old-fashioned loveliness.

But what fascinated Joseph the most about her was the big purse she clutched to her bosom. Why, he wouldn't think a filly that puny would have the strength to lug something that huge around.

It was so big and bulky, you could hide a saddle in there and never miss it. What possessed a gal to carry a purse like that?

He was still musing over the girl and her purse when the hymn ended.

11:00 a.m.

The knell of church bells, put into play by a small console at the pipe organ, floated through the sanctuary calling the faithful to worship.

A hush fell over the crowd, punctuated by a cough here, a clearing of a throat there, the scurrying footsteps of the latecomers rushing to find a seat.

The brilliance of the lights for television blazed down on the platform, their glare hiding the sea of faces from Malcolm's view. But as he sat in his chair, Malcolm knew the house was packed. He could feel the people and hear them despite the dazzling brightness, and his heart rejoiced.

As the last chiming toll died away, Gil Anderson rose from the seat next to Malcolm's and moved to the pulpit.

Malcolm looked up toward the balcony. The television lights could not overpower the circular glow of Joseph Holmes' window. To the left of it, Malcolm saw the tiny red light that came from the shadows beneath the glare. It was the light which announced that the television camera was on and watching.

Gil Anderson had been waiting for that cue, and launched into the welcome in his informal style.

Glancing at his bulletin, Malcolm anticipated the

declaration of the first hymn, and found the page before Gil could give it.

Malcolm responded to Gil's uplifted arms and stood as Gil stepped back from the podium and Allen Lloyd, the minister of music, took his place and gave the downbeat.

> *Amazing grace! how sweet the sound, That saved a wretch like me! . . .*

The swell of the voices was overwhelming. The music bounced from the windowless marble walls at the side of the hall and magnified the sound until the thousand voices echoed as ten thousand.

> *'Twas grace that taught my heart to fear, And grace my fears relieved . . .*

As the second stanza began, Malcolm stole a sideways look at Harold Thomas. The young man's lower lip trembled as he sang, but his eyes glistened with confidence. The boy would be all right.

> *. . . We've no less days to sing God's praise, Than when we first begun. A-men.*

The hymn came to its conclusion. It had certainly been the right note on which to start the service, Malcolm thought. The old familiar hymns were always the best, particularly when the congregation was spotted with so many visitors.

Allen Lloyd ducked his head to the microphone. "Please remain standing."

The minister of youth, John Swallow, was up next. Malcolm liked to give all the pastoral staff an opportunity to participate in the Sunday morning exercises. It not only familiarized the membership with their pastors, it gave the junior men a chance to feel they were making a valid contribution to the church's most public hour.

"Let us bow our heads and unite our hearts in prayer," Swallow said, after clearing his throat.

Malcolm winced. John's introduction sounded a little too pompous, a little too trite. He made a mental note to speak to John and give him a few pointers.

Yet, the prayer itself was well formed and not too long. Malcolm was pleased. A service, he had lectured his assistants, must begin quickly. The opening exercises must move briskly to get people involved. There must be pace to keep them interested, to make them forget their troubles and cares and concentrate on the act of worship.

When he was finished praying, John Swallow smiled toward the audience. "Before you sit down," he said, "turn to those around you and extend the hand of fellowship. Introduce yourselves and make everyone feel welcome."

Additional lights flooded the auditorium for the sake of the television cameras. There was a murmur as people exchanged names and handshakes.

It was the first opportunity Malcolm had to really see the crowd. It was every bit as large as his ears had already told him it was. And, it was particularly gratifying to see so many clean-cut young people present. Such bright, all-American appearing young men and women they were, like the young couple who were shyly accepting Kate Holmes' greeting.

Suddenly, he heard Harold Thomas gasp, "They're here."

Malcolm swung toward Thomas, his eyebrows arched in an unspoken question.

"Sir, the Brotherhood is here," Thomas choked in a whisper.

Malcolm looked back at the audience, but John Swallow was already saying, "You may be seated."

The house lights were turned off and the platform lights

blinded Malcolm once again. This time, the wash of light was not quite as appealing. This time, it seemed to menace.

He fought the sudden, cold trepidation gnawing at the pit of his stomach, and he was acutely aware of the audience watching them, of his responsibility toward them. Above all, he must maintain a normal Sunday platform demeanor. He must keep Thomas and himself from doing anything which might telegraph needless alarm to the congregation.

"Let's not panic," Malcolm whispered as much for himself as the boy. "Now, think carefully, Harold. Are you sure they're really out there, or are you just afraid they are?"

"When the lights were on, I thought I recognized some of their people," Thomas insisted.

"Thought? The mind can play tricks when you're nervous." And to himself, Malcolm said, *Yes, that's probably all it is. This boy is scared to death of the crowd, of speaking before it. Please, Lord, let that be all it is.*

"Maybe you're right." Thomas admitted shakily.

"I know I'm right," Malcolm flashed a confident smile. "Besides, God is with us."

"Yes, He is, sir," Thomas nodded, the fear still evident in his face.

Malcolm settled back in his chair while the choir sang, praying silently, *O Jesus, help this young man to be strong. Calm his fears—and mine, too.*

After the anthem came the responsive reading. Malcolm watched Harold Thomas carefully as the lights in the auditorium were brought up for that. But Thomas did not look back out at the onlookers, nor did he participate in the reading. He kept his head down, his eyes closed in a silent prayer of his own.

He was still praying when Malcolm entered the pulpit for the formal pastoral prayer and to read the scripture from Jude.

In former days, the offering would have come between his prayer and the Scripture reading in the order of worship. However, since the church had begun televising its services, the offering had been moved to come after the sermon. The change had been Malcolm's idea. It insured that the TV public would hear all of his message, without having it cut by the demands of the clock just as he reached his most important point.

The reading completed, Malcolm began his prepared introduction of Harold Thomas.

"This morning, I chanced to meet with our newspaper boy," he opened. He told them how the boy had asked what a cult was, and he gave them his definition, the one over which he had labored only hours before.

He told them why he believed religious cults posed a threat not only to the organized churches of America, but to her individual citizens as well. He quoted some of the statistics and documentation developed during the recent congressional investigations. He expounded on the things the Bible said about false teachers and those who followed them.

The time he had was all too brief. He wanted to say more, but glanced at his watch and knew he had to bring on Thomas. The young man's words would be more effective than his own, he felt, for Thomas had experienced a cult firsthand.

"I have received some criticism this morning," he said, "from some of you who believe our promotion of Cult Sunday has been too strong.

"Some of you would rather a church didn't promote and advertise what it was doing at all. But, I'd like to remind you that it was the church that first introduced the use of a musical jingle to the world of advertising. The church bell."

He paused for the twitter of laughter that ran through the auditorium. "That's right," he continued, "church bells were urging people to attend church long before newspapers or radio or TV were ever invented.

"As someone has said, 'It pays to advertise. So, advertise your praise.'

"Be that as it may, I wish you could've all been in my office this morning and heard the testimony I heard. I wish you could've all been in the High School and College departments during Sunday school this morning. It was a beautiful experience. One our young people profited by, and so did I—thanks to the presence of the young fellow I'm going to introduce to you now.

"Listen to him. Pray for him. Some of what he says will shock you. But, know that what he says is the truth. And know, also, that 'Greater is he that is in you, little children, than he that is in the world.'

"Here, as advertised, is Brother Harold Thomas . . ."

As he stepped aside to motion Harold Thomas to the microphone, Malcolm heard a strange commotion in the audience. What was going on?

Instinctively, he shielded his eyes and tried to see what was happening. He caught only a blur of movement, then a clicking sound.

"What's the matter? Is someone sick?" he asked.

His words were drowned out by a scream.

11:25 a.m.

Peloubet poked his head into Master Control. "Hey, Wally, do you need a break? I'll watch things for awhile, if you want."

"Naw, I'm okay. But I got some coffee left. Want a cup?"

"Sounds good." Peloubet pulled up a chair and dropped down beside Wally at the console. He was a dapper little man whose waxed black mustache matched his French name. He yawned and stretched while Wally poured two cups from the stainless steel Thermos.

The 11 o'clock hour was a lazy time on Sunday morning for the two men. Because of the hour-long church service, there were no breaks to load, no buttons to push. All Wally had to do for those sixty minutes was to occasionally cast an eye on the monitors to make sure KBEX was still on the air.

"Got a brain twister for you," Peloubet said, sipping at his coffee. Riddles and brain twisters were Peloubet's weakness. He was famous for them in virtually every bar in Grunnell.

"What is it?" Wally asked, mildly interested.

"How can you make eights add up to an even thousand?"

Wally sipped his own coffee, mulling the problem over

in his mind. "Say that again, slowly," he said.

"How do you make eights add up to an even thousand?" Peloubet enunciated each word with overexaggerated lip movement. His pencil-thin mustache bobbed with every syllable.

Scratching his head, Wally shrugged. "I give up. How do you make eights add up to an even thousand?"

"Come on, Wally, it's no fun if you don't try to work it out."

"I'm tired. My brain can't take it," Wally protested.

"You're an engineer. We're supposed to be good at math." Peloubet turned over Wally's log to the blank backside. He tapped the paper. "Come on, Wally, put your pencil to use. Get the brain cells to functioning."

"Sadist," Wally chided with a grin. Lethargically, he began to write down a series of figure eights.

"You'll never get it that way," Peloubet said impatiently.

"Give me a hint, then."

"I just did. And that's all the help you're going to get from me."

Wally tried another tack. He wrote down the number *1000,* studied it a second, then scrawled, *1000 ÷ 8 =*

"Uh-huh," Peloubet grunted.

"Oh, for pete's sake." Wally slammed the pencil down.

Peloubet laughed. "Throwing in the towel so soon?"

"Can't we just drink our coffee and visit a little? Why do we always have to play games?"

"Okay, I'll show you and then we'll talk." Peloubet picked up the pencil and set about jotting down the solution.

He was interrupted by Roger Uttenmeyer's distorted voice on the shortwave.

"They got guns!" Roger shouted. "They got guns!"

"What did he say?" Peloubet looked up.

"Aw, don't pay any attention to him. Just Roger's sick idea of a joke," Wally dismissed.

But Peloubet was staring at the monitor. "Crime-in-Italys, that ain't no joke."

Wally blinked at the screen. His eyes were playing tricks. They had to be. Stansfield and two other men stood at the pulpit. One of the men held a weapon, a strange looking cross between a pistol and a rifle.

11:28 a.m.

She had known something was wrong the moment they entered the auditorium. Brother Bartholomew was not at Position 7, holding their seats for them, as she had been told he would. And, yet, by some miracle, no Infidel had occupied the position.

Brother Andrew, her escort, had also felt there was something amiss. While they were still several pews up the aisle from their assigned post, he had grabbed her arm, his strong fingers digging into the fabric of her dress until her skin hurt, and had whispered in her ear, "I don't like it. Maybe it's a trap."

It had still been early then, at least twenty minutes before the service was scheduled to start. Only a few other people were in the sanctuary. Brother Andrew had looked around as if he were a caged animal, scenting the wind for a sign of danger.

Warily, he pushed her into the nearest pew and when they were seated turned to look around again. He nudged her, and with a tilt of his head directed her attention to the left and slightly behind where they sat.

There, she saw Brother John and Sister Joy in Position 13, exactly where they were supposed to be.

"What do you make of it?" she asked.

He put his arm around her and leaned close as if they were lovers exchanging romantic secrets. It gave her an odd feeling. She had not been so intimate with a man since before she joined the Brotherhood.

"Laugh and tell me you love me," he whispered. When she had done it, he smiled for the benefit of any who might be watching. Then he whispered, "It seems all the other Brothers and Sisters are where they should be."

"But where is Brother Bartholomew?" She said it a little too loudly, and he put his finger to her lips to warn her.

"Where is he?" she repeated much more softly.

"I don't know, but I'm going to find out. Tell me you're cold."

"What?"

"No time to explain, just say you're cold. And say it so that anyone who is curious can hear you."

"I'm cold," she said.

"Louder. Call me 'honey'."

"Honey, I'm cold."

"You're right, darling, there is a draft here. Come on, let's move. I wouldn't want my little wife catching cold on our honeymoon."

He pulled her to her feet. "Let's move down there and get out of this nasty breeze."

They moved then to Position 7 and took their proper place. "Isn't this better, darling?" Again it was loud enough for others to hear.

"Much," she said, following his lead.

He then bent down and gave her a peck on the cheek. Under the cover of that motion, he whispered, "Tell me you're still cold. Ask me to go and get your sweater out of the car."

She did as commanded. He gave her another kiss and said, "Wait here. I'm going to look for Brother Bartholomew. If I'm not back by the time the service starts, get yourself out of here."

He was gone for the better part of five minutes. She waited nervously, praying to Abba for courage. The time dragged by.

Then, Brother Andrew came back. "I'm sorry, darling, your sweater isn't in the car. Here, snuggle up to me. I'll keep you warm. That's what husbands are for, you know."

As she moved closer to him, he put his arm around her and dropped a folded note into her lap. Nonchalantly, she opened it and read:

> *Trouble. Nothing to worry about. One Infidel slain. Foul-up. Brother B. never told to hold this position for us. No trap.*

So that was the answer! Somehow, the plan had been garbled in the individual briefings. In a way, that fact worried her more than Brother Bartholomew's absence from Position 7.

What if his assignment wasn't the only thing which had been wrongly relayed? What if events didn't transpire from here on out as they had been outlined?

She longed for the safety of the Temple. Then she felt the touch of Brother Andrew's hand on her shoulder and it comforted her. Idly, she reached over and caressed his long fingers. He looked at her and smiled, not a smile for the others, but a smile for her.

It reminded her of Abba's smile. She realized that, although the seats at Position 7 had not been held for their arrival by Brother Bartholomew, they had still been empty when they came. It had been Abba's doing, she realized. Abba had willed to keep them vacant as he willed success for their mission.

Only once more did she have any further misgivings. It had been when the balding usher came down the aisle and asked them to move.

Brother Andrew refused, of course. And then came that other man, the old man with the white hair and silver-headed cane. She knew he was evil fortune from the instant she laid eyes on him.

He did not just ask them to move, he demanded it. She had argued and almost given herself and Brother Andrew away.

Wisely Brother Andrew stopped her foolishness in time. He had urged her to give in, even calling her by her old name. She was surprised and pleased that he had cared enough to remember, had noticed her that far back. She didn't know why it pleased her, it just had.

Still, the old man and his wife had bothered her. They were the kind of people she remembered from the times her carnal mother had taken her to church. They were proof that Christianity in the traditional sense was a false religion. They were like the Infidels and the Pharisees which Abba had condemned since the beginning of his creation. She would take pleasure in teaching them the hard lessons of the true Abba. After that, she did not worry. She eagerly looked forward to the thing which would soon come to pass.

In a very little while, she thought, her purse would give forth its secret. She took delight in that during the long, boring hymns and prayers to a god she did not know and could not believe in. And while they worshiped their false god and prayed to him, she worshiped Abba and sought his power.

It became somewhat more interesting when their preacher, a tall, thin man with a kindly face, stepped to the podium to lecture on what he termed "The Danger of the Cults."

There was no denying that he possessed some charisma of his own. Nothing like the inspiring quality of Abba, naturally, but he did have a certain authority.

His arguments were very persuasive, especially when he

used portions of Abba's word. The girl was thankful that Abba, himself, had explained the real meanings to his disciples. Otherwise, she might have been misled by this counterfeit prophet.

He had spoken of "the love of Christ as reflected in them that believe." The girl scoffed. How could he speak of such a thing when the audience to whom he spoke was filled with hypocrites? The old man on the other side of Brother Andrew was proof enough of that.

To think that she had tried to keep this preacher Stansfield from conducting his sham service with a telephone call! Better he spoke. With every breath he revealed himself a liar. Praise be to Abba.

"Here as advertised," the preacher had smugly said, "is Brother Harold Thomas. . . ."

The girl saw Thomas, the creep, stand. That was the signal! Her hands went to her purse. It was as if the Chief Priest were there, calling the cadence. Her fingers responded to the count. They closed on the automatic carbine and its clip. She had made her moves perfectly.

Brother Andrew was standing. He had the weapon now. All over the auditorium, she saw the other Brothers and their weapons rising, rising as the army of Abba should. She heard the metallic clatter of cocking weapons. Her heart pounded. It was ecstasy.

"Stay where you are," Brother Andrew shouted. "We are not here to hurt you."

On the platform, the preacher peered through the lights into the audience. "What's the matter? Is someone sick?" he asked.

And she saw that something was wrong. Very wrong. Brother Andrew was pointing the carbine toward the platform, where he focused his full attention. He did not see the old man come to his feet. He did not see the old man's cane swing back in an arc.

"Watch out!" she screamed.

The cane whipped down toward Andrew's skull. But her warning had come in time. Brother Andrew wheeled and caught the cane in mid air. He gave it a sharp tug and the old man lost his grip on its silver head.

It was now Brother Andrew who used the cane, bringing it down in a sharp, short blow into the old man's face.

The old man dropped heavily to the pew without making a noise. His eyes rolled up and his head dropped forward on his chest.

His wife shrieked and Brother Andrew turned on her, backhanding her across the mouth. It stunned her. She fell silent, her hand pressed to her lips, her eyes following Brother Andrew in horror.

Paying the two old people no more heed, Brother Andrew pushed past them to the aisle. The girl stumbled after him, almost tripping over the old man's booted feet.

Already one of the Brothers was on the platform, his gun leveled at the preacher.

In the aisle, the girl spun toward the crowd, expecting further resistance.

"Hit the house lights!" one of the Brothers yelled.

And the sanctuary was flooded with light. She could see now that there would be no resistance. Some of the spectators laughed as if they thought the whole thing a joke. Others sat dazed. And others cowered like sheep.

On all sides, in every aisle, at every door stood the Brothers.

We are in control, Sister Courage rejoiced. *Praise be to Abba. We are in control!*

11:29 a.m.

Some men react quickly and surely to danger. Malcolm Stansfield was not one of these. The screams, the guns, and the young people in the aisles shouting orders broke upon his brain as phantom images from a chaotic nightmare.

He blinked his eyes, feeling momentarily that it would all vanish. And when it did not, he felt unreal, detached from his body in time and space.

A young man in a blazer materialized on the platform. Malcolm saw the gun in the young man's hands, the savage visage of his features.

As Malcolm watched, unable to move, the gunman attacked Harold Thomas. Thomas saw it coming, raised his hands as if to protect himself, and in the next instant, was doubled as the assailant drove the butt of his gun into Thomas' stomach.

Thomas' head came forward, then snapped back as the attacker delivered another blow to the chin. Thomas was propelled backward. His feet lifted off the floor and he fell unconscious near the choir rail.

Repulsed by the sudden violence, Malcolm started forward to help him, but was met by the vacant stare of the unraised gun in the attacker's grip.

The message of the gun barrel was clear. Malcolm

backed away from it until he could back no further. He was pressed against the pulpit.

It was then that he came to himself again. It was then he realized that what he was caught up in was not a nightmare, but real. Once he had come to grips with the reality, his first immobilizing fear ebbed. His mind began to function again.

Deliberately, not out of fear but out of wanting to know exactly what he faced, he turned his back on the gun and its hypnotic presence. He faced, instead, the congregation. *God, help us,* he prayed silently. *Help me. Let no one else be hurt. Let me know what to do.*

He did not remember the lights in the auditorium being turned on. But they were on. His eyes swept the room.

Thank Heaven, most people were reacting as slowly as he had. They looked stunned, not quite comprehending yet what was happening to them.

He picked faces out of the crowd. Mrs. Markus was giggling hysterically. Pete Malko was praying. Miriam Stansfield had her arm around each of the children. Thank the Lord, they were still all right.

As nearly as he could make out, there were perhaps twenty to twenty-four gunmen, all young, all neatly dressed, blocking the aisles and the doors. Who were they? What in Heaven's name did they want?

Then he remembered Harold Thomas' terrifying words. *They're here.* The Brotherhood.

His attention was attracted by the sharp movement by one of the gunmen who guarded the door immediately to the right of the platform. The man had stepped aside to allow two other men to pass through. They carried one of the boxes of flowers which had been mistakenly delivered to the church.

The men placed the box on the floor just in front of Malcolm's vantage point. Quickly the lid of the box was torn away to reveal more guns and gas masks.

The rifles were the futuristic type of weapons Malcolm had seen on the television newscasts when the report dealt with Vietnam and other war fronts. They were dark and lethal looking.

Several young women descended on the box and tore the rifles from it, brandishing them as seasoned veterans. It was a sight ghastly and fascinating all at once.

Before the first box was emptied, a second was brought in and the action repeated. Forcing himself to look away, Malcolm went back to seeking out faces in the crowd.

Stan Brown was angry, his face red. He seemed about to explode in action. And a few pews in front of him, Kate Holmes was weeping as she dabbed at a bloody bruise on her husband's face.

Joseph Holmes was sullen. He ignored his wife's ministrations. He stared into space, his eyes squinting, his mouth working as if he was chewing on something very bitter.

"Be calm," Malcolm heard his own voice urging. "Be calm. Don't panic. I don't think they'll hurt us, so long as we don't try anything foolish."

Behind him, he heard Thomas' attacker say, "You're doing the proper thing, Stansfield."

"I'm only trying to keep my people from being injured," Malcolm said. He felt witless saying it, but he thought he had to say something.

Out in the audience, a woman's voice began to recite the Twenty-third Psalm. It was more a weeping, sobbing plea than a true recitation.

"The Lord is my shepherd; I shall not want."

It was Miriam, and how he loved her for it. He picked it up.

"He maketh me to lie down in green pastures: he leadeth me beside the still waters . . ."

Other members of the congregation were joining in. One by one, voice by voice, the recitation grew.

"He restoreth my soul: he leadeth me in the paths of righteousness for his name's sake . . ."

The words had a calming effect. Hysteria left Mrs. Markus as she took up the Psalm. Pete Malko looked up from his praying and joined in. Stan Brown's anger seemed to quiet.

But Joseph Holmes remained sullen, and continued to stare into space.

He heard the words of the Psalm. He heard the preacher urging calm.

Calm? How could he be calm? The pain of his jaw had begun to make itself felt. He looked at the guns, at the young hoodlums who dared to mock First Church with their intrusion, and his anger grew. It churned and became rage.

He was not going to let any young pups buffalo him. Guns or no, they weren't going to tell Joseph Holmes what to do in his own church.

He shoved Kate's hands away from his face. Mustering all the strength, all the dignity left in him, he stood.

"Joseph, no!" Kate trembled.

"Come on, Kate. We're getting out of here."

The young man who had hit Joseph with his own cane was hovering a few feet away in the aisle. He wheeled on Joseph, the rifle leveling at Joseph's stomach.

"Sit down, old man. We don't want any more trouble out of you," he barked flatly.

Joseph stared him down. "You ain't gonna' shoot me sonny." And to Kate, "Come on, Mother, let's go."

He turned his back on the young man and lurched up the aisle. He walked without his cane. He walked in the short, high-kneed steps of the aged, but he walked with purpose and with pride.

"I'm warning you, sir," the young man said.

"Go on and shoot," Joseph Holmes jeered. "But mind you, you'll be shooting me in the back."

There was a fusillade of gunfire. It drowned out the screams on both sides of the aisle. It roared in his ears.

There was no sensation of having been shot, for in fact, he had not been. The shots had been high over his head.

A smile formed on Joseph Holmes' lips. At the same instant, his eyes looked up toward the balcony to see where the bullets had gone.

He saw it then. The window. The beautiful stained-glass window was shattering. The lavenders and pinks and the blood red exploded, and he saw it as in slow motion—the shards tumbling, floating down as autumn leaves blown from an old oak.

He saw it and all that it represented. His father. The Holmes tradition. The Holmes pride. Shattered. Broken. Destroyed.

And his pride and his courage were broken with it. He slumped against a pew. Slowly, ever so slowly, he slid down the armrest to his knees. He gaped at the hole where the window had been. It was gone, and something in Joseph Holmes was gone, too.

The echo of the gunfire died. The auditorium was deathly silent, except for the mourning sobs of Joseph Pardee Holmes.

11:28 a.m.

In the instant it took to perceive the image on the monitor, Peloubet was running from Master Control. "I'll throw a program reel on VTR Two," he shouted as he ran. "We'll be recording in ten seconds."

Wally didn't bother to acknowledge his fellow engineer. There was no need. A newsmaking event was unfolding before KBEX's camera. The newsroom would want as much videotape on it as they could get for later reports. That much was S.O.P.

The problem Wally Nichols faced next was not as cut-and-dried. Should he continue to let the disrupted church service go out for public consumption, in spite of the potential for brutal violence? Or should he cover the picture with the "Technical Difficulties" slide and ask Peloubet to ready some standby programming?

The argument was renewed each time some shocking incident developed before the cameras—the assassination of President Kennedy; the murder of his brother, Bobby; the Watts Riot; the violence surrounding the Democratic Convention in Chicago. Critics said television had fanned the flames, worsened the effects by its very presence.

Should he dump to the slide and spare the station the inevitable faultfinding? If he went to the slide, there would be criticism from the other side that he had rejected the public's right to know.

His finger hesitated over the button. What to do? He looked up at the screen. One man was already down on the church's platform, and the gunman was bearing down on Malcolm Stansfield.

Wally bit his lip. It was too big a decision for him to make on his own. He'd have to wait for someone who had the right to make a news judgment. He let the church service continue to air.

"Speed," Peloubet's voice said over the intercom breathlessly. "We're recording."

Wally punched up VTR Two and watched the picture lock in on the proper monitor. Certain that they were recording, he reached for the phone and dialed the newsroom.

Three . . . four . . . the phone was ringing at the other end. "Come on, come on, pick it up," Wally snarled.

Five . . . six . . . wasn't anybody up there? Somebody had to be on duty up there. Sure, on Sunday there was never more than a skeleton crew, but someone had to be assigned to come into the station early and pull the overnight news copy from the wire service teletypes. Someone had to be—

"Newsroom," a voice finally said.

"Who is this?" Wally demanded.

"Sprague. Eleanor Sprague." Wally cursed his luck. Eleanor Sprague was a youngster barely out of journalism school. She hardly knew enough to come in out of the rain, never mind making a major news decision. But, she'd have to do.

"What do you think, Sprague?" he asked. "Should we continue to cover it?"

There was a pause. "Who is this?"

"Wally Nichols down in Control, sweetie. Should I cover, or keep it on the air?"

Another pause. "Keep what on the air?"

"Look at your monitor." The newsroom was equipped with a bank of television sets which allowed them to view not only KBEX's telecasts, but those of the other stations in town as well.

"I don't understand," Eleanor Sprague said sweetly.

"Your television set!" Wally yelled into the mouthpiece.

"I . . . I don't have it on."

"You what?"

"Don't get huffy with me," she sniffed. "I forgot to turn my monitors on this morning. What's the big deal? It's only some lousy religious program."

Wally stifled his urge to swear at Ms. Eleanor Sprague. "Well, that 'lousy religious program' may be your biggest story of the year right now. Turn your monitor on and then get ahold of your boss. Ask Barry what he wants me to do."

"I don't take orders from you," Eleanor Sprague argued.

"Do it!" Wally banged the phone down and turned back to the monitor. The camera was on a wide shot. An old man was running up the center aisle of the church. Another man was shouting something at him. There were puffs of smoke and flame spitting from the gun in the second man's hands.

Pandemonium broke loose on the screen. People were ducking behind pews, throwing themselves out of the line of fire. The camera shook, then bobbed crazily. The auditorium disappeared from view and the next picture Wally saw looked like a piece of the ceiling. The cameraman had either ducked with everyone else, or—Wally gasped—had been shot.

Wally leaped from his chair and grabbed up the shortwave microphone. "Roger? Roger, come in!"

He forgot about call letter identification. He forgot about everything else, except getting an answer from Roger Uttenmeyer.

"Roger? Roger?"

Nothing. Only static.

"Roger! Come in!"

More static and then, Roger's voice.

"We're okay, Wally. I mean, I think we're okay." Roger sounded strange, his response forced.

"What's going on over there, Roger?"

Static again. Wally glanced up at the monitor. The camera was steady again. The picture was of the old man slumped in the aisle. Wally couldn't tell if the man was alive or dead.

Roger's voice came over the speaker once more, and Wally jumped at the sound of it. "Wally, listen, I got . . . I got some company with me in here. She's got a gun. I think we better do what she says. She wants to talk to you."

William D. Rodgers

11:37 a.m.

Burch Zimmerman lit his seventh cigarette in two hours and flipped the page of the Sunday comics spread on his desk. The comics weren't as funny these days, but he read them religiously anyway, especially *Little Red Writing Hood.* It had been Sandy's favorite.

When she was small, she used to sit on his lap after Sunday breakfast and he'd read the funnies to her. He'd invent silly voices for each character in every strip, and she'd laugh and clap her hands in glee. And always, always, they'd save *Little Red Writing Hood* for last for the same reason kids saved the cherry on a chocolate sundae for last. It was the best part.

Burch still saved *Little Red Writing Hood* until he had read all the other comic strips. *Little Red Writing Hood* seemed corny and not humorous as it had in those long ago times. However, it was a link with his dead daughter which he could not quite break.

He was just about to turn back to it, when the Com-key telephone on his desk rang. It was Fran in Communications.

"Burch, it looks like we have a hostage situation," she informed him.

He expected her to tell him it was some drunk down in the low rent district who had tied one on Saturday night and was now threatening his missus with a rusty twenty-two. But then, Fran said, "It's First Church. Some kind of suspected terrorist activity."

He wasn't prepared for that. The cigarette slipped from his lips, the hot ash burning a hole in his trousers before he could slap it out.

"Burch? Did you hear me?"

"Yeah, Fran, yeah, I heard you." He rubbed at the cigarette burn, his mind racing. Terrorists? First Church? Naw, couldn't be. Terrorists were something you found in New York or L.A., or maybe even Chicago. But you didn't find them in Grunnell. Not in a church. Not on a Sunday.

"Give me the status, Fran," he finally managed to mumble.

"Adam-3 has been dispatched to check it out."

"Good, good. What's their ETA?"

"They should be on the scene in approximately three minutes."

"That's fine, Fran. Let me know." He made as if to hang up, had second thoughts and said, "Oh, Fran, when did the complaint come in?"

"There's been no lag time in responding, if you're checking up on our efficiency, Captain," Fran said coolly.

"Naw, Fran, that's not what I meant to ask at all. I mean, who called it in?" A piece of undigested bagel had suddenly become persistent in his stomach.

"The first call came from a little old lady. A Mrs. Peabody. They're still coming in. The switchboard is jammed."

"It's no hoax, then?"

"Hoax? It's on television!"

Of course, Stansfield's Cult Sunday. Burch remembered the phone call earlier, and the advertisements. Terrorists? No, it was probably one of Malcolm Stansfield's stunts. Well, this time the good pastor had gone too far.

"I see," he said. "I don't suppose you tried calling the

church to find out what's going on over there?"

"Burch, this is Fran Goldman, remember? I've been on the dispatch desk for a lot of years. Of course I called the church."

"And?"

"There was no answer."

"Fine. Let me know what the squad reports when they get there," Burch said and hung up.

So that's why Malcolm Stansfield had called this morning requesting police protection. He was setting the department up to be unwilling participants in a showy little demonstration.

Burch didn't know, couldn't guess, what Stansfield's motives might be in attempting a charade such as this. Publicity, probably.

Still . . . maybe he'd better see for himself. He went down to the watch lounge where a television set had been provided by the Police Auxiliary for the pleasure of any personnel who happened to be on a coffee break.

The lounge was deserted as Burch walked in. He flipped on the television set and then went to the coffee vending machine while the tube warmed up.

He put fifteen cents in the slot. A paper cup dropped into the opening behind the plastic shield and was filled by a stream of hot, black liquid.

As he pulled up the shield, Burch glanced over at the TV set. The screen was lighted with a picture of the auditorium of First Church. There was a young man in the pulpit beside a gentleman Burch recognized as Malcolm Stansfield.

Wait a minute! What was this? The young man was holding an authentic looking AK-47. He had to give it to Malcolm Stansfield again. He had armed his play terrorists properly enough.

Aw, but that was no terrorist. Give Stansfield poor marks there. The young man was too clean-cut. He should have had long hair and a beard. He should be wearing Levi's if he was supposed to be what he was pretending to be.

Burning his fingers on the coffee cup as he took it from the machine, Burch crossed to the TV set and turned up the sound.

"We are the Guardian Angels of Abba," the young man with the AK-47 was saying. "We have been sent by Abba to catch you up and redeem you."

Burch snorted. That dialogue was straight out of a grade-B movie. His suspicions were confirmed.

He reached for the phone on the wall and buzzed Fran. "You should see this show," he said. "It makes *Starsky and Hutch* look like literature."

Fran did not laugh. "I was just trying to reach you, Captain. Adam-3 reports they are on the scene and shots have been fired."

"Blanks," Burch observed.

"No, Burch. Shots. Adam-3 is under fire!"

11:40 a.m.

At the first sharp clatter of gunfire, Malcolm Stansfield's involuntary reaction had been one of self-preservation. He had dropped to his knees behind the solid oak protection of the pulpit.

But in the next instant, he thought of Miriam and the children, and his concern for them overrode all instincts of safety for himself. He came back to his full height, his eyes searching the wild kaleidoscope of panic spreading through the auditorium.

People were screaming, throwing themselves out of the way of the bullets. Joseph Holmes was down in the aisle and Malcolm wasn't certain whether the old man was alive or dead. The stained-glass window was gone, shattered. And Miriam? Where was Miriam?

He started to take a step forward, to leap from the platform to find her.

"Hold it!" a voice commanded before his limbs would move, and he felt the cold muzzle of a rifle against the base of his skull.

"But my wife!" Malcolm protested. It was a prayer and an outcry of helplessness rolled into one.

"Forget it!" the young voice behind Malcolm commanded. There was no sympathy in his tone. Malcolm yielded, feeling trapped, useless, angry with himself that he did not possess the courage to do what must be done.

"Step aside," the young man ordered. He leaned forward and shouted into the microphone. "Everybody take your seats. I said, take your seats now!"

Tentatively, the people began to climb up from behind the pews where they had thrown themselves when the shooting started. There was some murmuring, some choked sobs. And then, Malcolm saw Miriam.

She looked pale and shaken and so did the children. Yet, they appeared to be physically unharmed. Malcolm breathed a tiny prayer of relief.

"No talking!" the man beside Malcolm barked.

An uneasy hush fell. The only sounds were the scrapes and rustle of people settling in their seats, and the sobbing of Joseph Holmes. The old man lay where he had toppled. For a short while longer, he wept. Then he grew quiet, staring upward at the jagged, gaping hole where once the stained-glass masterpiece had been.

Malcolm's heart went out to Joseph. He understood, a little, how much that window had meant to the man. He understood, but was powerless to comfort him.

The apprehensive stillness ended in slow degrees. There were new murmurs and whispers and sobs. One woman, a woman Malcolm did not recognize, began to shake uncontrollably, crying out in long, agonized wails.

A girl who looked not more than nineteen or twenty, but who now shouldered a vicious automatic weapon, stepped in front of the woman and slapped her. The wails stopped abruptly.

"I warn you, do as we say," the man at the microphone sputtered. "We are not here to harm you, only to teach you the Truth."

His words were lost in the rising din of fear and it made him angrier. "Shut up!" he bellowed.

When the response was not what he desired, he turned to

Malcolm. "You'd better shut 'em up, preacher, or . . ."

He let the threat trail away. It had its effect. Once again overtaken by a sense of unreality, of being a participant in a hallucination, Malcolm took the microphone. His mouth was dry, his tongue stiff, almost unwilling, as he spoke.

"We must be quiet," he said. "Please, listen to me." Over and over he said it until the words seemed to lose their meaning.

But the crowd responded, bit by bit. The auditorium was again silent.

"Yes. Yes . . . we must . . . keep ourselves in . . . control," Malcolm had difficulty in finding the right words. "We must . . . cooperate and . . . do as these . . . people . . . say."

He had them with him, now. They were looking up at him, waiting for his next sentence, waiting for him to tell them what to do, to lead them.

He wanted desperately to comfort them, to pray with them, to assure them that everything would be all right. The only thing he could repeat was, "Cooperate."

A man's voice from somewhere in the assemblage yelled, "There's more of us than them. Let's take 'em."

"Try it and your preacher dies." The man beside Malcolm shoved his gun against Malcolm's temple. No one moved.

"In the name of God, man," Malcolm pleaded, certain that these words might be his last. "Take it easy."

He was pleading not so much for his own life, but for the lives of his congregation, and particularly for the lives of his wife and children. For one dark instant, he thought of his son and daughter and was painfully aware that more than anything else, he wanted to live to see them grown.

"These people—we—will do whatever you say."

"I know," the man replied with a confidence that was unnerving. "We are the Brotherhood. We come with the power and blessing of Abba."

The Brotherhood. And their presence was his own fault, Malcolm was thinking. He had been the one to bring Harold Thomas to First Church. He had been the one to insist upon such heavy promotion. He had been the one who had ignored the telephoned warning, who had made light of Harold Thomas' request for police protection, who had allowed his small doubts to be appeased by Dick Whiting's assurances, who had pushed all thought of danger back into the recesses of his mind. He, Malcolm Stansfield, was the architect of Cult Sunday, and now, they were all reaping his folly.

The man at the microphone proceeded with his statement. "I am Brother John, and these—" he indicated the young people with the guns—"are the true apostles and servants of the Lord of All, Abba, who you sometimes call Yahweh, and sometimes Jehovah, who you mock with your false worship of his son who was called Christ. Abba, who has come to dwell again on earth, to gather the chosen unto himself at the end of the age."

"Blasphemy!" Malcolm gasped. He had not meant to say it. It just came out.

The young man who called himself "Brother John" whirled on Malcolm. "You say anything else without my permission, and you'll be the first to die."

"I won't let you speak satanic lies from this pulpit," Malcolm threw caution to the wind. He didn't know why he was doing it, except perhaps to make amends somehow for letting this thing happen.

Brother John's eyes grew hard. His rifle came up. His finger tightened on the trigger.

"No, John!" Another member of the Brotherhood stepped in and shoved the barrel of the weapon downward. "Remember, not in front of *those*." It was clear he meant the television cameras. "Not yet. The time will come, but not yet."

Brother John glared at Malcolm for a full minute before

completely lowering his rifle and turning back to the microphone.

"And you," the other Brother said to Malcolm, "had better do exactly as you're told. You can only push so far. There will be no stopping it, then."

He backed away, leaving Malcolm pondering the portent. Malcolm felt sick, weak, afraid. Afraid to let the blasphemy go unchallenged; afraid to protest against it. Afraid, he told himself, not for himself, but for all the others.

What would Paul do? What would Christ do? Malcolm forced himself to inventory the Scriptures he knew so well. At least, he tried to do that, but the only verse that would come was the one he had quoted to Harold Thomas before, "Greater is He that is in you . . ."

Yet, now, he failed to find the comfort in it.

"We are the Guardian Angels of Abba," Brother John took up where he had left off. "We have been sent to catch you up, to stop the lies you were being told this morning, to lead you into the Light."

Out of the side of his vision, Malcolm caught the motion of Kate Holmes as she suddenly stood and moved as if toward her husband. Malcolm was as surprised as Brother John seemed annoyed. Only moments ago, he had seen Kate sitting in her pew, stunned, almost catatonic, a fearful and bedraggled old woman. But now she was a woman in possession of herself, the Kate he knew her to be, a woman acting with purpose.

Brother John broke off his speech in mid-sentence and barked, "Brother Andrew!"

At the shouted warning, Brother Andrew saw Kate and placed himself so as to deny her exit from the pew.

Kate stopped, but did not sit down. A tall, commanding figure of a woman more used to intimidating than being intimidated, she said simply, "I am going to my husband."

Malcolm cherished her courage, had to admire her for it,

but was terrified by it. They were hostages of madmen. The slightest act of insubordination could provoke a slaughter. He swallowed hard against the bile the thought brought churning from the pit of his stomach.

"Make that woman sit down," Brother John ordered.

"I am his wife. I will not sit down, young man," Kate Holmes addressed the platform. "You will have to kill me to keep me from going to my husband."

She took a step toward the Brother blocking her way. He held his ground, but there was confusion written on his face.

"Brother John?" he appealed.

John shifted in the pulpit uncomfortably. An indecisive glimmer flickered across his face. He studied Kate and she rebelliously answered his stare.

To Malcolm, the deadlock seemed interminable. At any second, he expected to see Kate beaten or gunned down. "*Sit down, Kate. Please, sit down!*" he wanted to implore, but he dared not speak.

And then, the deadlock was broken, and it was Kate who broke it.

"What's it going to be, young man? If you're going to shoot me, you'd better be done with it."

Brother John suddenly relaxed. An expression which might pass for a smile played at the corner of his mouth.

"Show these Infidels the compassion of Abba, Brother Andrew," he said.

It seemed to startle the man who stood in front of Kate Holmes. He hesitated.

"I said, let her help the old man," Brother John repeated sharply, the smile gone.

Brother Andrew stepped aside. In the aisle, Kate knelt by Joseph.

"Are you hurt, Father?" she asked gently.

"The window, Kate. The window." Joseph Holmes said, his voice breaking in a low whine.

"I know, Father. I know," Kate soothed, lifting his head and shoulders and cradling him against her bosom. "Well, you don't seem to be harmed otherwise."

"The window."

"It's going to be all right, Father. All right," Kate stroked his cheek. "Do you think you can make it back to the pew?"

Joseph Holmes gave no response.

Kate got to her feet, then bent down and tried to pull her husband to his. He did not fight against her, but he made no attempt to rise.

His dead weight was too much for her. She lost her footing and went down on top of him.

Malcolm started forward.

"Where do you think you're going?" Brother John restrained him.

"She needs help," Malcolm mumbled.

"No," Brother John said coldly. "She wanted to help him, she's gonna' have to do it by herself."

Malcolm knew his cause was hopeless. He looked back at Kate Holmes. She was up, wrestling her husband to a standing position, coaxing him. "Come on, Father. I can't get you on your feet by myself. Come on. That's it. Yes, that's it."

By her sheer will and with great difficulty, Kate Holmes managed somehow to half drag Joseph to an erect position and back to their pew.

Before they were reseated, Brother John put his hand over the microphone so the others could not hear what he said next to Malcolm.

"Yes, preacher, Abba teaches compassion. But, he also teaches punishment. By Abba's compassion you live. Yet, from this moment on, you must do what we say. If you do not, I will have them all killed while you watch. Understand?"

Malcolm reluctantly nodded. It was the only thing he

could do. And, still, he hated himself anew. He was failing his God and his Lord. He had failed his faith.

Malcolm was still feeling that failure when he became aware of a new sound filtering into the auditorium. It was so faint, so far away, that he could not be certain it was even there.

However, it was there. Growing louder, growing closer—the whine of a siren approached rapidly and with it came hope again to Malcolm Stansfield.

The police! Of course, the police were coming. Thousands of viewers must have witnessed what was happening on their television screens. Someone among them must have phoned the police. They would be rescued. He knew it. It was only a matter of time.

Brother John heard the siren, too. He cocked his head, listening. But if he was afraid of the siren and the police it was bringing, he did not show it.

Malcolm wondered at it, that lack of fear, as the siren halted directly outside.

There were shouts, and then the sharp echo of new gunfire.

11:44 a.m.

"She says, if we don't keep telecasting their crusade—that's what she called it, a crusade—without interruption, they'll kill the crew." Wally Nichols was on the telephone to the home of F.G. Bronson, KBEX-TV's programming director.

"Say what?" F.G. gulped incredulously, reverting to the street expression of his youth. "Is this some kind of a joke, Wally?"

"No way!" Wally snapped, offended that F.G. would even think he might be capable of engaging in a hoax of any kind where the serious business of television was concerned.

As calmly as he could, he explained it all again to F.G. He told him how the services at First Church had been invaded before KBEX's own cameras by a gun-toting group of terrorists, how at least one of those terrorists was in the remote booth with Roger Uttenmeyer, how she had demanded, via the shortwave, that KBEX continue to telecast the event without commercial interruption or even station breaks.

"And what did you tell her?" F.G. asked.

"I said, I couldn't do it on my own, that I didn't have the authority. I said only two people had the authority to suspend regular scheduled programming, the station manager, and you, F.G."

"What did she say to that?"

"She said she didn't care. She said they were watching, and if for any reason we took the telecast from the church off the air, they'd kill everybody."

"Well . . . uh . . . have you checked it out with the police?" F.G. said, thinking out loud. "Have you confirmed the authenticity of the threat?"

"I don't need to check it with the cops," Wally responded in an agitated tone. "For cryin' out in the night, F.G., all you have to do is turn on a television set to see it's for real."

"I don't like it," F.G. said. "We can't have terrorists telling us how to run our station. It could set a bad precedent."

Wally groaned and said, "Look, F.G., we don't have time to debate the morality of the thing. This is life and death. Just give me permission to ride with it."

"Did you try to get Darrell?" Darrell King was the station manager, a vice-president of the corporation which owned KBEX.

"Yes. His line was busy."

"Uh . . . well, for something of this nature, I think I'd better clear it with Darrell," F.G. stammered.

"At least, give me permission to dump the noon break," Wally complained.

"No, I'll get back to you."

"What do I do if I haven't heard from you by twelve?"

"What the log says you're to do," F.G. said.

"But that could kill the crew—" Wally realized he was talking to a dead line. F.G. Bronson had already hung up.

Cursing Affirmative Action for putting men like F.G. Bronson in positions of management before they were ready, Wally looked up at the air monitor.

Nothing in the church had changed. The people with guns were still there. It looked like a prison camp in a state of siege.

The digital clock beside the monitor read, *11:47:38.*

Peloubet would be loading the next break, the break that F.G. had ordered Wally to take, unless . . .

How long could it take for F.G. to get hold of Darrell? A few minutes? Not more than five. There was time, Wally told himself. Not a lot of time, but time.

Impulsively, Wally went to the shortwave and called the remote.

Roger Uttenmeyer sounded strained, tired as he acknowledged the call.

"Is she still there?" Wally asked.

"I'm here." The feminine voice was almost sultry.

"We're working on your request," Wally said as calmly as he could. "These things take time, though. We may have to cut away at noon just for a few minutes, but we'll be back on the air from your site as soon after that as we can get it arranged."

"I said there are to be no interruptions of the broadcast," the woman said flatly.

"Don't panic, lady, we're doing what we can." Wally wiped the sweat from his forehead.

"So you will understand," the woman said, "I am holding an M-1 rifle. It is pointed at your friend's head. I will not panic. I assure you, if you force me to, I will serenely pull the trigger."

"In the name of Heaven—"

"Yes, in the name of Heaven," she replied dryly. "In the name of Abba."

"Just don't panic," Wally said, knowing further argument was useless. "I'll be back to you."

He signed off. The digital clock read *11:52:20.*

The telephone was silent. Wally regarded it. "Ring, darn you! Ring!"

The more he looked at the telephone, the angrier he became. He seized it and dialed Darrell's home number. A busy signal.

He depressed the button and dialed F.G. Bronson's. Another busy signal.

He jammed down the receiver. *11:53:17.*

There was a flurry as Eleanor Sprague came tearing into Master Control, neatly tailored in a gray tweed skirt and man-shirt, as if she had just come from doing a commercial for hairspray.

"I talked to Barry," she announced breathlessly.

"Hallelujah!" Wally exclaimed bitterly.

"He wants you to get some videotape for us," she said, not at all cowed by his remark.

"It's already rolling," Wally said.

"And, I'll need some background from you." Eleanor Sprague didn't even thank him for anticipating the newsroom needs.

"There's your story!" Wally jabbed a finger at the monitor. "You're the reporter, I'm only the engineer."

Eleanor Sprague looked so hurt by his short harangue, he immediately felt sorry for her. She was so young and inexperienced.

"Look," he said more softly. "I got my own troubles right now. I didn't mean to jump down your throat."

While she scribbled notes on her yellow pad, he capsulized the situation as he understood it.

She nodded and reached for the control room phone.

"Put that down!" Wally screamed.

"I'm calling Barry to get his OK to do a bulletin cut-in," she explained, beginning to dial.

"Like fun you are. I need that phone kept open." He didn't bother to tell her why.

The fierce expression in his eyes must have had the intended effect, for she recradled the phone and without another word, left the room.

The red numerals of the clock read, *11:56:00.*

Wally Nichols knew what he would do.

11:56 a.m.

It was like the eye of a hurricane as Malcolm had always imagined the eye of a hurricane would feel. The first whirlwind of fear had been passed through. There was a false peace, a sense of security, a time to collect thoughts and to pull jangled nerves together in preparation for the next assault which would surely come.

A good fifteen minutes had passed since the volley of gunfire and the first siren outside. There had been some shouted exchanges between the police and members of the Brotherhood, but nothing which Malcolm could distinctly make out, nothing which gave him further insight into the situation.

Occasionally, another siren would come screeching to a halt outside. There had been no more gunfire.

In the sanctuary, all was still except for the now and then cry of a baby and the small voice of a very young child which kept saying to its mother, "I want a drink, Mama, a drink."

The choir had been removed from the loft behind the platform, and forced to take seats among the congregation. That was for better containment, Malcolm guessed.

Allen Lloyd was with them. Gil Anderson and John Swallow, however, were still on the platform with

Malcolm, sitting as he was in the velveteen covered parson's chairs. From where he sat, Malcolm could see the mingled bafflement and horror on their faces.

Next to them, slumped in another parson's chair, was Harold Thomas, having been manhandled there by two burly cultists. Thomas' eyes were vitreous, blood oozed from his mouth and a deathly pallor hung around him, but he was conscious and breathing. Malcolm was grateful for that. The blows which had been delivered to the young man's body had been so brutally administered, Malcolm had feared him dead.

There were cultists on the platform, too, standing guard with their rifles, while Brother John, who appeared to be their leader, paced up and down at the platform's edge.

The heat from the television lights was stifling, almost as oppressive as the guns. Malcolm wiped the perspiration from his upper lip and shifted in his seat.

What are they waiting for? he wondered. *What kind of game are they playing with us? God, let this thing end.*

There were twenty-seven armed members of the Brotherhood now in the auditorium. Malcolm had counted them twice. Twenty-seven. They were easy to spot, for shortly after the takeover, they had all donned khaki-colored fatigue jackets from the boxes of "flowers"—men and women alike. Malcolm surmised that was so they could tell each other apart from the crowd if shooting started.

A few minutes after they had made their move, the three male cultists who had hidden downstairs in the boiler room had come into the sanctuary leading such people as James Hutchinson, the church treasurer, and the handful of others whose business kept them away from the worship hour.

They had deposited their prisoners on a pew down front, exited, and now they were back again, this time with the nursery workers. Recognizing the women, a young mother jumped to her feet screaming, "My baby! What have you done with my baby?"

Brother Bartholomew immediately pushed the woman down on her pew.

"Take it easy," Brother John announced from the platform. "All the babies in the nursery are being well cared for by Sister Tender and Sister Devoted."

"They're okay . . ." Mrs. Gillenson, head of the Nursery department, managed to interject before she was forced to settle beside the others on the front bench.

Brothers Bartholomew, Nathanael, and Philip approached Brother John and saluted.

"Building secure," Nathanael said.

"You're sure?" Brother John asked.

"Absolutely. We've swept it twice. Everybody in the building is now here with us."

"Good," Brother John smiled. Nathanael moved closer to his superior and whispered something Malcolm could not hear. The two conversed in low, urgent tones for several moments, and Brother John gestured toward the center door at the rear of the auditorium.

Nathanael snapped another salute, did an about-face and marched away with his two Brothers to follow orders.

Two blocks away, the chimes on the clock at City Hall marked the noon hour. Brother John looked at his own wristwatch, then went to the pulpit microphone.

"The hour of your deliverance has come," he said. He closed his eyes and lifted his rifle upward, until it was above his head in a curious attitude of prayer.

"O, Abba," he began, "sanctify them through thy truth: thy word is truth. And for their sakes I sanctify myself, that they also might be sanctified through the truth."

Malcolm started. He recognized the prayer as John 17:17.

". . . Then shall the eyes of the blind be opened, and the ears of the deaf unstopped. Then shall the lame man leap like a hart and the tongues of the dumb sing for joy, for waters shall break forth in the wilderness and streams in the desert of the conscious mind."

More scripture in perverted form, this time misappropriated from the thirty-fifth chapter of Isaiah. Malcolm knew that the Brotherhood used scripture, of course, but to hear it come tumbling from the mouth of a thug with a gun astounded him. It was chilling.

"Be with us, Lord Abba, that we might deliver these Infidels from their destructive pathways, for you, and you alone, are the truth and the way and the light. Amen."

From the Brotherhood members came a chorused "Amen!"

Although his prayer was complete and his eyes opened, Brother John kept the rifle aloft, a grotesque offering to an angry god.

His next words came as a low moan, and the next with more intensity, each sentence building upon the last, until his manifesto reached a climax and what he said crashed through the sanctuary as peels of thunder.

"Behold," he opened, "the lord, Abba, cometh out of his place to punish the inhabitants of the earth for their iniquity: the earth also shall disclose her blood, and shall no more cover her slain.

"For, Abba has said, 'Thou shalt have no other gods before me.'

"Their sorrows shall be multiplied that hasten after another god. And, so, Abba will execute vengeance in anger and fury upon the heathen, such as they have not heard or seen.

"'He that worketh deceit shall not dwell within my house: he that telleth lies shall not tarry in my sight,' Abba says.

"And that is what you, in this house, have done. By inviting the evil son of Satan, the lying Judas, Harold Thomas, to flaunt his untruthful falsehoods against the love of Abba, you have sinned mortally.

"Abba has said, 'Be ye afraid of the sword: for wrath bringeth the punishments of the sword, that ye may know there is a judgment.'

"In other words, the punishment for the blasphemy is death.

"But Abba is also merciful. Do not the Scriptures declare, 'Turn unto the Lord your God: for he is gracious and merciful, slow to anger, and of great kindness, and repenteth him of evil. Then will the lord, Abba, be jealous for his flock and pity his people.'

"Thus, Abba has commanded that the sheep be separated from the goats, the wheat from the chaff. And, thus, today, that separation begins, a separation that will soon be made throughout all the world.

"Today, you shall be given a choice. You will renounce your false and misguided worship of Jesus Christ. You will proclaim your devotion to Abba, now and forevermore. You will give up your earthly possessions which bind you to evil. And you will join the army of Abba.

"But, if ye refuse and rebel, ye shall be devoured with the sword: for the mouth of Abba hath spoken it!"

"Praise be to Abba. Praise be to Abba," the Brotherhood repeated.

"Meditate on these words, believe them and you will be saved this day by the mercy of Abba." Brother John lowered his rifle and turned abruptly away from the microphone.

From the misused Bible verses, a pattern of meaning seeped into Malcolm's understanding. His insides squirmed.

No, this couldn't be happening. Not here. Not in America. Not in Grunnell. Not in First Church.

It happened in Russia. It happened in Eastern Europe. It happened in the Germany of World War II. It happened to six million Jews. It happened to other men in other times, in other places.

People were not martyred for their faith in this time and country. Martyrs were men such as Paul and Peter and the Christians who died in Rome, and Stephen.

Stephen! Malcolm choked back the ironic laughter which welled within. Only two weeks ago at this very service, he had preached a sermon on the first Christian martyr.

Yes, Stephen was prepared to die, he had told his listeners. He knew he was going to die. But he was not afraid. He had the Holy Spirit with him. The Holy Spirit who abides with all true believers, even today, even in the 1970s.

As Stephen kneeled naked, because they had stripped away his garments, and felt the jagged stones tearing at his flesh, crushing his life away, he'd had no concern for his own safety. Instead, he prayed in a loud voice—as recorded in Acts 7:60—that the Lord would not charge the men who killed him with the sin of that murder! Even at the moment of death, Stephen was following the command laid down by his Master and ours. He was loving his enemies as himself. He was praying for those who persecuted him.

We can have the same kind of inner strength which belonged to Stephen, Malcolm had promised his congregation. All we have to do is believe in the Triune God—Father, Son and Holy Spirit. It is through the power of God, the blood of Jesus and the strength of the Holy Spirit that we can have the courage of Stephen.

"The Courage of Stephen." That was what Malcolm had entitled that message. It had been a good one, he knew.

Oh, yes, he could discuss martyrdom in a most effective cerebral fashion. But when it came to the real thing, when he sat staring at the guns of the Brotherhood, the courage of Stephen was failing him.

"You've meditated long enough," Brother John was saying, back in the pulpit again. "After all, we can't waste the very expensive television time with which we are so generously blessed."

He gestured toward the television cameras in the balcony and chortled at his own joke.

"Just to make sure it's clear to you," he continued, "what we're gonna' do, is march you up here one-by-one. You'll get down on your knees right here, in front of the pulpit where we can all see you. You'll be asked if you still believe in the false god, Jesus. You will answer, 'No.' "

"Then you will be asked to swear your belief in the Father, Abba. Those who comply will be instructed in a new way of eternal life.

"Those who refuse—and I have no doubts that among your number there are fanatics so warped by false teachings, that they will scoff at Abba's magnanimity—those who refuse, will be separated out to be shot at the conclusion of this holy crusade."

A shock wave of cries and whispers engulfed the crowd.

"Silence!" Brother John's face flushed with anger.

"I see some of you still have your doubts," he said when order had been restored. "Brothers, bring in the proof of our intention."

The doors from the narthex on the center aisle were opened and Brothers Nathanael and Bartholomew marched toward the pulpit bearing between them a large, canvas-wrapped object.

As they came forward, Malcolm could see that the canvas looked like one of the old paint tarps kept stored in the basement.

"Bring it up here," Brother John urged. "That's right. That's right. Now, hold it up so everyone can get a good look while I pull away the shroud."

Malcolm gasped. In the tarp was George Washington Isaiah Perkins. The two Brothers stepped away and the lifeless, bloodied body toppled to the floor.

12:02 p.m.

Where do they come from? Burch Zimmerman wondered about the mob of onlookers already gathered at the hastily erected barricades two blocks from the church. There was never any foot traffic on the downtown streets on Sunday morning, yet, at the first smell of blood, hundreds of people always managed to beat the police to the scene.

They must spring up out of the pavement and asphalt, he mused. He leaned on the horn and struggled to nose his cruiser through a corridor being created for him by two uniformed foot patrolmen.

Finally, he was through the jam and inside that coveted circle where the action was. He vented his frustration at the delay by gunning his engine, and the cruiser shot forward past the closed stores and vacant office buildings until he brought it to a screeching stop behind Lieutenant Max Vigeveno's unmarked car a half block south of First Church.

Max was standing on the sidewalk beside his vehicle shouting an order at a blue-suited officer who went racing off to follow the instructions.

Per procedure, Burch reached for his radio and let Communications know he had arrived and was assuming command of the situation.

It was Fran Goldman who took his call. "Hey, Zim," she cooed, "why don't you stop by the Purple Dragon on your way back in and get some of that beef chow mein and egg rolls. We can take it up to my place for a cozy dinner for two."

"Aw, Fran, what's a good Jewish girl like you want with Chinese food? It'll just slant your nose."

"Scratch the food then," she giggled. "That's not what I'm hankering for, anyway. Just bring yourself."

"Ten-4," Burch acknowledged. He felt his face flushing red. Suppose someone else was on that channel and overheard? He preferred to keep his private life private.

The redness was still in his face as he climbed out of his car and joined Max Vigeveno on the sidewalk.

Max was a short, stocky Italian who looked more Mafia hit-man than cop. His breath constantly oozed garlic, which was made worse by Max's habit of leaning in close to anyone he conversed with, as if whatever he had to say could only be related in strict confidence.

Burch did not care much for the Lieutenant. Aside from bad breath, Max had other maddening habits. For one thing, he was too accommodating. He was always striving too hard to ingratiate himself with his superiors, and you had a feeling he was insincere, that he was bucking for promotion via his favors.

Even now, as Burch took a package of cigarettes from his pocket and shook one loose from the rest, Max had a lighter out and flickering before Burch could put the tobacco to his lips.

Exhaling the first smoke from his cigarette, Burch took in the scene down the block. Two patrol cars were parked at angles across the avenue from the giant antique house of worship. Several officers were crouched behind them, service revolvers and shotguns drawn and ready.

The pavement in front of the church was full of broken

glass. Behind one of the pillars on the portico of the building, Burch thought he saw the protruding barrel of a rifle.

"So what's going down, Max?" Burch took another drag on the cigarette.

Pocketing the lighter, Max leaned in. Burch involuntarily drew back. It was a mistake, for Max only drew closer, showering Burch with the remembrance of last night's pasta with every word spoken.

"You know the score?" Max queried.

Burch nodded, blowing smoke out his nostrils, trying to wash away the garlic.

"Hostages. A thousand, give or take a few," Max mouthed needlessly.

"So tell me something I don't know." A ripple of impatience colored Burch's inflection.

"We got the building surrounded," Max announced brightly.

"SWAT?"

"On the way. But near as we can figure, the hostages are being held in the auditorium. The suspects have the doors in and out well covered. There's only one window that opens into the room. That big round one that's all busted out. Other than that, the place is a regular Bastille. How we gonna' storm the Bastille with a six-man SWAT squad?"

"You've obviously been thinking about it." Burch's impatience was fast becoming intolerance. "So, tell me, Max."

"I think we need more than one SWAT team. I think we should get the State Patrol to throw in theirs."

"Call them and request it, already."

Straightening with pride, Max said, "I have."

"*Schlubb!*" Burch said under his breath. He flipped his cigarette butt to the sidewalk and crushed it ferociously under his heel, wishing that it was Max Vigeveno's accommodating smile.

For his part, Max failed to mark the Yiddish insult and launched into his views about where to establish the command post (on the second floor of the Denton Building straight across from the church, where else?) and where to place the SWAT sharpshooters when they arrived.

He also said he had called the city engineer to get him down to City Hall and dig out any plans for First Church that might be on file. He said he had called the fire department and asked for them to stand by. He boasted that he had even thought of alerting the area hospitals and having them prepare to receive mass casualties in the event the situation got out of hand.

He went on and on in a nonstop lecture until Burch Zimmerman's head was swimming with details and his nose was filled with the stench of rotting garlic. He could take no more.

He held up his hand. "Max, shut up!"

The little Italian fell into a morose silence, a silence for which Burch was very grateful.

He rubbed his forehead wearily and reviewed the situation. Max was right. They would need two SWAT teams, and maybe more. But two was all that was available.

The Denton Building would make a good command post. They would have to go in from the rear entrance, of course, since the front entrance was plainly visible to the suspects on the portico of the church.

And then Burch thought, *Why does it have to be so complicated?* In the old days, they didn't worry about SWAT tactics and sharpshooter vantage points. They just charged in, guns blazing and devil take the hindmost.

But, in the old days, thugs with rifles didn't take over churches. They didn't hold a thousand hostages at a crack. They didn't make demands. . . .

Demands! He forgot the old days and turned to Max.

"Have there been any demands made?"

Max looked embarrassed. "Didn't I cover that for you, Captain?"

Burch allowed a dark, small smile to play over his face. "No."

"That's because there have been no demands yet," Max tried to cover himself. "It appears that the takeover has been engineered by a group calling itself 'The Brotherhood.' That's all we know."

"Yeah. It's a religious cult." Max was taken aback. Burch allowed his smile to grow larger. It was a pleasure to be one up on Lieutenant Max Vigeveno. A pleasure.

"It was on television," Burch said. "A regular spectacular."

"Maybe we should check with the FBI," Max suggested, in an attempt to recover his poise. "They might have a file on them, if they're a cult."

"Good idea, Max. So, do it." *That should show you, you little schlepp, that you don't know everything. That Captain Burch Zimmerman is still on the job.*

He continued to smile after Max as the stubby Italian beat a retreat to his car and its radio.

He was still smiling when he let his gaze wander back to the church and the patrol cars in front of it. It looked like a siege. It was a siege. An unholy, unthinkable siege.

The shadows cast by the tall skyscrapers surrounding him suddenly seemed chill. A thousand lives were hanging in the balance, a thousand taxpayers looking to him to break the siege and send everyone home safe and sound.

The truth was, he didn't have an idea of how he was going to do that. Not an idea. All he had was a skeleton Sunday complement of men, two SWAT teams and Lieutenant Max Vigeveno.

Cheer up, Burch, he told himself. *Somehow it will end and you can go to Fran's place. Think of Fran.* Maybe there *was* a chance for him with a girl like her.

But the more he tried to think of Fran, the more he thought about the thousand lives, and the SWAT teams and Max Vigeveno.

The smile faded. The game of waiting had begun.

12:03 p.m.

While Burch Zimmerman was worrying about his SWAT teams and the strategy for conquering the "Bastille," as Max Vigeveno had dubbed it, Wally Nichols was worrying about his own strategy in the KBEX control room.

He had not taken the noon station break and was now so noting on his log. It bothered him, for Wally Nichols was not a man given to making decisions on his own. His was a life governed by the security of schedules prepared by others, of policies set down by others, and of practicing the electronic principles discovered by others.

The decision of canceling a station break should not have rested with him. It was something to be dictated by F.G. Bronson. It was his job as the program director to rule on such things. Or, it was to be an order passed to Wally from the very top, from Darrell King, the station manager. But neither man had called in time.

Wally loathed them for it. A simple phone call was all that it would have taken. A simple call, and he would have been off the hook.

Yet, neither F.G. nor Darrell King had had the courage to call, the decency to dial the unlisted number which would connect them with Wally.

"Yes." That was all either one of them would have had to say. "Yes."

What choice did they have? The terms had been quite explicit—"Don't interrupt this telecast or your crew will die."

Maybe if they had heard that voice cracking out over the shortwave monitor, maybe then Darrell and F.G. would have known there was no other way but to dump the break and stay with the remote from the church. Maybe . . .

But they hadn't heard the voice. Only he, Wally Nichols, had heard it. Only he knew how desperately vital it was to follow the commands of the woman's voice to the letter.

He found some solace in that. He realized that he had not really made the decision at all. It was the woman at the church with the gun pointed at Roger Uttenmeyer who had made the decision for him.

His eyes focused on the air monitor. The picture was still there. The nameless faces, the people with the weapons, the stunning reality, were still airing in living color. That meant that Roger and the crew still lived, because he, Wally Nichols, had willed it.

No, that wasn't the truth. The girl with the gun had willed it. He was only following orders as he always followed orders.

But they should have called, Wally rebuked the console before him.

As if responding to that rebuke, the light on the unlisted phone line flashed before the bell even rang. The voice on the other end was none other than Darrell King.

"Sorry I couldn't get back to you sooner," Darrell began. "I was on the horn with F.G. when you took it upon yourself to dump that noon break without clearance. He's really hacked at you for challenging his authority and bowing to the demands of terrorists." The last was said with a mirthless laugh.

"What else could I do?" Wally demanded, not caring

how insubordinate he might sound. He was still angry with Darrell King for forcing him to take the matter into his own hands.

Darrell was soothing. "You did the right thing, champ. I told F.G. we had no other choice."

"Thanks for the vote of confidence." Wally's sarcasm was still heavy. "We ride it out all the way, right, Mr. King?"

"You tell me, champ. Is the crew really in danger?"

Wally's dander burned hotter. He fought the impulse to slam down the phone.

"I assure you, Mr. King," the words were angry, "that I'm not joking. It's no hoax."

"I didn't mean that, champ. I meant, did the person you talked with sound like they really would kill the crew? Could you tell that person's state of mind? What exactly did they say? Did you get to speak with Roger? Did—"

"Mr. King, all I know is, I believe that Roger Uttenmeyer and the others will be shot if we so much as break for a news bulletin."

"Come on, now, champ. There must be some way around it. How about feeding a false air picture to the church?"

Wally gave a disgusted groan, and not too patiently explained to Darrell King that the monitor in the control booth at the church was a television set. There was no direct line. The control booth at the church received their signal over the air just like the folks at home.

"That's good enough for me, champ," Darrell said. "You're in the driver's seat. Let's just hope the whole thing is over by start-time on the football game."

"Football! You're not suggesting that the game is more important than human life?"

"Easy, Wally, easy. I don't know why I said that. A little unhappy humor I guess. I just wish this was one Sunday when the hometown blackout rule was still in effect. The Quarterback Club will boil me in oil if they don't get to see their heroes romp the Broncs."

Again Darrell's mirthless laugh grated on Wally's ear.

For a moment, only for a moment, Wally felt a twinge of sympathy for the man.

People were always upset when regular programming was preempted by news, no matter how important the news might be. Football fans were the worst of all.

Darrell and his staff would spend a lot of time in the days ahead pacifying viewers and mollifying advertisers whose advertising had been canceled by the emergency.

But the sympathy faded as he thought of Roger and the girl and the gun.

"I'm gonna' phone up our beloved news director now," Darrell said, "and see if we can get a mini-camera crew down to the church to cover the police action outside. How about you, champ? You got all the help you need? The network will probably want a feed on this."

"Buddy is due in to relieve me at one-fifteen. I'll stay, of course. I've asked Peloubet to call in a couple of extra tape men for editing and dubbing if we need it. If you do get ahold of Barry, tell him we're really light in the newsroom. Eleanor Sprague is the only one up there."

"That dumb kid," Darrell snorted. Then more evenly, "Well, it sounds like you're on top of it, champ. Hang in there. I'll be there as quick as I can to direct things personally."

Great! Fantastic! That was all he needed, Wally thought. The big boss hovering over him, getting in the way. Wonderful!

He looked back over at the monitor. What was that? . . . Oh, good grief, it looked like . . . It was . . . a black man . . . No, not a man, a body . . . a body in a canvas tarp!

It was so unreal on the monitor. Wally's head felt light. The picture began to blur and distort.

He rubbed his eyes to clear his vision and looked again. And, he knew.

He knew it wasn't his eyes. The video rolled sideways, caught briefly and locked in, then tore and broke up altogether.

Horrified, Wally watched it dissolve and fade away. They had lost the signal from the remote!

Frantically, Wally twirled dials and pushed buttons. Nothing. The screen remained black.

"Roger!" Wally screamed. "Don't kill him! Please don't kill him! It's not my fault. It's not my fault!"

The only reply was a maddening silence.

12:08 p.m.

The girl watched Brother John as he stood in the pulpit at First Church and pronounced the judgment of Abba to the astounded and frightened people all around her.

She was in the center aisle of the auditorium, standing guard with the rest of the Brotherhood. The weapon in her hands was heavy, but she bore it without complaint. It was an instrument of Abba's will, a part of her as she was an instrument of Abba's will by his own choosing.

She was on a high, higher than she had ever been before, but not on the drugs of her generation. The marijuana and alcohol which once enticed her, no longer held any fascination. They were empty, as empty as the faiths of her mother and father, as empty as their love for one another and for her.

But she was high, giddy, almost out of herself. It was as if she stood holding the world at arm's length in the palm of her hand. She was in the world, but not of it. She saw and understood and perceived on two levels.

She was aware of the seeming reality around her, the molecules and the atoms which Abba's power brought together to give substance to mortality. Beyond the shadows which men mistook for fact, on a higher plane, she saw the metaphysical truth of eternity as projected by the transcendence of Abba.

She had been initiated into the inner circle of the universe. She had been selected to sit in the company of the true saints and angels of Abba's Court. This day, she had been taken out of herself and it was as if the knowledge of the heavens was hers.

To think she had almost been left out of this wonderful mission—that but for the illness of another, she would have remained behind in the Temple to miss being a participant and a witness to the fearful Hour of the Lord which had been prophesied for thousands of years. It would have broken her heart. But she had not missed it. That was how well Abba knew his children.

It was all going so beautifully and so easily. Why not? Abba had planned it. He had written it in the stars and in the heavens.

True, she had had her moments of doubt. They pricked her consciousness. It was mildly upsetting to remember how her heart had pounded when she heard the first police cars out in the street. Oh, but Abba had known the police would come. He had prepared special details to guard the entrances to this church building. Their orders were to keep the police at bay by shooting over their heads.

Even in the terrible hour of his glory, Abba had compassion. The girl softly praised his name. Only if the police charged were the special details of the Brotherhood to shoot to kill.

Besides, the police were powerless before the might of Abba. The Priest had told her so.

She felt so safe, so secure. She was doing the will of Abba and no man on earth could rise against it now.

The Priest had warned that blood would be shed this day, but not the blood of the Brotherhood. So she banished her doubts and watched Brother John and waited and drifted in and out of herself borne by the glory of the pageant in which she had so large a role.

While she watched, two Brothers came down the aisle past her, carrying an object wrapped in a yardage of cloth. They moved, dancing before her as images in a golden dream.

There was something about the bundle which riveted her. Perhaps it was the manner in which the bundle sagged between the Brothers in such a strange, limp fashion.

Something else, too. She could remember no bundle in the plan outlined to her by the Priest. None at all. Perhaps she had missed it, or forgotten it. There had been so much to learn in so short a time.

However, there was no doubt the bundle must have a special meaning from the way the two Brothers so gingerly handled it. They placed it carefully on the platform in front of the pulpit.

Brother John came around the pulpit and ordered the Brothers to hold the bundle up between themselves so all could see it clearly.

At another order, the cloth was taken away from the object inside, and the girl thought, "Oh, what's so special about that? It's just a man, a black man."

There was blood on the lapels of the man's ill-fitting suit. It did not repulse her, for she had seen blood on others, those who had been Caught Up and who had refused to accept Abba for what he was.

This man had obviously been Caught Up, too, the first of many this day. An Infidel brought to Grace.

She studied the man, the first fruits of their labor. His head was flopped at a crazy tilt. His eyes were frozen in a grotesque expression of horror.

The girl understood, then, that he was dead. She felt the awesome presence of Death. It washed over her.

She looked around at the people in the pews. They were transfixed by Death, too. They knew this would happen to them if they refused the loving mercy of Abba. They feared it. It showed in their features. She could smell the fear upon them.

But she was not afraid. She scrutinized the face of Death. She saw it for what it was, not something of which to be afraid, but proof that Abba's day had come, proof of his power of Life and Death.

This was the proof of Scripture. This was the fulfillment of Revelation. Abba had said, "I am he that liveth, and was dead; and, behold, I am alive for evermore, Amen; and have the keys of hell and of death."

The keys had been unloosed. The prophecy was coming true!

It was just as Abba had predicted so many centuries before. "Every eye would see . . . every knee would bow."

It was marvelous how he had foreseen the advent of television. Sister Courage was aware of the cameras in the balcony watching the unfolding of events on this great day. Yes, it was all happening exactly as Abba had said it would in his book.

She was spellbound by the enormity of Abba's reach. She did not see the anguish on the face of the man a few pews behind her. She did not hear the low cry of his anguish.

She did not know his name was Stan Brown. She did not see him rise, pushing away the hands of his wife which sought so vainly to restrain him. No one did. All eyes were on the lifeless form of the black man in front of the pulpit.

But Stan Brown did rise. Peggy Brown did reach out to pull him back to safety beside her, but he roughly pushed her hands away.

The outrage of seeing sweet, gentle, old George Washington Isaiah Perkins dead at the hands of these fiends did cause him to need to strike out, to strike back.

The rage twitched through his muscles and gathered in the calloused hands which so deftly laid brick five days a week. With animal instinct, he searched for one of them on which to inflict that fury.

His eyes fell on the girl a few feet away. Her back was to him. The little tart was holding a rifle. If he could get to the girl, if he could take that weapon from her, he would make them sorry for what they had done to George. He would make them all sorry they were ever born.

He lunged forward.

Sister Courage suddenly felt the life being crushed from her by two strong arms that wrapped around her from behind. She felt the hot breath on her neck.

The arms grew tighter. They forced the breath from her lungs, the spittle from her lips. Her tongue seemed to fill her mouth and throat. She could not breathe. She could not yell out. Darkness rushed up to meet her. The gun dropped from her hands and bounced on the floor.

The vise around her ribs closed tighter still.

Sweat stood out on Stan Brown's clean-cut features, on the skin browned by hard labor in the sun. The girl was struggling against him, but he did not think of her as a girl. She was one of them. That was all. One of them who had to be punished for what they did to George.

He paid no attention to the footsteps racing over the hard tile floor, the floor George had lovingly polished. The footsteps closed.

Stan heard it then, the odd song of a naked knife blade whistling through space. His eyes caught briefly the leering face of a man.

The pain exploded as the knife sliced home. It caught him in the back above the right shoulder blade.

Stan Brown's arms tightened with the thrust, then opened as the steel tore through flesh and severed muscle. He lost his hold on the girl.

The knife pulled free and poised for another jab. Hands ripped him away from his intended victim.

Stan tried to raise his right arm to fend off the knife, but his arm hung uselessly at his side. At the same instant, he saw the rifle the girl had dropped and knew it was his only chance.

He threw himself flat as the knife whizzed past, its target spoiled by his sudden move. He stretched his left hand out. His fingers brushed against the wooden gunstock.

His strength was going. He could feel it slipping away. He had to get that gun. It was the only hope.

Calling for every muscle in his body to respond, he dragged himself forward. His hand inched closer to the prize. His fingers locked firmly around its stock. Just a little further and he would own it.

A hard heel smashed sharply down on his fingers. He cried in agony. The gun was kicked. It was sliding away from him.

A heavy weight caved in on top of him. The knees of the man who straddled him pressed into his shoulders and pinned him.

He twisted his head and saw the fierce impression of the man, the young man who had fallen on top of him, the man whose knife came streaking toward his heart.

12:14 p.m.

Wally Nichols was sick. Every muscle in his body ached. He was feverish. Any minute, he felt he would vomit.

He glared at the air monitor carrying the slide, "Technical Difficulties. Please Stand By."

He glared at the KBEX console, at the racks of transistors around him, at the shortwave microphone in his hand.

All of these things were garbage. The picture from the church was irretrievably lost. The shortwave radio brought no reply to his repeated attempts to establish contact with the remote site. Nothing he could do—none of the so-called "Magic of Television"—had worked.

As a result, Roger Uttenmeyer and the people with him, the people Wally knew and sometimes even allowed himself to like, might at this very moment be dead or dying.

Wally's fevered brain began to conjure up the image of that tragedy. He saw Roger with a bullet through the head. He saw Roger's widow and all those children who would now be fatherless, because somehow he, Wally Nichols, had failed.

Wally shut his eyes against the ghoulish images, but they remained. He could not escape the fact that if Roger did die—or was already dead—he must assume a large part of the blame.

"Hey, don't take it so hard." Peloubet laid a conciliatory hand on Wally's sagging shoulder. "We've done all we could. There's nothing more anyone could've done."

Peloubet had come up to the control room when the signal first went out. Along with Wally, he had sweated blood to trace the trouble, and to no avail.

"It's like those crazy riddles of mine," Peloubet continued to philosophize. "Sometimes, there is no logical answer. Sometimes nobody knows why things happen, they just do."

Wally shrugged Peloubet's hand away. He was in no mood to be absolved of the blame. Oddly, he wanted it. There was a strange kind of comfort in it.

If it wasn't his fault, it meant that there had never been anything he could have done to help Roger and the others. It meant that he had been helpless from start to finish, an observer from the beginning, powerless to influence the course of events.

In the past hour, Wally had seen himself as much more than a mere observer. He had been a participant. The action had hinged around him. It was his one opportunity to rise above being a pusher of buttons and a builder of model trains. It was his chance to become the hero he'd always dreamed of becoming.

If Peloubet was right in his conclusion that Wally was guiltless in the failure to keep the remote on the air, it also meant that he would have had no claim to heroics.

"Things just happen," Peloubet repeated.

"Go away," Wally said. "Just go away."

Peloubet drew a deep, sad breath. "Sure, Wally. Sure."

Wally could hear the man's footsteps receding toward the tape room. Abruptly, they stopped.

"Wally, look!" Peloubet's voice was choked with excitement.

Wally saw why. The preview monitor from the remote was fluttering to life.

The shortwave speaker crackled. "Wally? This is Roger. We're sending video again, are you getting?"

Wally depressed the talk button on the microphone. He wanted to say, "Thank God, you're still alive!" Instead he acknowledged with, "Yes, Roger. Yes. What happened?"

"They pulled the plug." Roger put particular emphasis on "they." "There were . . . uh . . . certain things they didn't want telecast."

"That's enough," the woman's voice told Roger. Apparently, she took the microphone away from him, for her voice filled Wally's ears with, "Just see what we allow to be seen goes out over your station."

The shortwave transmission ended with that, but Wally didn't care. Roger was alive. Wally Nichols was still involved in the drama.

Quickly he dissolved from the Technical Difficulties slide to the church feed.

Beautiful! The picture was beautiful, clear and strong. The congregation were still in their pews. The people with the guns were still in view. But the body? The body was gone from in front of the pulpit.

So, that's what *they* didn't want people to see. Well, if that was the way they wanted it, that's the way it would be.

What mattered? Wally Nichols was still in the action. He still had a chance to be a hero.

Another pair of eyes watched the scene at First Church reappear on the screen. This particular screen was on an inlaid mahogany console in the inner chamber of the Holy of Holies.

The eyes sparked anger as they watched. The man to whom they belonged was highly agitated. Even his neatly trimmed beard seemed to bristle.

He rubbed his fingers nervously through the gray

streaks at his temples. He tore the aviator's scarf from his neck and threw it in a corner of the richly appointed room.

That fool! That fool, John! He had been given explicit instructions to let no evidence of capital violence appear on television until the separation of the wheat and the chaff had been completed.

But, there he had been, flaunting the dead body, pointing it out as "proof" of what would happen to the Infidels who did not join the fold.

It was a good thing that Sister Heedful had been detailed to guard the television crew. A good thing.

The bearded man took pride in that decision. He had personally seen that she was given that assignment. He had given her the secret instructions to keep any unexpected and unplanned violence from the eyes of the cameras.

He had done it, because he knew that if the police believed the hostages were in imminent danger, they would in all likelihood rush the church. There was no way the members of the mission could stand such an onslaught.

That fool John! He was ruining the carefully laid plans, the precisely laid-out timetable. If the police had seen that body . . . if they did launch a counterattack . . . there would be no time to carry out the demands, to receive the ransom.

Well, at least the station was telecasting from the church once again. That was the signal he had arranged with Sister Heedful. Everything was still all right. The police were still at bay.

Yet, one could never be certain that things would remain that way. Not after that body had been clearly shown.

The bearded man reached for the intercom beside his chair.

"Yes, Lord?" the voice of the High Priest answered.

"Has my treasure been removed?"

"To the storehouse, Lord."

"And the Seven Beasts?"

"Placed and armed."

"Then relay the demands to the authorities."

"But, it's not time."

"I *know* that!" The bearded man lost control for a moment. Then, more softly, "The timetable has been changed by that fool, John."

"I see."

"But I still think we can carry it off. After all, I am that I am."

The High Priest sniggered, "Praise Abba."

"Thank you. Oh, and my congregation?"

"In the Court of Adoration, praying for the success of the mission."

"Good. I shall have to address them soon. One last time. Be ready to prepare my way."

"Consider it done, my Lord."

For a long time after he had finished with the High Priest, the bearded man sat watching the television screen.

It was hard giving all this up, he lamented, but there was the promise of better things to come. What was it that was said in the scriptures?

"I go to prepare a place for you." How apt that description was. How very apt.

No more seedy hotels for a Temple. From this day forward, only mansions of gold.

12:21 p.m.

Four bodies had been removed from the auditorium of First Church during the television blackout and hidden from public view in the pastor's study. One of these was the Reverend Malcolm Stansfield himself, because in the instant of Stan Brown's desperate attempt, he had found the inspiration of physical courage.

The question of courage would be much argued in the press over the days and weeks to come. Repeatedly, it would be asked, why didn't the people in the sanctuary of Grunnell's First Church do more to resist their captors?

As one TV commentator would put it in introducing a TV debate on the subject, "There were almost six hundred able-bodied men in church that morning, and twenty-eight cult members who held them hostage. Six hundred to twenty-eight, not counting women and children. Surely, you would think that six hundred could overpower twenty-eight, even if those twenty-eight were armed.

"In the first two hours, though, only three of that great number of men displayed any will to resist. One was an old man who defied his tormentors by walking away from them. He didn't get very far. Another was a bricklayer who sought to take a weapon from one of the female members of the death squad. He was stabbed for his trouble. And the third was the pastor of the church. His fate has been well publicized. Not one other man in those pews so much as lifted a little finger. The question remains, 'Why?'"

Why? That was the question Malcolm had asked himself as he sat on the platform on that fateful Sunday.

George Perkins was dead. Why? Why was God letting this thing happen? It was not the dispassionate theological query Malcolm was so fond of putting forth. It was emotional, born of fury, written in wrath.

Nor could he reply to himself with the same kind of seeming logic which said only minutes before that he was unable to respond because his family could not survive without a husband and father. His family? They were his weak excuse for his own fear.

And then he had seen Stan Brown's brave assault and the contagion of it grabbed him. Malcolm sprang from his chair and threw himself at Brother John, whose attention riveted on the action in the center aisle.

Malcolm's charge was a blind rampage. His head down, he intended to catch his prey in the small of the back, bowling him over before the young man knew what hit him.

Yet, by some sixth sense, Brother John must have felt Malcolm's coming. Too late, Malcolm saw John twist away. Too late, Malcolm sought to dodge the rabbit punch that axed for his neck.

Malcolm's rage splintered into befuddlement as a hardness cracked against his skull and catapulted him into murky shadows.

In the audience, Miriam strangled back a cry and clutched her children to her. Peggy Brown was senseless in her grief, but no one else stirred.

From the balcony, a woman screamed, "Get those corpses out of here before I let these TV cameras be turned back on."

On the platform, Brother John squinted up at the lights

and yelled instructions. Six members of the Brotherhood stepped forward and hoisted Malcolm Stansfield, Stan Brown and George Perkins as so much yielding flesh.

"Take them out this way," Brother John barked. "There's an office where we can dump them."

As an afterthought, he jerked a stunned Harold Thomas from his seat. "You're a disturbing influence, too, *Brother*," he spat out in bitter disgust.

Not one of the six hundred men in the pews moved. They sat, watching dumbly as their pastor and two of their fellow churchmen were dragged away, not knowing whether Malcolm Stansfield and Stan Brown were alive or dead. Wondering only vaguely what might become of the former cult member they had come so eagerly to hear.

But Malcolm Stansfield was not dead. His consciousness was swirling in a place of deep darkness, and something, or someone, was calling to him through the veil.

He contended against the force which would turn him from the soothing blackness. "Let me go!" He thought he shouted it, but was not certain. He was not certain of anything.

A burning, stinging pain slapped against his cheek, joining with the throbbing hurt in his head and neck. He tried to lift a hand to the new injury, but his arm was restrained. No matter how he strived, he could not raise it.

He was slapped again. It was so pitch black here, he could not see who was doing it, who was holding his arms.

Far away, a dim, gray glow appeared in the curtain of night. The light grew in size and brightness. From beyond the light came an undertone.

"I think this one is coming around," it said.

Another slap. Malcolm cringed against it. The light was blinding. Sluggishly, his vision cleared and he could see he was in a room. His office! The blinds at the window were drawn, but the light still hurt his eyes.

He blinked. His head ached with a dull palpitation. The room was swimming. He blinked a second time and the room lost its momentum, gradually settling before him. He was conscious.

The first thing he saw clearly were his own arms, strapped with belts to the armrests of one of his side chairs. He was sitting up. How had he gotten here? The last thing he remembered beyond the void was the sanctuary and . . .

He turned his head, the effort setting the demons in his skull on fire, and came face to face with Brother John. John was smirking, his upper lip curled back to reveal his crooked, yellow teeth.

"Welcome back to the land of the living, preacher," Brother John snickered.

Malcolm tried to look away, but Brother John pinched Malcolm's jaw between thumb and fingers and forced him to meet his eyes.

"That was a stupid thing you pulled in there, preacher. Stupid! You're a very stupid man. See what happens to stupid people who do stupid things?"

He jerked a thumb over his shoulder at Stan Brown, who was sprawled on the carpet. Blood was seeping from Stan's wounds, staining the floor beneath with a bright pool.

"What have you done to him?"

"Don't worry, preacher. He's still alive. See?" Brother John moved to Stan Brown and toed his ribs.

Stan moaned weakly.

"Of course, he won't be with us for long. I think the poor old boy is bleeding to death."

"Get a doctor!" Malcolm strained against the bonds that held him to the chair. "Please, get a doctor."

"Hear that?" Brother John said to his three comrades with him in the study. "He wants us to get a doctor."

The others smiled stoically and stayed immobile.

"Then, let me help him. Please!" Malcolm struggled to rise, dragging the chair with him.

Brother John shoved him back with such force that the chair tipped and almost went over backwards.

"You are a pigheaded man, preacher," Brother John admonished. "Use your eyes. He's beyond helping by human hands. Only Abba can do anything for him. The same with this one."

He was standing over the corpse of George Perkins. George had been placed in front of Malcolm's desk and stripped of the tarp in which he had been wrapped earlier.

Malcolm gagged. "You animals!"

"Because we killed? No, preacher we do the will of Abba, our Father. That one is dying because he went against that will. And, this one died because he blundered into the place where some of us were waiting to execute that will." John advanced on Malcolm. "And you will die unless you cooperate with us."

"No! I will never cooperate with you." Malcolm spoke not so much with the newly discovered physical courage as with the conviction of repugnance. He was beyond reasoning. He had reached a primordial hatred, a hatred which he had thought was buried forever beneath his Christian belief.

"I think you will, preacher. I think you will." The undercurrent of intimidation was in the level tone with which Brother John delivered the line. He leaned down, putting his hands over Malcolm's arms. With a smile, he let his full weight come down, driving the pastor's flesh into the armrests, cutting off the circulation until Malcolm grimaced with pain.

"What's the matter, preacher, got a cramp?" Brother John taunted.

Malcolm spit at him.

John drew back sharply, regarded the spittle on his jacket, then slapped Malcolm viciously.

"Spit on me again, preacher, and you won't have the chance to cooperate!"

"Listen to them, sir. Please, do what they say. They're insane."

For the first time, Malcolm was aware of the figure of Harold Thomas in a corner of the room. He, too, was strapped by belts in a chair. His eyes bulged with fright. Tears stained his cheeks.

Brother John turned on him. "Liar! You are so filled with evil you don't recognize the sanity of Abba's judgment."

Harold Thomas made no reply. He stared at John with those bulging, tormented eyes.

Brother John stalked toward him. "You see? You don't deny you are a liar, a Judas. You sat at Abba's table. You accepted Abba's blessings. You have seen the truth, and still you appoint yourself to slander our Father.

"Why are you doing it, Thomas? Because Abba did not make you High Priest? For revenge? Is that it? Or, maybe it's for money. The devil take you, answer me!"

Harold Thomas appeared on the breaking point, but when he spoke, his words were clear and strong. "For Christ. For Jesus Christ, my Lord."

That the response was unexpected by John was plain. Indecisiveness crisscrossed his features and then quickly passed.

"Abba is your Lord!" The statement was rabid.

Harold Thomas said nothing.

Brother John clawed the .45 from the holster under his jacket. He shoved the muzzle into Harold Thomas' face.

"Say it! 'Abba is my Lord.'"

Closing his eyes, Harold Thomas began to pray. "Our Father which art in heaven . . ."

"Say it!"

"Hallowed be thy name . . ."

"Look at me, Thomas. I'm going to pull the trigger."

"Thy kingdom come . . ."

"'Abba is my Lord.'"

"Thy will be done . . ."

"You're going to die, and that scares you, doesn't it, Judas?"

". . . in earth, as it is in heaven . . ."

"'If a soul sin, and commit a trespass against the Lord Abba, and lie unto his neighbor in that which was delivered him—the holy word of Abba—then it shall be because he hath sinned and is guilty.'"

"Give us this day . . ."

"Brother Thomas, I have judged you in the name of Abba . . ."

". . . our daily bread . . ."

". . . and have found you guilty of heresy!"

"Forgive us our debts . . ."

"I sentence you to death."

Harold Thomas opened his eyes and looked directly into the eyes of Brother John. ". . . as we forgive our debtors."

Malcolm wanted to scream out. He wanted to stop it, but it was past stopping.

The other members of the Brotherhood strained forward. If they sought to halt it, they could not.

Brother John's finger pushed against the trigger.

"Lord, lay not this sin to their—"

Harold Thomas was repeating Stephen's prayer when his voice was lost in the lethal explosion, a single, flat hammering sound which singed the sensibilities.

Bitter tears flooded Malcolm's eyes, grief and shock of seeing a human life snuffed out, encouraged by the saturation of gunpowder released into the air.

"Praise be to Abba," Brother John said, and stepped away from the body.

"Praise be to Abba," the others reprised.

Through the lingering smoke fogging the room, Malcolm saw the bloodied, shredded flesh and bone that had been the face of Harold Thomas. He retched, the sour smell of his nausea mingling with the acid vapor of the gun.

In the midst of the shock, Brother John was at Malcolm yet again.

"Have you seen enough, preacher? We're going to go back to the sanctuary, you and I, and you're going to get on your knees. Then, I'm going to put this gun to your head and you're going to say, 'Abba is my Lord.'

"You're going to be the first Caught Up today, preacher. As Abba has commanded, 'Bell the goat, and the sheep will follow.'"

Malcolm dared him with a contemptuous stare.

"'Abba is my Lord.' See how easy it is to say, preacher?"

"Kill me. Go ahead, kill me and be done." Malcolm heard himself saying it, and wondered if he really meant it.

The .45 crept closer.

Let me be as brave as Harold Thomas, Lord Jesus, Malcolm silently petitioned. *Don't let me cringe.*

The gun pressed against his forehead.

"Don't make me do it, preacher."

"Kill me. Please!" Yes, he did mean it. He did want the strength of death. He didn't know how much longer he could cling to his resolve.

"You're a fool." Brother John's voice was burred with disgust. His jaw worked with ire. He rammed the gun harder into Malcolm's skin. Then, he hesitated. Something seemed to be rolling through his brain. His mouth set as he reached his decision.

Without warning, he lowered the pistol.

"To kill you before we're through would be too easy for you."

He holstered the .45 and swung to the others. "Anybody have any ideas how we can redeem this fool?"

Numb with the strain of the last minutes, Malcolm slumped forward. Only the fact that he was tied to the chair kept him from collapsing completely. Another test was surely coming. How could he take any more? His courage was seeping away.

"Hey, what about this?" One of the Brothers, a stocky, blue-eyed man was standing by Malcolm's desk. In his hands was a silver-edged picture frame.

Malcolm stiffened. The man was holding the portrait of Miriam and the children, given him on his last birthday by the church. Miriam had conspired with the congregation, keeping the studio sitting a secret from him. How that portrait had delighted him. It was the only professional photograph he owned of his family.

"Leave that alone!" He hurled it viciously through clenched teeth.

"Let me see that," Brother John said. He took the picture and made a great show of examining it.

"They're out there in the auditorium," the man who had discovered the photograph said. "I saw them sitting near the front."

Brother John nodded and smiled. "Is this your family, preacher?"

Malcolm refused to answer.

"Of course they are. An important man like you should have a picture of his family on his desk. Nice looking. I wouldn't be so ashamed of them, if they were mine."

"*They're not my family,*" he wanted to say, but he knew the lie, just like his silence, would be useless.

"Pretty wife. Cute kids. How old are your kids, preacher? You don't need to tell me. I can guess. Mind if I take this out of the frame? I want to get a better look."

He popped the easel back from its clips and yanked the photograph roughly from the frame, tossing the latter carelessly over his shoulder.

"Oh, yes, now I can see everything very well. The boy favors his mother, but the girl looks like you, preacher. Want to see?"

He thrust the image in Malcolm's face. "A man like you

must put great store in his wife and children. You wouldn't want to see anything happen to them, would you?

"Don't look so scared. We wouldn't want to harm them, either. Unless . . ." he paused. "Unless you fail to lead in their salvation, and the salvation of all the others."

The smile faded. "Say it, preacher. 'Abba is Lord.'"

Malcolm blinked through the tears at Miriam's lovely features, at the grinning faces of teenaged Malcolm Jr. and innocent Beth.

"Abba is Lord." Brother John shrugged and purposefully tore Beth from the portrait.

"I can't!"

"Sure you can, preacher." Malcolm Jr. was ripped away. "Abba is Lord."

"Don't make me!"

"It's for your own good, preacher, and for theirs." One-by-one, Brother John crumpled the torn pieces of the photograph and dropped them in Malcolm's lap.

"Abba is Lord," John said, and the first piece fell.

"Abba is Lord." The second piece was dropped.

"Abba is Lord." The third fell and with it, Malcolm's last shard of resistance.

His body shook with a shuddering wail. There was no choice, no choice at all.

Brother John laughed. "Brothers, the goat is belled."

12:32 p.m.

In a borrowed office at the Denton Building, Burch Zimmerman lit a cigarette with a gold-plated lighter from the polished desktop and experienced pangs of jealousy.

This office to which the building caretaker had guided them was fancier than Burch's own office—far fancier—and it belonged to a man who was third vice-president of a second-rate import company.

There has been no justice in the world from the beginning, Burch mused. He, Zimmerman, was only a heartbeat—well, maybe a couple of heartbeats—from being Chief of Police and his office was gunmetal-gray-government-schlock. But the third vice-president of a sleazy importer—a man whose largest contribution to the welfare of society was bamboo puzzles from Hong Kong—had a richly appointed office with a gold-plated desk lighter.

Burch admired the lighter, rolling it in his hand, feeling the substance of its surface. It was a nice piece of workmanship. He couldn't help visualizing how it might look on somebody's coffee table . . . maybe even his coffee table. It would certainly give his lonely bachelor's apartment a little class.

A cigarette lighter of this quality was rare, indeed, he

observed. Perhaps he should put it in his own pocket to keep some other light-fingered cop from lifting it. It would be a terrible thing for a citizen who donated the use of his office as a command post to get his desk-top lighter stolen by the police. No doubt, it would be safer in Burch's pocket. And if he should accidentally carry it home, well . . .

"If you're going to do something, do it!" The voice of Sergeant Shaw intruded on Burch Zimmerman's meditation.

Burch was caught, his only crime thinking about committing a crime. He dropped the lighter as a hot potato and guiltily shoved it away before he realized that Sergeant Shaw was standing beside the windows, binoculars trained on the circular window directly across the street from this second story office. Shaw's comment had been rhetorical, addressed to the terrorists who couldn't hear it in the first place.

Burch exhaled a cloud of smoke and relief. If anyone had seen the look on his face as he toyed with the lighter, they would have "made" him, so it was a good thing he and Shaw were alone. Otherwise, his reputation as an honest cop would be down the drain. And for what? A gold lighter? In all the years on the force, he had never taken more than a cup of coffee and free meal from any citizen. What was so appealing about the lighter anyway?

The truth was, it wasn't the lighter at all. It was this office, and his jealousy of the schlepp that owned it.

Deliberately, Burch pushed the tempting lighter behind a chrome water pitcher and turned his attention to the small TV set on one corner of the desk.

The caretaker had borrowed the Sony Trinitron from another office in the building. It was a honey of a set. The nine-inch screen gave a sharp, clear picture with very life-like colors.

"Hey, Shaw," Burch called, "why are you burning your eyeballs on those glasses, when you can come over here and watch it all close-up?"

"I prefer my crooks in person," Shaw said.

"Yeah? What do you see? In person, I mean?"

"Not much," Shaw admitted. "A little bit of the balcony. The top of the pulpit. Once in awhile, I catch a glimpse of one of the subjects. They're better armed than we are."

"Then why keep straining your eyes?"

"I don't know. It helps the waiting, I guess."

"Yeah," Burch said. He leaned forward and cupped his chin in his hands as he studied the TV screen. "Well, they aren't showing much more on the TV."

He watched as the camera panned the sanctuary. It all looked as quiet as it had been for the last twenty minutes. Yet, something about it bugged him. There was something missing in that picture. But what?

Max Vigeveno popped his head in the door. "Agent Clymer is on line one, Zim. He's got the file on the Brotherhood in front of him now."

Burch waved Max Vigeveno on into the room as he picked up the telephone.

"How's my favorite G-man this morning?" he said.

Clymer laughed. "You're the only man I know who still persists in calling us G-men, Zim. We call ourselves 'agents' at the FBI these days."

"Okay, *agent,* what you got for me?"

"You have something to make notes on?" Clymer interjected.

Burch clapped his hand over the receiver. "Give me some paper, Max."

Max took a notebook from his coat pocket and flipped through it. He found a blank sheet and tore it out, handing it to Burch.

Burch grabbed a fountain pen from a desk set in front of him. Balancing the phone between his ear and shoulder, he told Clymer to go ahead.

"It's not much, Zim," Clymer said, "but here goes.

"The Brotherhood was founded by one Jackson Bails, also known as Jack Bailey, also known as Bailey Jackson, also known as—"

"Skip the preliminaries, Clymer, I don't have that much paper."

"Yeah, sure." There was a rustle on Clymer's end, a pause, then Clymer cleared his throat and resumed reading. "This fellow Bails has nineteen priors, mostly petty. He took the big tumble over—get this, Zim—bigamy. Five to ten in Chino, served eighteen months.

"He came out claiming he had found religion in prison. He was ordained by one of those mail-order churches and set up 'The United Church of the Brothers in Christ.'

"Somebody staked him—one of his former wives we hear—and he began to attract a small following. Mostly youngsters.

"At first, his theology was pretty straight. Not for long, though. He got pretty weird in his teachings. Took to calling himself 'Abba.' Some of his followers dropped out. Said he had taken to thinking he was God.

"Anyway, he bought a bus and for the next three years, traveled all over the country. He continued to call San Francisco his headquarters, but that was only a mail box.

"His followers traveled with him, regular gypsies.

"Then Bails blew into town here. He bought an old skid-row hotel over on Seventeenth and Welsh and renamed his church 'The Temple of the Brotherhood.'

"The religious con must be pretty good, because he paid cash. There's been talk on the street that he's dealing in arms and drugs. We've never been able to catch him at it, though."

"Hey, G-man, give me a break," Burch said. "I'm running out of paper."

"You've about got it all," Clymer said. "We've tried to get an undercover agent into Bails' church, but he's smart. So far, we've had no luck.

"We've tried for search warrants a couple of times, but the courts don't want to be accused of stepping on First Amendment rights. Makes it tough for us to do our job."

"Got a description of the crumb?"

"Just a second . . . Yeah, here. Bails is five-nine, one-sixty-five. Well-built. Fifty-three years of age. Brown eyes. Gray hair. He has a beard. No other distinguishings. Forceful personality. Likes young girls."

"Have you been keeping up on the situation we got here?" Burch asked as he scribbled the last of Clymer's description.

"Since your man called," Clymer said, "I kept the TV set on while I dug out this file."

"Did you see Bails in the church?"

"No. I don't think so. Of course, it's hard to tell. But if he's there, he's been keeping out of camera range.

"It's not his style to be there, anyway. He probably sent his henchmen, while he sits back somewhere waiting to run, if things don't go his way."

Burch drummed the pen on the desk pensively. "I want your opinion, G-man—what do you think they'll do to those hostages?"

"Have you had any ransom demands?"

"Not yet."

"If I know Bails, you will have."

"But, what do you think they'll do to the hostages?"

"Let me put it this way, Zim. Every place the Brotherhood has been, bodies suddenly turn up. Always young people. Always, they've been tortured. Usually, they're very hard to identify."

"Yeah, we've had a few of those around here, lately," Burch said. But he was thinking of his own daughter, Sandy. He was remembering the trip to California to claim her body. He wondered if the Brotherhood had anything to do with her murder.

No, that would be too much coincidence. He rubbed his

forehead, banishing the remembered agony.

"So, you're telling me you think they'll kill the hostages."

"That's what I think, Burch."

Burch swore softly.

"Would it help if I came down there?" Clymer wanted to know. "Officially, the Bureau can't get involved yet, as you are aware. Technically, they haven't broken any Federal laws. But I'd like to be in on it as an interested citizen until they do."

"Welcome, I'm sure."

"What do you think, Zim?" Max Vigeveno asked after Burch had finished the call.

"I'd rather be the chief," Burch said. "He's out of town, fishing."

Burch got up from the desk and moved over to the window. He took the binoculars from Shaw and zeroed in on the view through the church's broken window.

"You can see better on the TV," he finally said, handing the binoculars back to Shaw.

"Max, get the SWAT commandos up here for a meeting, and do it now." And, then, as an afterthought, "And send as many squads as we can spare over to the Temple of the Brotherhood on Seventeenth and Welsh. I want them to arrest everyone there."

"It's as good as done," Max said, springing toward the door.

"Discretion. Tell 'em to use it, Max. It may be the only chance we have to stop a bloodbath."

Grimly, Max nodded and exited.

Burch went back to the desk and sat down. He stared at the Sony. Something was still missing. A way to break into the Bastille, that was what was lacking.

"Well, Reverend Stansfield," Burch said to the screen, "you sure have your Cult Sunday."

Then, it came to him. He bent down closer to the small

screen. Stansfield. He wasn't in the picture. He wasn't on the platform. A tingling chill worked its way up his back.

Maybe the bloodbath had already begun.

1:00 p.m.

The girl was petrified. She was still shaking inside from the awful attack she had sustained. Her ribs still ached. The man had squeezed so hard. She had been so humiliated. And now, for the second time in one day, she had officially been singled out. She must have done something grievously wrong to be relieved of her assignment as one of the guards of the Infidels and ushered from the sanctuary by Brother Bartholomew.

Perhaps they had discovered that it was she, after all, who had made the improper early morning telephone call to Stansfield. In any event, being singled out twice by the Brothers did not settle well.

The blood still glistened on Brother Bartholomew's clothing as he led her to the hall. Blood from her attacker, blood Bartholomew had shed in saving her.

Once in the hallway, Brother Bartholomew pointed her in the direction of a door with a little sign above it: *Pastor's Study*.

"Brother John is waiting for you there," he said.

"But why? I'm being more care—"

He cut her off. "No time for questions, Sister. Do what I tell you."

And so she went, afraid, her own footsteps echoing as a

counterpoint to her anxiety.

Bartholomew watched her from the distance, standing by the side entrance of the auditorium. When she stopped by the appointed door and looked back at him, he nodded curtly, and waited until she knocked. Satisfied she had done his bidding, he disappeared into the sanctuary.

She knocked again, timidly. A muffled voice came from behind the door. "Who is it?"

"Sist . . . Sister Courage." She stumbled over her own name, a clue to how frightened and shaken she was.

"Be right there, Sister Courage." Brother John's voice was as muffled as the first, but it did not sound angry. The fact did little to ease her alarm.

The door opened just enough to allow Brother John to step out beside her. He closed it quickly, as if the room held a secret he did not want her to share.

"Thanks for coming so promptly," he said.

"If I've done something wrong, I'm sorry. I didn't mean—"

He laughed, putting his arm around her. It was like her carnal father used to do. It felt so strong and comforting.

"No, Sister. You haven't done anything, have you?"

"The man. I didn't know he was—"

"That. Forget it. I didn't know Brother Bartholomew was going to send you. I mean, I just told him to send one of the Sisters to me."

"I don't understand," she managed.

"You will," he smiled mysteriously. "But first, tell me, how's it going in there?"

"All right," she answered, wanting to be helpful, needing to make amends. "Some of them are getting restless, and some kids have to go to the bathroom. I heard several adults whispering about their pastor. They wonder what we've done with him."

"I'll just bet they do." He was obviously pleased by her report.

Still, she could not rid herself of the idea that all this had something to do with the way she had allowed herself to be disarmed.

"Brother John, if you're angry with what happened in there . . ." tears filled her eyes, "it wasn't my fault. I didn't see that man until he grabbed me. I . . . I . . ."

"Stop blubbering, Sister. Didn't I say this had nothing to do with that?" He was losing patience with her. "No one is blaming you. No one saw that fool before he jumped you."

He took his arm from her shoulder and pivoted away. "You'd better go back and send another Sister. You're too upset for what I have in mind."

"No, please! If you want me to do something, I can do it."

He looked at her, disbelieving what she said.

"Whatever it is. Please."

He pulled at the lobe of his ear, contemplating her. "I don't know," he sighed.

"I want to make it up to you and the others," she pleaded. "I don't want you to think I can't handle things like that man."

"Do you love Abba?" he demanded.

It hurt her to think that any Brother might think otherwise. "Yes. Oh, yes."

He softened. "And Abba loves you."

He approached her and gently kissed her on the cheek. It was so good to have someone kiss her, for while much was said about love in the Brotherhood, there was little physical affection displayed. Her tears quit flowing. The love of Abba was with her once again.

Tenderly, Brother John reached up and pushed a stray lock of her hair away from her forehead. He kissed her again.

"Praise be to Abba," she whispered.

"Sister," he said tenderly, "I'm glad Brother Bartholomew sent you. Because, what I want done, demands a perfect love for Abba and his Brotherhood. You love like that, don't you?"

"Yes."

"Yeah, I feel it in you." He withdrew the fingers that caressed her hair. She was quivering. She wanted him desperately to touch her again, to show her how much she was loved and wanted.

The tenderness was gone. He was showing her some torn and crumpled pieces of a photograph.

"Do you recognize this broad and these kids?"

She nodded. "I think I saw them in there."

"You did. I want you to go back in and find them. Sit next to them. Keep your rifle up. Point it, casually, at the woman so we can see what you're doing when we're up on the platform."

She took the pieces of the picture from him and looked at the woman. An Infidel, one of them. Attractive, but not of Abba's fold.

"If I point to you, I want you to bring the lady and her kids up to me on the platform."

"To you, on the platform," she repeated. She wanted him to know she understood his instructions.

"If anything happens before that," he said, "I mean, if the police come busting in or something, I want you to . . . kill them."

He gazed intently into her eyes, testing her. "Do you think you can do that, if you have to? Kill them?"

She started to reply, but he put his finger to her lips to stop her.

"Not too fast, Sister. Think about it. Can you really do it?"

He took his finger from her lips. She tilted her chin until her eyes met his.

"For the love of Abba," she said.

1:05 p.m.

For awhile after Harold Thomas had been shot and Brother John threatened Malcolm Stansfield with the death of his family unless he cooperated, the preacher had slipped back into unconsciousness.

He was submerged into a half-world. His mind, weary of the pain and horror of the last two hours, was drifting in and out of focus. He saw and talked to Harold Thomas, and as he was talking to the boy, Harold Thomas dissolved before his eyes and became a skeleton, a skeleton with only half a skull.

And the skull turned and became a window, a stained-glass window of brilliant design with lavenders and pinks and, in the center, red.

Malcolm reached out to touch the red pane and found it not glass, but blood. He recoiled at the wet stickiness that cleaved to his fingers.

He backed away, and the tiny red pool became wider, a sea, a wall. It covered the pinks and the lavenders. They fractured and were swallowed into the wall and the wall changed shape and became Brother John.

Brother John's face was maniacal. His eyes were like a cat's eyes, with slitted pupils. He laughed soundlessly and pointed his finger into the distance. But the finger wasn't a finger, it was a gun, spitting flame.

Malcolm turned to see what the gun was shooting at. Miriam and the children. Blood ran from their wounds. They reached out their hands to him, begging him to save them.

He ran toward them, but the faster he ran, the further away they were. They kept receding until they vanished altogether, and he was alone in the darkness. Alone. He saw and heard no more.

He awakened with a start. Immediately, he knew where he was. In his own office, strapped to a chair, back to a real world as nightmarish as his feverish dream.

His mind cleared. The darkness had refreshed him. He had no idea of how long he had been out, but it could not have been long. The light coming through the window indicated it was still early afternoon.

There were three members of the Brotherhood in the room with him. They were talking among themselves, their backs to him. He couldn't be certain, but Brother John seemed to be missing.

Someone had mercifully draped a jacket over Harold Thomas, hiding the gruesomeness of his murder. Stan Brown was still sprawled on the floor, his labored breathing degenerating to a shallow, irregular rattle. It was a sign his end was near. He needed medical attention, and soon.

Be with him, Lord, Malcolm prayed, then lowered his gaze to the belts around his arms. Whoever had placed them had done a very good job. They were tight enough to prohibit movement, but not tight enough to completely cut off the circulation.

For a moment, Malcolm panicked. How could he help Stan—how could he help anyone if he could not free himself from the bonds?

I've got to get ahold of myself, he contended with his panic in thought. *I've got to think. What can I use against them? What have I got that I can use to press an advantage?*

The answer did not come swiftly. It formed slowly, an abstraction at first, which became knowledge, a comforting realization.

He smiled in spite of himself at it. If anyone could see him now, they would think he had gone mad. Here he was, trussed to a chair, without a gun, while his enemies had many. Here he was, in a room with two dead men and another on the threshold of death, his family threatened, his parishioners captive, and he was no longer afraid.

For, he realized, it was time for his faith to show its strength. This was *war*. He had something better than the weapons of the Brotherhood. He had Christ and the Holy Spirit.

"*Greater is he that is in you.*" At last, he truly understood that fantastic passage of scripture.

But, now, what must he do? What did the Lord want?

The conversation among the three members of the Brotherhood grew louder.

"I don't like it," one was saying. "I wish we could get it over with and get out of here, before the cops outside decide to take matters in their own hands."

"What's the matter, Brother Nathanael? Don't you think Abba can get us out of here?"

"Sure, I do. But, I would feel better if Abba was with us. I don't like the way Brother John is handling things."

"Brother John was chosen to lead by Abba," the third Brother broke in.

"Then why doesn't he lead?" Nathanael seemed exasperated. "Why doesn't he quit playing games with these poor people and get on with the Catching Up?"

"Abba has ordained that the ceremony cannot begin until at least 1:30."

"Yeah? Do you know what that means?" Nathanael complained. "Do you have any comprehension of how long it's going to take to process a thousand Infidels?"

"It'll take as long as it takes," the second Brother said rigidly.

"I figure a minimum of three minutes per person," Nathanael explained. "That's three thousand minutes. What's three thousand divided by sixty?"

While Brother Nathanael drew the equation in the air with his finger and tried to find the answer, the second Brother said, "The longer it takes, the better. Didn't you hear what Abba said? The more time we give him, the better he's gonna' be able to deal with the cops."

Nathanael whistled, "Fifty hours. At three minutes per, it'll take fifty hours. There's no way those cops are gonna' wait that long."

"Don't you believe it's in Abba's power to keep them waiting?" The second Brother's voice was cold.

"Brother Nathanael, keep it up, and so help me," the third Brother warned, "I'll bear witness against you before Abba's Sanhedrin."

The portent seemed to have a powerful effect on Brother Nathanael. He blanched. "No. No, I love Abba. I serve him. It's just that . . ."

"You're a Doubter," the third Brother upbraided. "There is no room for Doubters in Abba's legion."

"I'm not a Doubter!" Nathanael contradicted, as if the louder he disavowed it, the more certain the refutation would be. "I . . . I . . . This place gives me the jitters, that's all."

He began to pace. "I have the right to be jittery, don't I?"

He started to turn to confront the others again, but in the turning he tripped over Stan Brown's form.

Stan Brown gave a long and feverish groan. Brother Nathanael stared down at him with open rancor.

"It's things like this creep that give me the jitters," he spluttered. "I ought to put a bullet in him and put him out of his misery."

"Then, do it," the third Brother prompted.

Nathanael swung the slinged rifle from his shoulder.

"Leave him alone," Malcolm said flatly, surprised by the strength of his own voice.

It surprised Brother Nathanael, too. His head snapped up. His eyes flared.

"Maybe I ought to put a bullet in you, instead, preacher," he threatened.

"Just leave him alone," Malcolm repeated.

In a low, commando-like crouch, Brother Nathanael crossed toward Malcolm. His face twisted with enmity.

"All right, you can shoot me," Malcolm said with a curious bravery that surprised even himself. "But what would it prove? That you're not a Doubter? No, it would prove only that you can kill me."

Brother Nathanael flinched. He didn't quite know what to make of Malcolm's sudden temerity.

Long ago, Malcolm had learned in his counseling ministry that sometimes irrational men could be talked out of their intentions by a logic which pandered to their emotions. He had once talked a man out of suicide. This was not all that different, except the life he was battling to save was his own.

He took a deep breath and consciously ignored the rifle which was pointed at him.

"It would seem to me," he ventured calmly, "that the best way to prove you don't have doubts is to convince me that I should believe in your Abba."

Nathanael's eyes narrowed. "What are you trying to pull, preacher?"

"Nothing," Malcolm bluffed. "I only want you to tell me why Abba is so special."

For a millisecond, he thought he had lost his gamble. *Whatever I do, I can't show fear,* he told himself. *I've done too much of that already.*

But the moment passed. "I've been informed that I'm

essential to your plans for converting the others," he said. It sounded stiff. He had to lighten up, to make it more conversational.

"Look," Malcolm said, "all I'm trying to do is find out what I'm supposed to say when we get back out there."

"He's stalling, Nathanael," the third Brother chimed in.

"Or, maybe Brother Nathanael doesn't know what to tell him," the second Brother scoffed.

"Stay out of this," Nathanael rebuffed them. "It's between him and me."

"You're right," nodded Malcolm. "It is between us. I don't think those two really understand, do they? But we do. I understand you, Brother Nathanael."

Nathanael looked quizzical, but the rifle remained firmly in his hands. He made no move to lower it.

"Please, tell me about Abba," Malcolm adopted a pretense of really wanting to understand.

"You don't really want to know," Nathanael became hostile again. "You're just playing me along, stringing me out."

"I'm not in a position to do that. I really want to know."

"I really could kill you, you know," Brother Nathanael mouthed savagely.

"Yes."

"Bang. It wouldn't matter."

"You have the gun," Malcolm mollified.

"And I have the love," there was a prideful ring in Nathanael's statement.

"You call what you're doing to us, 'love'?" The moment it was out, Malcolm was sorry for it. It was a tactical error.

"Abba is love, preacher," Nathanael rejoined. "That's what this is all about—love."

"I see," Malcolm said, not seeing at all.

"Aw, you're just like the others. You don't understand. Why waste my breath on you?" The rifle inched up.

"I'm trying to understand," Malcolm said quickly,

pressing himself to remain unperturbed.

"You think love is all that sweetness and light stuff, don't you, preacher? It's not. Love sometimes has to hurt. You have to hurt people to make them learn. Sometimes, you even have to kill."

"How . . . uh . . . how do you know that?"

"Abba says so!"

"What does he say, exactly?"

"He says you have to punish some people to make them see the error of their ways."

"You mean, like when I punish my children?" Malcolm was groping for something, anything, to make Nathanael forget pulling the trigger. "To correct them?"

"Yeah, like that. Like Abba has said, 'Foolishness is bound in the heart of a child; but the rod of correction shall drive it far from him.'"

"Proverbs 22:15," Malcolm added. "You know the Bible, Brother Nathanael."

That pleased Nathanael. "Sure. My carnal mother made me memorize many verses when I was a kid. Many. But I never understood them, until Abba told me what they meant."

"Abba certainly seems to have a lot of wisdom," Malcolm said. The words almost choked him, but he said them as if he believed them.

"Right on, preacher. More wisdom than anyone. And more than wisdom, love. Do you know what the Bible says God is, preacher?"

"God is Love."

"And Abba is Love, so Abba is God. It makes sense, doesn't it?"

"But, how do I know?"

"You can see it, preacher. You can see it at the Temple. There's so much love there, it's almost unbelievable."

"I've been told that," Malcolm said, remembering sadly what Harold Thomas had said about that love. "But I've also been told that it isn't the right kind of love."

"Who told you that?" Brother Nathanael stiffened. For another moment, Malcolm thought he had gone too far.

"Harold Thomas," he said bluntly, praying it was the right tack.

"That Judas," Nathanael drew out the last syllable in the same way all members of the Brotherhood did when speaking of their betrayer. "He was using you, preacher.

"Everybody on the outside uses people. My carnal parents used me, and I used them. My girlfriend used me, I used her. Nobody loves anybody."

"What's the answer, then?" Malcolm attempted to draw the conversation back along more reasonable lines.

"Abba. He is the only answer." The response was by rote. Nathanael said it as if he had been programmed to say it.

"Well, that's interesting, but—"

"But you thought Jesus Christ was the answer, didn't you, preacher? He's not. I was taught that, too. But, he's not."

"Who is a liar but he that denieth that Jesus is the Christ?" The quote was on Malcolm's lips before he could squelch it. However, he did not regret it. It was something which had to be said, something he needed to say.

"You calling me wrong, preacher?" The question was heated.

"Just quoting the Bible."

"That's not in the Bible."

"First John 2:22," Malcolm held his ground.

"Not in Abba's Bible. You see, preacher, that's another myth foisted upon a gullible world for thousands of years." Nathanael's vehemence took on a vengeful glee. He thought the argument was won.

Malcolm frowned. "So, you believe that for two thousand years, everyone who read the Bible was fooled? That only you and the Brotherhood have, at last, been given the Truth?"

"You dig, preacher. You dig."

"But, if Abba is truly Love, as you say," Malcolm was carefully laying the trap, "how could he let people be misled for two thousand years? Love wouldn't allow all of them to die without a chance at the truth, would it?"

Frenzy transgressed Brother Nathanael's eyes. "I don't want to talk anymore."

"Why? Because you know you've been brainwashed? Because you know how false your Abba is?" Deliberate mocking accented Malcolm's rebuttal.

He saw it coming, then. The rifle barrel flashed higher. Malcolm threw his weight against the side of his chair. It hung for a split second on two legs, then the chair and Malcolm both tumbled to the floor.

The impact was harder than Malcolm expected. With his arms bound as they were, he had to absorb the landing on his shoulder. The pain numbed his arm.

Brother Nathanael adjusted his aim. His anger was demonic. He squinted at the sights.

Malcolm gasped and braced himself.

"Uh-huh, preacher," Nathanael suddenly grinned. "You can't trick me into killing you. That's what you were trying to do, wasn't it? Well, I'm not gonna' do it. You deserve every torture we're gonna' give you."

He swiveled away.

Malcolm knew he had hit a nerve. There was something in the way Nathanael had reacted, something more than the gun and the menace, something that—maybe—could be used for deliverance.

This was what he had been waiting for. If only he could have the faith to put it together. If only he could do it in time.

1:17 p.m.

Master Control at KBEX was no longer the private domain of Wally Nichols. It was jammed with people pushing, shoving, shouting, rushing in and out. It reminded Wally of Grand Central Station in the Golden Age of Steam.

A half dozen station executives, including F.G. Bronson, had already arrived by the time Darrell King came in on the heels of Wally's relief man, Buddy Dickinson.

Darrell was dressed in tennis whites that accentuated his copper-bronze tan. His sunstreaked brown hair was tousled just enough to give him a harried appearance, but not too harried. Wally decided Darrell looked as if he belonged in a clothing ad in *Town and Country* magazine, and wished that were where Darrell had remained, so Wally could flip the page and forget him.

Buddy Dickinson, on the other hand, was a dull-fashioned, puny kid of twenty-one. He was a fair-to-middling television engineer, but Wally had no intention of turning the board over to him. As far as Wally was concerned, this was his action, and he was going to ride it through at the helm all the way.

Instead, he put Buddy to work patching the air signals of

the other two commercial stations in town into the monitor bank. Darrell had requested it so that he could keep tabs on the way KBEX's competitors were covering the story.

"Pot up the sound on KDOR," Darrell ordered, shouting above the hubbub of confusion that surrounded them.

Wally checked to see which monitor the KDOR signal was on, and turned the proper volume controls.

The KDOR reporter faced the camera with Grunnell's First Church in the background, while policemen ran past.

"This is Mitchell Ames with KDOR-TV 3 action camera coming to you live from just outside the First Church of Grunnell," the reporter announced. "A little less than two hours ago, terrorists seized control of the church service, holding over a thousand people hostage. Here is the way things were in the sanctuary just minutes ago."

KDOR cut to a videotaped shot of the interior of the church.

"Where did they get those pictures?" Darrell bawled. "We're the only station with cameras inside, aren't we?"

As if in answer to his question, a superimposed legend appeared at the botton of the KDOR picture. *Courtesy KBEX-TV,* it said.

"I'll sue those dirty—" Darrell swore. "Where do they come off, pulling a stunt like that?"

"Uh . . . Darrell," F.G. Bronson said softly, "they're well within their rights under the agreement."

"What agreement?" Darrell withered F.G. with a look.

"The Reciprocal. The one that gives them the right to tape excerpts from our news and sports programming, just like we have the right to tape excerpts from theirs."

"I know what a Reciprocal is," Darrell blustered. "But that's only for sports. Not news. Only sports. Isn't that right?"

"Well, uh . . ." F.G. stammered.

"You signed that agreement," Darrell said. "It better say only sports, or I don't care if you are the only one of your race on our executive staff, Bronson. I'll can you. You hear me? I don't care about the Civil Rights Commission, or Equal Opportunity. If that agreement says *news*, you're through."

"Uh . . . I'll go check the agreement right away, Darrell. Yes, sir. Right away." F.G. retreated from the control room.

On the screen, the KDOR reporter added insult to injury by saying, "In an exclusive interview which will be aired in its entirety on the Channel 3, 5 p.m. news tonight, Captain Burch Zimmerman of the Grunnell police force said—"

"Turn it down! I've heard enough," Darrell yelled. "Look at that! Those KDOR—" and he used a descriptive obscenity—"are beating us with our own picture. The viewers will think we're idiots. Our ratings will go down. We can't even do a voice-over bulletin because *she* won't let us!"

The female terrorist in the remote control booth with Roger at the church, had become *"she."* That was the only way anyone at KBEX was referring to her, and it was enough. No other term was needed.

"I've tried repeatedly to get her to give a little ground on her demands," Wally affirmed defensively, at the same time feeling important in his role as the station's unofficial negotiator in the matter. "But she's adamant."

"Get her on the shortwave. Let me talk to her," Darrell said.

Wally didn't like the implied put-down of his own abilities. "I don't even know if she'll answer my call," he mumbled.

But he knew the look on Darrell King's face meant he had better try. As he reached for the microphone, Barry Howell, the KBEX news director, made a hurried entrance.

"I thought you'd want to know, Boss," he puffed at Darrell, "the police are on their way to an old hotel down on skid row. It's tied in with the thing at the church somehow."

"Do the other stations know about it?" Darrell posed the question with intensity.

Barry shrugged. "It's on the scanner, but I've got another one of our insta-cam units rolling on it. We'll get some footage for the news."

"Great!" Darrell snorted. "KDOR and KERH won't wait for their newscasts. They'll blast the thing live, if it's important, while we give our audience the same thing we've been giving them for two hours. We've been left holding the bag on this one, and I don't like it."

A little hazily, Barry said thinly, "What else can we do? It isn't my fault, you know."

"I'll show you what we can do," Darrell said. "Wally, have you got her on the shortwave, yet?"

"I've been waiting until you were free to talk," Wally justified his failure to comply with Darrell's request. But there was no further excuse for delay. Reluctantly, Wally pushed the mike button.

To his amazement, the radio cracked with an immediate comeback.

"What do you want?" *She* was plainly irritated.

"I have someone who wants to talk with you," Wally stammered. Before he could say more, Darrell ripped the microphone from his hand.

"This is Darrell King, Vice President and General Manager of KBEX Television." Darrell said it importantly.

"So?" the woman asked with insolence.

"I thought perhaps you'd appreciate hearing from someone with authority," Darrell turned on the charm.

"Abba is the ultimate authority," the woman stated.

As if he hadn't heard it, Darrell said, "To whom am I speaking?"

"Abba's representative."

"Yes, but what is your name?"

"It doesn't matter. If you have something to say, say it, Mr. Veepee."

"Well, you see," Darrell dripped charm in spite of her snippiness, "we have ourselves an unfortunate situation. We are in the business of communications. We have an obligation to report all the news. Now, this is a very big story. There's more to it, much more, than what's happening there in the church. We have a responsibility to our viewers to present the other facets. So, you see, in the interest of fair play, you have to let us cut away to show—"

"I don't have to let you show anything, Mr. Veepee, but what I want you to show."

"You listen to me, you little . . ." The charm was gone.

"No, you listen to me. Do you want your man to die? Because, if I see anything on the screen but what I'm seeing now, I'll kill him."

Darrell's face was red. "You're bluffing, lady."

"Try me."

"There's a death penalty in this state for murder. You think about that, girlie!"

Dead air was the only riposte Darrell received.

He banged the microphone on the counter. "She's bluffing. Did you hear her? She's not more than eighteen. She won't kill Roger, or the crew. She's bluffing."

The others in the control room scurried to find something to do, embarrassed by the spectacle Darrell was making of himself.

Wally became engrossed in his switcher. He tweaked dials that weren't connected to anything at the moment.

"Barry!" Darrell virtually accosted the news director as he scurried for the door. "Get ready to go on the air. I want it to be a complete report. Everything you've got. The more blood and guts, the better."

The news director gave a thumbs-up sign. "We'll be ready in five minutes."

Wally couldn't believe his eyes and ears. Darrell wasn't serious, was he? He couldn't be serious. He wasn't planning to—

"Wally!" Darrell hovered over him. "I want you to stand by to take a live feed from both insta-cam units."

"She'll kill them, Mr. King." Wally's voice trembled.

"We've listened to that kind of namby-pamby garbage long enough," Darrell was seething. "She's pushed me too far. Now, we're gonna' air those reports. Stand by."

1:26 p.m.

They finally knew what they were dealing with. The ransom demand had come into headquarters an hour ago. Through a foul-up that would never be completely explained, it had not been relayed to Captain Burch Zimmerman until a few minutes before the scheduled meeting with the SWAT team leaders.

Even the meeting was not happening as soon as Burch had wanted it to happen. However, Burch was philosophical. Despite emergencies, the wheels of government ground slowly. And who could find fault with that? Especially in a system which always encouraged you to blame the other guy?

But, at least, they finally knew the bottom line, a ransom of $200,000. The demand was authentic, Burch could feel it in his bones.

Two hundred thousand was not much, as ransoms went. Yet, it was a practical amount. It could be raised quickly, without much fuss. One bank could probably handle it.

In fact, the man who had phoned in the demand had made a point of just that. Burch had been told the caller admitted frankly that some of their plans had not worked out quite as they had hoped. Thus, they were willing to settle for far less than they had originally contemplated, *if* the ransom was gathered and paid quickly. The deadline was 3 o'clock.

Fred Clymer of the FBI was listening as one of the SWAT leaders, a Lieutenant Kelly, filled him in on some of the physical background. From time to time, Kelly indicated the blueprints of the First Church which were spread on the importer's polished desk.

Burch scratched his head and wondered why they were going to all the trouble to plan an assault on the church when they could pay the lousy ransom and forget it.

The ransom was being assembled, of course, as a contingency. Burch had given the order to have it ready with the bills marked.

Prudent police procedure dictated, however, that every effort be made to free the hostages without acceding to criminal demands. It was especially prudent for the elected city officials who would have to answer to the taxpayers when they shouted that crime was not supposed to pay.

With the economics of politics involved, it was a better course to free the hostages by shedding a few drops of blood than giving away a dollar of city money.

Burch reached into his pocket for a cigarette. The pack was empty. Irritated, he wadded the empty cellophane and tinfoil package and disposed of it in a too-full ashtray.

He thought for a moment of sending Max Vigeveno out for another pack, then remembered he had detailed Max to handle the Press down on the street. His real intent was to keep the meddlesome klupper out of the way.

"Hey. Anybody. Got a cigarette?" he butted into the conversation between Kelly and Clymer.

The G-man looked askance at Burch over the horn-rimmed half-glasses perched on his FBI nose. "'Smoking is dangerous to your health,'" he scolded. The schtoonk was serious.

"I know," Burch baited, "but have you got a cigarette?"

"The director frowns on smoking," Clymer said gravely,

"and, I hope none of these good police offers practice such a bad and filthy habit."

"Oyvey," Burch grunted. There went his hope of bumming a smoke. Who, in his right mind, would admit to using yenmens in front of Clymer after a sermon like that?

The G-man adjusted his glasses smugly, rubbed his balding pate, and turned back to Kelly. "Now, Sergeant Kelly, what were you saying?"

"It's *Lieutenant* Kelly, and I was saying tear gas is out."

"Why?" Clymer inquired.

"It's dangerous to your health," Burch groused. No wonder Clymer was stationed in Grunnell. It was not exactly a prize assignment for a G-man, but then, Clymer was no prize himself.

Patronizingly, Kelly spelled it for the kvetch from the FBI. "The suspects all have gas masks. You can see that on TV. If we lobbed gas in there, they'd whip on their masks and wait it out.

"The hostages, on the other hand, have no protection. Exposed to the gas for any length of time, some would die."

"I agree," Sergeant Lopez, SWAT Commander for the State Police, nodded.

"I can see you local gentlemen are well trained," Clymer smiled, as if he had known why gas couldn't be employed all along, as if he had been testing them.

Burch stifled a temptation to tell the G-man what a schlepp he thought the Bureau had put in Grunnell. Instead, he yawned. It wasn't as satisfying as a smoke, but, at least, it gave his mouth something to do besides antagonizing Clymer.

"Carry on." Clymer waved as if he was in charge.

Kelly looked to Burch. "Captain?"

"By all means, Sergeant, carry on," Burch said acidly, waving his own stubby hand in the same way the FBI agent had waved with his more delicate member.

Kelly pointed to the blueprints. "There are five stories of classrooms, but I think we can forget them. As far as we've been able to determine, everyone in the church is in or near the sanctuary.

"As you can see, the sanctuary itself is like a box. There are no windows, except for that big round one in front that's all broken out. Discounting the window for a moment, there are five ways in or out."

Tracing each on the blueprint as he spoke, Kelly went on, "There are three doors that lead in from the narthex at the front of the building. Those doors and the narthex are well-covered by a half dozen suspects. In other words, forget it.

"The second way into the sanctuary is on the second floor. A door on each side of the balcony. I think we have to assume those are being guarded, too.

"The balcony extends from the second floor and rakes across the ceiling of the hallway. It abuts the exterior wall on the third floor, and, of course, except for that big window, there are no other openings."

"Doesn't this city have a fire code? Don't you require exits at the back of the balcony?" Clymer interposed.

"Yes, sir," Kelly said, "but, it's an old building, built prior to the present ordinances."

"A good point it is, though," Burch said. "What about fire escapes?"

"The only fire escape is on the far side of the classroom wing, Captain," Kelly said. "It's a possibility. However, the hall on the second floor doesn't offer much cover. If there are guards posted on the balcony doors, they would have a clear field of fire at anyone who tried to take their positions."

"A thought, no more," Burch tapped his forehead with a finger, making light of his own brain power. "A bad thought at that. Go on, Lieutenant."

"Now, at the back of the sanctuary—the front from the

audience—there is a door on each side of the platform. Those doors open on two hallways that run the length of the auditorium and end at outside entrances at the back of the building."

"That's the way you boys are going in, then," Clymer exclaimed, looking so proud of himself for guessing that.

"Afraid not, sir," Sergeant Lopez took over the briefing. "If the terrorists have guards posted at the platform doors, they also have a view of the back entrances."

"It's the same problem as on the second floor," Kelly said. "No real cover. They'd cut us to pieces before we got five feet."

"The Bastille," Burch muttered.

"Beg your pardon, sir?" Kelly asked.

"Nothing," Burch said. "Nothing."

"The fifth way in is the best way," Lopez cleared his throat. "Look here, behind the choir loft above the platform. The baptistry."

"It's too big for that," Clymer said.

"You a Catholic, too?" Lopez smiled.

"I'm Lutheran," Clymer replied.

"You still baptize by sprinkling. But, in this church, they baptize by immersion."

"Huh?"

Clymer was so perplexed, even Burch had to laugh.

"They're dunkers," he said.

"So the baptistry is like a large tub or small pool."

"Oh," Clymer said.

Lopez tapped the blueprint. "There are steps on each side of the baptistry to connecting dressing rooms. And the dressing rooms are reached by a stairway from the basement level.

"The stairway makes a sharp turn, and where it turns is a basement window. That's our way in."

"But isn't it covered by the suspects?" Burch licked his lips and wished for a cigarette.

"No, sir," Kelly was triumphant. "Lopez and I scouted it out a little while ago. It was clear then, and I'm betting it'll be clear now."

"Here's the way we figure to work it," Lopez said. "Kelly and me will take the two gassers on his team. We'll arm them with M-16's, of course. We'll go in through the window and come up the stairs to the baptistry.

"When we're ready, we'll signal on Tac 2. The sharpshooters upstairs in the Denton Building, here, will each take out a suspect at the platform or as near the platform as they can. Between the two teams, we got four sharpshooters, so that means four suspects go down.

"At the same time, the gassers from my team will go for the big window from the street with grappling hooks. We'll need help from your boys, Captain, to keep the suspects in the narthex and on the portico at the front of the church busy. We'll need cover fire."

"You'll get it," Burch said. "I'll command that part of the operation myself."

"Good," said Kelly. "Between the grappling hooks and the cover fire, the suspects should think we're coming in the front. It'll give us just enough diversion to come through the baptistry into the choir loft and get the drop on them."

"When the sharpshooters take out four of their number, it should really confuse 'em and shake 'em up, so we can do our thing," Lopez added.

All was quiet then, as each man thought it over.

Burch was the first to speak. "What do you think, Clymer?"

The G-man removed his glasses. "It certainly is bold."

"It has to be," Lopez observed. "We think it will minimize hostage casualties. Some might get caught in the cross fire, for sure, but there's nothing we can do about those."

"We could always pay the ransom," Burch said softly.

The eyes in the room stared at him as if he had suggested

treason.

"Another bad thought," he said, thumping his forehead with his index finger.

The telephone rang, sparing him more chastisement from the eyes of his peers.

Sergeant Shaw answered the ring and held out the receiver toward Burch. "It's for you, Captain."

"Burch, I know we shouldn't be bothering you at a time like this—" Something was wrong with Fran Goldman. She always called him Zim. "But she came to the station looking for you. When you weren't around, she insisted I get ahold of you. Here, I'm putting her on . . ."

"Zim . . . Zim, I saw her!" It was his ex-wife, Gerry. She was crying so hard, she could hardly talk.

"Gerry, for the love of Abraham!" Burch censured. "I'm in the middle of a very important operation. I've got no time for your female hysterics."

"Don't hang up on me, Zim! Please! I saw Sandy!"

"Sandy is dead, Gerry. A million times I've told you, our daughter is—"

"No, Zim. Our daughter is alive. I saw her."

"You didn't see her, Gerry, because she's dead."

"I did. In the church."

"All right," Burch said wearily. "What church?" He was acutely aware the others were looking at him oddly. He would humor her. The sooner he let her spit it out, the sooner he could get back to work.

"The church," she choked. "The one on TV. The one where the terrorists are."

"First Church?"

"Yes. She's there. She's with *them.* She has a gun, but they're making her help them."

"Gerry, you're imagin—"

"They had a close-up of her," Gerry insisted. "She doesn't look like herself. She's lost weight. Her hair's longer—and she's so pale. But it's her!"

"Okay, Okay. You saw her. Or you *think* you saw her."

"I don't think, Zim, I know. A mother knows her own baby."

"Sure, Gerry."

"You don't believe me. You think I'm insane."

"I—No, I've just got a lot of things on my mind. I gotta' go, Gerry. They're waiting for me."

He wanted to hang up the phone, but she was weeping uncontrollably into his ear. He couldn't cut her off, not like that.

"Stop crying, Gerry, Stop that, you hear me?"

"Don't take my word, Zim. Look at the TV. See for yourself."

"All right, Gerry. I promise, I'll look at the TV," he said rashly.

"And promise me you won't let her get hurt. Promise me you'll take care of her until I get there."

"What? No, Gerry. Don't come down here. You hear me good. Don't come down. You'll just make things worse."

"But, it's Sandy, Zim. Our Sandy."

"Yeah, well, if it is Sandy, I'll find her and keep her safe and sound. But, don't you come. I mean it, now, I do. Put Fran back on."

"Yes, Captain?" Fran's voice was still strained.

"Don't you make with that 'Captain' stuff with me. And don't you ever call me for her again, when I'm in the middle of something like this."

"Yes, Captain."

"You latch on to her and keep her there. Handcuff her, or throw her in the lockup. Anything. But, don't let her come down here. That's all I need."

"Yes, Captain."

Slowly, Burch recradled the phone. Was Sandy ever going to be put to rest? Finally and completely put to rest?

He was staring at the screen of the Sony before he knew

it. Getting as close to it as he could, he studied the picture.

It was a long shot. You couldn't tell anything from a long shot. But what was he doing? Sandy wasn't there. Maybe, a girl who looked like Sandy. But Sandy was not there. Sandy would never be anywhere again. He had the rusty locket, plucked from the ravaged skeleton, to prove it.

"Captain?" Kelly ventured.

They were all facing Burch expectantly.

"Do we go with what's been laid out?"

"What?" Burch said blankly, his eyes drawn back to the television set.

"Do we have your approval on our attack plan?"

"Oh, . . . uh . . . yeah. Sure." Burch shook his head to clear it of the ghosts. "But, I got a couple of squads on the way over to the headquarters of the Brotherhood bunch. They might turn something that will help us. We'll wait for their report. It should be coming through in a couple of minutes."

"And if they don't turn anything, Captain?" It was Lopez who asked it.

"We go." Burch looked at his watch. "Thirty minutes give you enough time to get your acts together?"

In unison, Kelly and Lopez said, "Check."

"At 1415 hundred hours then, we go." Burch announced it with a finality.

The two SWAT leaders grabbed their gear and bolted out the door.

Fred Clymer pocketed his horn-rimmed spectacles, patting the pocket a couple of times as if to make certain they were safely stored.

"Would it be all right if I went up to watch with the sharpshooters?" he inquired.

"Yeah." Burch waved him away.

Only Sergeant Shaw was left.

"Got a cigarette, Shaw?" Burch appealed.

"Naw. Like the man said, smoking is bad for you."

"Go get me some."

"You're in charge, Captain." Shaw said, disdainful of the role of a "gofer."

He sauntered out. Burch reached for his pocket transceiver beside the gold-plated cigarette lighter on the desk. He switched it to Tac 2, the band the SWAT teams would be using.

As soon as Shaw came back, he'd go down to the street and brief his men. As soon as . . .

His eyes strayed back to the TV set. He watched it, unblinking, for a long time.

"Sandy," he whimpered softly. "If only you could be there, like your mother thinks. If only I hadn't seen you laid to rest."

1:42 p.m.

Max Vigeveno was exhilarated more than he'd been at any time since being assigned under Captain Burch Zimmerman. Max was in the shotgun seat of a squad car running Code 40—silent—toward the old hotel on Seventeenth and Welsh.

A sense of destiny was his, made doubly sweet by his secret knowledge that he had, at last, outfoxed the Jewish brass-hat who had been sandbagging a certain Lieutenant Vigeveno's career for years.

Max didn't care for Zimmerman any more than Zimmerman liked him. The fact was, lately, Max had grown to hate his superior.

Burch Zimmerman was a dinosaur, a has-been biding his time for retirement. In Max's opinion, the good captain should have been kicked off the force long ago. Zim was a rotten police officer, a man who lacked the talent for command.

Max had reached this conclusion based upon his own relationship with Captain Zimmerman. It seemed to Max that the captain always went to great lengths to deny him a chance at the glory.

Well, Max was finally having his revenge and it was piquant. What made it so savory was that he had been able to use Zimmerman's own orders in a way the captain had never intended when he issued them.

Captain Zimmerman had ordered Max to handle the Press. He had also ordered him to dispatch all available squads to the headquarters of the Brotherhood.

Max knew that the captain had meant for him to deal with the Press personally, a thankless, detestable duty. Max also knew the cars sent to the Brotherhood's Temple were to be led by some other officer. That had been the intent of Captain Burch Zimmerman's directives.

However, Max chose to misinterpret those intentions. Oh, he had handled the Press, all right. He had assigned Sergeant Gries to take care of the reporters and camera crews. The rest had been easy. He simply got in a car and told the plainclothes officer at the wheel to drive.

Actually, it had all taken more time to arrange than he had planned. If he had done it all as Zimmerman had wanted, this Temple place would have been surrounded ten minutes ago. But what was ten minutes for a chance to help crack one of the biggest cases in the history of the Grunnell Police Department?

He could see the commendation in his file, his picture on the front page of the newspaper. He could almost hear the reporters clamoring to interview him for the Ten O'clock News. Maybe he would even get the Mayor's Medal of Honor as Officer of the Year.

Why not? He would be the policeman who had recognized the fact that the key to the case was not at First Church, but at the old hotel on Seventeenth and Welsh. The goons at the church had to be getting their orders from somewhere. They were probably getting them from the head man of the cult. He was believed to be at the hotel. No, not "believed," Max mentally corrected himself. He was!

"There she is," the driver said. He was a crusty, middle-aged man who had his own bone to pick with Burch

Zimmerman. The captain had reprimanded him for accidentally destroying evidence in another case, and had busted him in rank.

The hotel was still a block away, but Max could see it looming up out of the two-story dives and abandoned pawnshops which nestled against it.

"Yeah. There it is," he said, licking his lips in anticipation.

He twisted in the seat and through the squad's rear window saw the file of four other police cars that followed him in the lead vehicle. As they passed through the last intersection before the hotel block, the two black-and-whites at the end of the line swung off to cover the alley.

Max faced back to the front. "Pull up there," he told the driver.

The car squealed to a rocking halt in the street in front of the Temple of the Brotherhood. Except for the squad cars, the street was vacant.

Before the car was fully stopped, Max was out of the door, a bullhorn in his hand. While other officers clambered from their cars, he walked around the hood and stood proudly with his legs apart. It was a stance of authority.

"You, inside!" The bullhorn amplified his voice. "This is Lieutenant Max Vigeveno. You are surrounded. There is no way out. Surrender peacefully and you won't be harmed."

A Hollywood cop on *Police Story* couldn't have said it better, Max thought. If the captain could only see him now.

"Surrender. You have only sixty seconds." He enjoyed the way the bullhorn magnified his voice.

But no response came from inside the flea-bag building. The only sound was the slamming of the door on one of the black-and-whites.

By this time, his plainclothes driver had joined him, a riot gun at the ready.

"It looks deserted, Lieutenant. Nobody at home," he said.

"They're there, Suggs. I know they're in there." Max studied the facade with its pigeon-weathered bricks, its fly-specked windows.

He thought he saw a shadow behind the closed venetian blinds. Yet, when he looked again, the shadow was gone.

He lifted the bullhorn. "Time's up. You've had your chance. We're coming in."

Placing the bullhorn on the hood of the car, he waved his men forward. "Follow me, men!"

He didn't notice the glances they exchanged, the reluctance some of them displayed. He was marching toward the building.

"But, Lieutenant," Detective Suggs complained, "shouldn't we be more careful? We're sitting ducks out here in the open."

"They're religious freaks, Suggs," Max smiled. "They aren't going to kill anyone."

"Their friends are armed at the church, sir," said Suggs.

"You don't understand, Suggs," Max derided. "The thing that's going down at the church is just another in a long line of demonstrations by a bunch of hippies."

They had reached the front entrance. "See, Suggs? Not a shot. No resistance. Stick with me, and you'll get your rank back."

It wasn't a boast. Max knew what he was doing. He rapped on the peeling wooden door frame, rattling the glass.

"Police! Open up!"

Nothing.

Max tried the latch. The door creaked open. He drew his own service revolver for the first time and stepped into the lobby.

It was empty, save for the desk. Max gestured with his revolver. Suggs eased toward it, then suddenly threw himself around it.

No one.

The door behind the desk was Suggs' next target. He loosened the latch, hugged the wall and shoved the door open.

"Unoccupied," he announced.

Several uniformed patrolmen and two plainclothes detectives had come in behind them. Max signaled five of them to check upstairs.

They did as ordered, much too warily for Max.

"What do you think, sir?" Suggs asked.

Max heard it then. The mumble of voices. It came from the ground floor hallway that led toward the rear of the building.

"Shhhh! Listen," he said. "They're down this hall."

Strutting toward the voices, he indicated that he wanted the others to join him.

"Shouldn't we be more careful?" Suggs whispered again.

"Can the caution," Max was impatient. He could see now that the hallway dead-ended at a set of ornately carved double doors. They were going to do it. He was going to do it. Take this place without a shot. He knew it.

But Max didn't know about the Seven Beasts Abba had ordered placed and armed. Max didn't know the Seven Beasts was the name Abba had given to the massive charges of dynamite hidden at strategic structural points in the Temple.

Max didn't know any of these things. He only knew about citations and medals and revenge for the wrongs Burch Zimmerman had done him.

He stood at the doors. Suggs took a position on one side of them, another officer did likewise on the other. Max stood squarely in the middle.

He nodded to each of them, and with bold daring, threw open the doors, as John Wayne might in one of those Hollywood adventures Max admired so much.

He was standing at the threshold of the ballroom. What a sight it was. More than two hundred young people were on their knees praying. Above them, on the wall over a crude platform was the Star of David pierced by a Christian cross.

On the platform, facing a crude altar under the strange symbol, were several men in prayer shawls and beanies. The leadership of the group, no doubt, Max observed.

He did not observe the men with the AR-15's, the M-62/S' or the M-16's. He did not see those automatic rifles leveling at his men and himself.

It didn't matter. For at the precise instant, the Seven Beasts roared. The building shook. It swayed, and fell in on itself.

Max saw only the ceiling plummeting toward him. He threw his arm up to protect his head, but his arm was forced downward by the crushing, grinding action of a heavy weight from above.

And, then, he couldn't breathe. The dust and weight pilfered the oxygen. His vision blurred. And he saw it.

A medal. The Mayor's Medal. As blackness rushed in on him, he reached for that medal.

"*It's mine, Captain!*" he laughed in his mind. "*I guess I showed you!*"

They would find him buried in the rubble three days later, his hand still clutching the glass bauble from the massive ballroom chandelier that had caved in his skull.

1:53 p.m.

There had been a delay which Malcolm Stansfield did not quite understand. He had previously gathered from the conversations of his guards that 1:30 was the hour set for Malcolm to make his public declaration on behalf of Abba. Yet, it was going on 2 o'clock, and they had still not untied him and led him from his office.

There had been much coming and going on the part of the members of the Brotherhood for the last twenty minutes or more. The remarks which they exchanged between themselves indicated the delay had something to do with Joseph Holmes' shattered stained-glass window.

Apparently, the police were across the street in the upper floors of the Denton Building, using the broken window as a means of observing the goings-on in the sanctuary. This disturbed the Brothers for two reasons.

First of all, they were upset because no one on the outside was supposed to see the happenings inside, except by television. The Brotherhood evidently had control of the cameras.

But what disconcerted them the most was that the police had scoped rifles. There was a fear the police might decide to start shooting directly into the auditorium.

One of the Brothers, a Brother Thaddeus—Malcolm

was beginning to pick up their names—suggested that the window be covered with a blanket or a piece of canvas. His proposition was eventually discarded as being too impractical. The window was too big and too high up.

And still the Brothers pondered what to do about the police, reticent to start the Catching Up with the enemy so visibly at hand.

The delay was both Malcolm's blessing and curse. A blessing, because it had given him time to think things through and decide firmly what action to take when he was led back to the sanctuary. A curse, because Stan Brown was in bad shape. The longer it took to get him help, the less likely it was that help would come in time.

A little while ago, Stan had screamed out in delirium—a single, anguished cry. After that, his breathing seemed to moderate. He seemed to be resting more comfortably. Malcolm thought that might be because some of Stan's wounds had begun to clot, although Stan was far from out of danger.

Brother John came back from another scouting trip to the auditorium. From the grin on his lips, Malcolm sensed the delay was ended.

"I don't see the cops anymore," John said. "Besides, even if they're still up there with their rifles, they won't start anything. They'd be afraid they'd kill one of our hostages instead."

The other Brothers seemed reassured by John's conclusions. Two of them quickly undid Malcolm's bonds and pulled him to his feet.

While Malcolm rubbed his arms to get the blood flowing to his fingers again, Brother John stepped next to him.

"Remember, preacher, you've got a nice family. Make sure you keep them." He gave Malcolm a shove toward the door.

The sanctuary was the same as they had left it. The bright television lights. The frightened faces in the pews.

Gil Anderson and John Swallow along with Dick Whiting were still sitting in platform chairs.

As he was led past Whiting, Malcolm heard the agent murmur, "Where's Harold? What have they done with Harold?"

"Shut up!" Brother Nathanael told Whiting.

Brother John took the pulpit and pointed Malcolm to a spot beside him.

Malcolm singled out Miriam from the sea of faces. She gazed at him and he at her. Her arms were wrapped around the children. She attempted a brave smile for his benefit. Malcolm returned it with a wink and continued to gaze at her. He wanted to remember her, just as she was, always. No matter what the next few minutes brought, he wanted her to know how very much he loved her.

Leaning his rifle against the inside of the pulpit, Brother John unholstered his .45 and laid it conspicuously on the opened pulpit Bible.

The lean, hungry fingers of fear tightened their grip on the auditorium again. Malcolm sucked in a deep breath. The final trial was beginning.

"This is the hour of your Catching Up," Brother John said into the microphone. "For, it is written, 'When Abba shall come in his glory, and all the holy angels with him, then shall he sit upon the throne of his glory: and before him shall be gathered all nations: and he shall separate them one from another, as a shepherd divideth his sheep from the goats: and he shall set the sheep on his right hand, but the goats on his left.

"'Then shall Abba say unto them on his right hand, "Come ye blessed of the Father, inherit the kingdom."

"'Then shall he say also unto them on the left hand, "Depart from me, ye cursed, into everlasting fire, prepared for the devil and his angels."'"

Brother John indicated the automatic pistol on the opened Bible. "This is the weapon of Abba's judgment."

"May I say something?" The loud interruption had come from a man standing in the midst of the congregation. It was the reporter from *Newstime*.

"Sit down!" Brother John sneered.

"I think you should know," the reporter said, undaunted by John's rebuke, "that I am Warren, a reporter for *Newstime* magazine. A member of the Press. I am here to observe and report, not participate. On that basis, you can see, I should not be subjected to—"

"Brother Andrew, make the fool sit down!" John roared.

"The Constitution of the United States of America guarantees freedom of the press," Warren insisted. "I demand that I be allowed to function as a reporter, without interference or intimidation."

"Do like Brother John says." Brother Andrew leveled his rifle. "Sit down."

"But the law—" Warren argued foolishly.

"Abba is the law," Brother John yelled. "And, I am Abba's voice."

Warren ignored Brother Andrew's gun. He said coldly to Brother John, "But, as a member of the Press—"

"There are no members of the Press in this auditorium," John replied, "only sheep and goats. The sheep will live. The goats will be slaughtered. What's it going to be, Mr. Reporter? Are you a sheep or a goat?"

"I resent—"

"He's a goat," John said. "Shoot the goat, Brother Andrew."

Warren's jaw dropped with the sudden awareness of the precarious situation he was in.

"No!" he gasped. "No. I understand now."

He dropped back to the pew, his face colorless.

"Forget it, Brother Andrew," Brother John called off the rifleman with a snickering disdain. "He won't give us any more argument. Will you, Mr. Reporter?"

Warren lifted a shaking hand to his sweating brow. "No. No, I'm sorry."

It was barely audible on the platform.

"I didn't hear you, Mr. Reporter," John ridiculed.

"I'm sorry!"

"Excellent, Mr. Reporter," John laughed, and then in an extravagant tone of conciliation addressed the rest of the congregation. "Is there anyone else who feels we are being unreasonable? Who has a valid excuse for being let out of this ceremony? Anyone else who is not a reporter?"

What is he doing? Malcolm wondered. *Why this cat and mouse game now?*

"Come on," Brother John was saying. "Don't be afraid. The Brotherhood wants to be your friend."

At the rear of the congregation, a man held up his hand.

"Yes. You there, in the back." Brother John's smile was lavishly warm.

Tentatively, the man rose. He was young, expensively dressed. "I don't want to cause you trouble," he apologized, "but my wife is expecting a baby. We're only visitors here today."

"A visitor?" John said ruefully. "You make a good point. How many visitors are there here?"

Hands shot up all over the auditorium. Some of those who held up their hands were recognized by Malcolm Stansfield as regular members of the church. He was ashamed for them.

"Wooooo!" Brother John exclaimed, "look at that. All you good people, no doubt, were enticed here by the devil's lies."

A few nodded eagerly.

"We can't let you all go," Brother John said. "We'd have nobody left to Catch Up, would we?"

"But, my wife . . ." the young man in the back appealed.

"Well, now, if we can't let the others go, we can't let her go. It wouldn't be fair, would it?"

The young man looked down at the floor.

"Sit down," Brother John said, suddenly harsh again. "You disgust me. Abba offers you Life, and you reject it. Sit down!"

So that was the game. Malcolm recognized the technique. The alternating gentleness and cruelty. It was part of brainwashing. It was being used to break down any resistance still in his people.

Brother John's words were barely out before a fat man jumped to his feet and bolted for the door on the outside aisle.

"I'm getting out!" he screamed. "I'm getting out!"

He lumbered only a few feet when he was caught by a short spurt of gunfire. The bullets tore into his stomach, hoisting him off his feet. He fell hard on his buttocks, sitting down, his legs straight out in front of him.

Several cries of surprise and anguish joined the dying reverberation of the rifle fire.

The fat man put his hand to his stomach. "Dear Jesus, I've been killed," he said with quiet amazement, and fainted into death.

The girl who had done the shooting patted her weapon and said, "Praise be to Abba."

Malcolm looked at the body. He did not turn away. He had seen too much killing this day to be shocked and repulsed by more.

There was no time for lamentation and mourning. Not now. He only hoped the fat man had known and trusted in Jesus. If so, he was free. If not, it was too late.

"When are you people gonna' learn?" Brother John was berating them. "We showed you one dead fool. Wasn't that enough? No, you force us to go on killing. We offer you the love of Abba, and you throw it in our faces. I've had it. I'm through with you. Kill them all!"

"No! Don't shoot me. Please don't shoot me!" A teen-age girl was running up the center aisle, her hands above her head.

It was Della Ritchie. Malcolm had baptized her when she was nine. Malcolm Jr. had had a crush on her when they were both in the seventh grade.

"Please, I want to go with you!" she wept.

"Leave her alone, Sister Solace!" Brother John barked at one of the young women who tried to grab Della as she ran toward the platform.

"Please, I agree with you," Della pleaded. "Let me come with you."

"Go back to your mother, Della," Malcolm said sternly. He wanted to protect her if he could.

"Preacher, keep your mouth shut!" John flared.

"I'm only trying to help you," Malcolm alibied.

"And don't forget it," John said.

Malcolm's insides were churning at the charade. But it had to be done. He had to gain their confidence if his plan was going to work.

Della pointed at him. "He lied to me!" she shrieked. "He made me say I believed in Jesus. He made me do it."

Brother John stepped from the pulpit and moved down the platform steps to the teenager. "But you don't believe in Jesus that way any longer, do you, little girl?"

"No!" Della shook her head, her long brown curls flying emphatically with the movement.

A lump came to Malcolm's throat. He cast his eyes away from the girl he had baptized. He could not watch her do this thing.

He saw Brother John's rifle then, leaning against the pulpit. He saw the pistol on the Bible. In one quick leap he could lay hold of them. One jump and . . .

And what? It was too risky. They would cut him down the way they had cut down Harold Thomas and the fat man.

No, he would wait. He would wait.

In the aisle, Brother John was embracing Della, holding

her close, comforting her.

"You know Abba is the only true God, don't you? You know Abba loves you," he said, the passion in his voice akin to love.

"Yes," Della sobbed.

"But you must be worthy of that love," John said. "You must be willing to do whatever Abba says."

"I am," she cried.

"Yes, I know you are. Sister Solace, come, love our new Sister."

Sister Solace, a large-boned woman, put down her rifle and gathered Della in her ample arms. She led the teenager to a front pew where they both sat, the Sister continuing to cradle Della's head against her breast.

John watched them benignly, then turned to the congregation. "See? This is the welcome that awaits those who come to Abba. Peace and security.

"This girl has made me change my mind. We will not kill you all before each one of you has had a chance to receive the glory of Abba."

A collective sigh rippled through the audience. The manipulation was complete. As complete as it could be. John seemed satisfied.

He remounted the platform and took the pistol from the pulpit.

"Okay, preacher. It's your turn." Then, in a stage whisper he added, "Look at your wife. Your kids. Sister Courage is taking good care of them."

The girl next to Malcolm Jr. raised her rifle to make certain Malcolm could see it. Miriam shifted uneasily. The children eyed the gun. They looked so defenseless, so small.

Malcolm permitted himself one last glimpse of these loved ones and got to his knees. His every nerve tingled. His every sense was alert.

Could he do it? Could he really say it?

Brother John's pistol was poised at Malcolm's temple waiting to bark its dark dirge if he failed. He swallowed.

And, then, came the flat bang of an explosion.

1:58 p.m.

KBEX-TV was not on the air "in five-minutes," as News Director Barry Howell had promised when he left the control room. It had taken him a good fifteen minutes just to finalize his script. Thus, he became an unwitting accomplice to Wally Nichols' plot to keep telecasting the picture from the church as demanded by the woman who held a gun on Roger Uttenmeyer.

He was flying in the face of Darrell King's orders, Wally knew, but he could not bring himself to squander human life for the sake of ratings. As far as Wally was concerned that was what it boiled down to in the final analysis. All Darrell's high sounding platitudes about "freedom of the press," and "calling her bluff" was flak to justify abandoning the fate of Roger Uttenmeyer to a girl with a gun. Wally was going to prevent that as long as he could.

Thus, when the mini-cam unit arrived at the old hotel ahead of the police, Wally feigned trouble in receiving their signal. It had taken some deft gymnastics with the buttons and levers on his switcher, but Wally had pulled it off.

Although Darrell was stewing, he was very understanding when Wally looked up innocently and said he thought the trouble might be in the monitor bank itself.

"Fix it," Darrell blustered, proving to Wally that the

general manager of KBEX-TV didn't know much about the technical side of the station.

Wally got up, opened the cubbyhole that led to the narrow passageway behind the bank of monitors and squirmed his way through it.

Once there, it took him only a few seconds to disconnect the air monitor altogether.

"Good grief!" Darrell howled from the other side of the monitors. "We're off the air! Wally, we're off the air!"

Wally grinned to himself, but by the time he had crawled out of the cubbyhole, his face was suitably grim.

"No, Mr. King. It's only the monitor. It was acting up. I patched the air picture into the preview monitor, see?"

Darrell narrowed his eyes at the video on the preview screen. The signal from the mini-cam unit was crisp and clear.

"It's about time," he bit. "Call Eerdmans and cue him. Tell him to talk. He's on the air and we need a sound track."

Swiftly, Wally jacked up the preview sound, then reached for the shortwave, switched it to the proper band, and called the technician in the mini-cam van.

"Cue Eerdmans," Wally said. "You're on the air right now."

"Hurry up!" Darrell coached behind Wally, his eyes glued to the monitor he thought was live. "The cops are about to storm the building."

The preview sound popped as the van's microphone was activated. In the background, you could hear the cops talking to each other as they crossed the street toward the old hotel.

This went on for a long count of eight and nearly sent Darrell into a choleric fit. There was some additional microphone noise and finally, Eerdmans' plangent voice.

"This is Henry Eerdmans," he said, "on the scene with KBEX TV's Newscene Camera. As you know, KBEX-TV has been following developments at the old First Church since a group of terrorists attacked during the morning service, shortly after 11 o'clock. Moments ago, several police cars pulled up in front of this hotel some ten blocks from the church. The hotel is said to be headquarters for a bizarre religious sect called the Brotherhood. The Brotherhood is believed to be behind the happenings at the church.

"As you can see, the police are now entering the hotel . . ." Eerdmans was ad-libbing in a smooth and masterful fashion.

"Beautiful! Absolutely beautiful!" Darrell was as happy as he had been angry. He gestured toward the monitors carrying the air signals of the competing stations. "Look at that. We're the only station at the hotel. I wonder how the boys at KDOR and KERH are taking it? We've scooped 'em. We've beaten them."

Wally experienced a small pang of conscience. Darrell didn't even suspect that the preview monitor he was watching was only that: a preview being fed to a tape machine in the film room next door, and not to the transmitter.

Nor did any of the other observers gathered in the KBEX control room seem to suspect that the picture which was actually being beamed to TV sets all over Grunnell was the same picture they had been seeing all morning—a view of the auditorium at First Church.

That picture was on the small, secondary monitor for VTR 1. And it was that small monitor by which Wally kept track of the real air signal, while the others raved about Eerdmans' report and congratulated each other over the supposed KBEX exclusive.

It was an unprofessional deception. Wally disliked himself for perpetrating it, but it was the only way he knew of keeping Roger alive.

It was ironic that in a manner of speaking the deception had been Darrell King's idea. Hadn't he been the one who suggested feeding a false air picture to the church? Wally had merely reversed the sham and was using it on Darrell instead.

On the small monitor, Wally could see activity on the church platform. Preacher Stansfield was being escorted back into the sanctuary by a little knot of gunmen.

One of the gunmen took the dais. Stansfield was forced to stand next to him. The preacher looked a mess. His suit coat was rumpled and stained, his face swollen and his hair ruffled.

The gunman at the pulpit took out a pistol and laid it where he could reach it, then said something to the congregation. Wally wished he could turn up the volume so he could hear, but that might be a dead giveaway to Darrell and the others who were absorbed in Henry Eerdmans' every phrase.

A tall, thin man in the audience stood up and said something to the gunman on the dais. Words were being exchanged when suddenly, the signal from the church was punctuated.

What was it *she* didn't want telecast this time? Wally only hoped it had nothing to do with Roger's safety.

Punching up the "Technical Difficulties" slide, Wally reached over and flicked the shortwave band back to the proper frequency to pick up a call from the church remote, just in case.

At the hotel, Eerdmans had completed ad-libbing a summary of the day's events as he understood them, and the camera zoomed in on the entrance to the building.

"The police have been inside the Temple of the Brotherhood for several minutes," Eerdmans said. "Thus far, we have had no indication that they have met resistance. If any shots had been fired, surely we would have heard them from this vantage point but a few yards away.

"I'm going to ask my cameraman to zoom out to a wide

shot of the street here, so you can get an idea of the location of this building. It's in the heart of the skid row district, a neighborhood crumbling with neglect.

"If you'll bear with us, ladies and gentlemen, we're going to try to move in a little closer and see if we can't get some pictures for you of what's taking place in the hotel at this moment."

The camera jerked from side to side as the man carrying it began to walk.

"We're crossing the street toward the Temple of the Brotherhood," Eerdmans explained. "This reporter doesn't mind confessing to an eerie feeling as we approach. Some of the rumors which have been circulating among the police as to what goes on inside the temple are gruesome, indeed."

On the preview screen, large white puffs of smoke bellowed unexpectedly upward from the foundations of the building. The needles on the VU meters in the studio pegged the high end. Speakers distorted with the overload.

The picture shook. The front wall of the hotel teetered and fell in on itself. It reminded Wally of the stories he had seen of buildings being purposely demolished during the heyday of Grunnell's urban renewal.

As the blast subsided, Henry Eerdmans' normally deep-toned air presence was high pitched and staccato.

"Oh, no . . . no! It's horrible," he cried. "It just exploded. Ladies and gentlemen . . . I don't know what to say . . . It's horrible . . . We were walking toward the building and . . . and . . . it was suddenly gone. Debris is raining down everywhere. . . . Give me a minute please, ladies and gentlemen, to pull my thoughts together . . . Policemen were in that building . . . We saw them go in . . . We did not see them come out . . . Oh, my word, ladies and gentlemen . . . They've been killed. No one could have been inside and survived that . . . that . . . terrible explosion. The shock wave almost knocked us off our feet . . . We've been pelted by falling bricks . . . It's a wonder we weren't killed! . . .

"Incredible . . . completely unbelievable . . . The police went in to rout a reported two hundred cultists and their leader . . . Oh, my word, if those reports are true, ladies and gentlemen, we've just had the worst disaster in Grunnell's history . . . The police . . . two hundred cultists . . . and their leader . . . may all be dead or seriously injured . . .

"Oh . . . oh . . . I'm sorry, ladies and gentlemen . . . I can't go on . . . I . . . I . . . words fail me. . . ."

Eerdmans broke down. He was weeping into his microphone.

Muted shock stunned the KBEX-TV master control room.

Darrell King kept repeating, "What a story! What a scoop! What a story! Stay with it. Stay with it."

Wally watched the dust swirling up around the camera to intermittently hide the rubble, but to the credit of the mini-cam operator, he kept his picture steady and focus clear.

Eerdmans could be heard choking, then he asked, "Are we still on the air? . . . Are we still on? . . . I don't know if you can hear me, ladies and gentlemen, but I'm going to keep broadcasting anyway . . . To summarize the incredible catastrophe which has just occurred here in lower downtown Grunnell . . . The police believed that the cult leader responsible for the takeover of the First Church of Grunnell this morning was in this hotel at Seventeenth and Welsh along with a great number of his followers. The police broke into the building just moments before a tremendous explosion leveled the structure. If the facts were as the police thought them to be, the mastermind of the raid on First Church is now buried under the rubble of the building that was his headquarters. To repeat . . ."

What was that Henry Eerdmans was saying? The mastermind of the raid on First Church was dead!

Wally seized on those words. Maybe he had seen too

many movies when he worked the late shift. Maybe.

But in those movies, when the warchief of the marauding Indians was killed, the Indians always abandoned their attack on the wagon train. Kill the leader and the Indians gave up.

It was a silly, desperate idea. A long shot. But it might work. Maybe it was in the power of Wally Nichols to stop the murder of Roger Uttenmeyer once and for all.

Wally depressed the lever on the intercom. "Peloubet, rewind Eerdmans' report."

"But, he hasn't finished it yet," Peloubet objected.

"Never mind. Do as I say and stand by!"

"What are you doing, Nichols?" Darrell was livid with surprise.

"I'll tell you, if it works," Wally shot. He grabbed up the shortwave microphone and called the church remote.

There was no answer. He didn't expect one.

"Get Eerdmans on the air NOW!" Darrell yelped.

Into the shortwave microphone, Wally said urgently, "I know you can hear me. Watch your air monitor. I want you to see something that just happened."

That brought a reaction from the remote. "Listen, turkey," the woman hissed, "you put anything on the screen but what I've said, and your friend is finished."

"You listen, lady," Wally summoned all the authority within him, "I'm trying to help *you*. Watch!"

He rolled the VTR playback before he could change his mind.

"Recognize it, lady?" he said to the shortwave microphone. "That's your Temple, isn't it?"

In replay, Eerdmans' report was as overwhelming as it had been the first time. After a while, even Darrell King quit demanding that Wally quit telecasting the report and return a live Eerdmans to the air. He watched in sullenness.

When the videotaped Eerdmans said, ". . . the mastermind of the raid on First Church is now buried under the rubble . . ." Wally pushed the transmit button on the shortwave mike.

"You hear that, lady? Your leader is dead. Where does that leave you? . . . Lady . . . Lady . . . Answer me!"

But the woman could not answer. The control room at the remote was empty.

And at KBEX, Wally stopped shouting into the microphone, thinking he had failed. He turned to Darrell King and slowly, haltingly, began to explain what he had done.

2:00 p.m.

In the sanctuary of First Church, the implosion from the hotel blocks away rattled doors and caused the floor beneath to shudder.

For a suspended millisecond to Malcolm Stansfield on his knees, it seemed the .45 in Brother John's hand had erupted. Instantly, Malcolm felt foolish. He was not shot. The texture and the sound of the blast were not those of a small firearm.

The hollow, short-lived "whump" had an unsettling effect on the members of the Brotherhood at First Church, too. While some of them milled about, wondering what the noise had been, a handful were dispatched to determine if it had something to do with the police. The unspoken implication was that Grunnell's finest were trying to dynamite their way into the building.

Brother John, for his part, kept insisting the explosion was outside and at some distance. "Hey, I was in 'Nam, remember?" he said. "I got so I can tell about bangs like that. You might say I'm an expert. And I say that racket was a long ways from here. It's got nothing to do with us or the pig cops."

If John was as convinced of that as he was attempting to sound, he had an odd way of displaying it. He paced the platform from side to side in a stiff, military gait. Every so often, he would stop and grin a mordant comment such as, "Maybe one of the pigs blew himself away with his own ammo," or he would jam his pistol in Malcolm's direction as if to reassure himself and others that he, Brother John, was still in complete control of the situation.

There was a different sense in the auditorium also, among the people in the pews. The jarring blast had somehow parted a little of the incubus in which they found themselves ensared by revealing that life did still exist beyond the marble walls of their temporary prison. It said to them that someone was out there, trying to get in and free them.

Kate Holmes, for one, smiled to her catatonic husband and whispered, "The police are coming for us, darling. Everything's going to be all right."

Mrs. Markus clutched her purse to her. She didn't want to lose it or leave it behind when they were rescued.

Pete Malko had been wondering what it would be like to die at forty-three. When he heard the explosion, he stopped wondering about death and thought, instead, about how good it would be to get out of there. He was almost giddy at the prospect, until he heard the child in the pew ahead.

The child was pointing at the body in the aisle. "Daddy, why doesn't that fat man get up?"

Pete went back to thinking about death. He didn't want to die, not at forty-three. He was in his prime. He didn't want to die.

Minutes ticked away. The hope that the police were on the verge of a daring rescue drained away. There were no police, no spurts of gunfire.

Malcolm Stansfield's knees began to ache from being bent to the hard platform. His thigh muscles were cramping and his lower legs were turning numb. He shifted.

The .45 in Brother John's possession waved his way. "Stay on your knees, preacher."

Malcolm sank back. John watched him a moment longer, then swung back to his nervous pacing.

More uncomfortable minutes, and then, the scouting Brothers came back. They had found nothing. The cops were still barricaded behind their squad cars across the street. The blast was a mystery. But certainly there were no cops pounding on the church doors.

Brother John was overjoyed. He embraced each of the Brothers on the platform, laughing praises to Abba.

Malcolm was not disappointed by the news. He hadn't expected the police to attempt anything drastic yet. He had read accounts of other hostage situations. He knew the authorities might wait up to two days or more before doing anything violent which might endanger the lives of victims.

So, while others worried about the explosion and hoped for the police, Malcolm's mind was racing ahead to the showdown which could be only a clock tick away. The fright in him was gone. He was calm.

Another man might have reasoned that because he had seen so much killing and violence that day, killing and violence had no effect on him any longer.

But Malcolm was not another man. He was a pastor, a preacher, a servant of the Lord God and of Jesus Christ. Christ had never failed him. Christ would not fail him now.

He removed his hands from his aching thighs and folded them in front of himself in an attitude of prayer. It wasn't because he was praying consciously. Rather, he was thinking about what the Lord wanted him to do, and the attitude of prayer came naturally for that.

Since he had been brought back to the platform, the message of Acts 1:8 had come to mind. It said, "But you shall receive power when the Holy Spirit has come upon you; and you shall be My witnesses . . ."

Plainly, he was to deliver a message about Christ.

Perhaps it would be his final sermon. If that was what God willed, so be it. Malcolm was going to make it count.

Methodically, Malcolm sized up each member of the Brotherhood as he watched them on the platform and in the auditorium.

What was it Harold Thomas had told him? That love was the basic tenet of the Brotherhood faith. Love was going to be Malcolm Stansfield's weapon.

Brother John was too preoccupied in his own Napoleonic posturing to be affected by such a message. He would resist it, try to prevent Malcolm from delivering it, no doubt. There was no way to stop Brother John, no power available to Malcolm, save the power of the Holy Spirit. He would trust that power.

And the other Brothers? Most were as fanatical as John, or they wouldn't have been sent to the church. He reviewed what he knew of each one until he came to Brother Nathanael.

Nathanael was a few feet away on Malcolm's right. He was regarding Brother John soberly as the latter continued to praise Abba and congratulate the members of his command.

Nathanael seemed as brainwashed as the rest. Back in the office, though, he had shown Malcolm signs of weakening. Their exchange had had an agitating effect on him. The scripture Malcolm had quoted seemed to unsettle him.

Yes, Malcolm decided, Nathanael was his best target. He would address as much as he was allowed to say to Nathanael.

If he got through, perhaps, Nathanael would turn on the others. Divide and conquer. Perhaps . . .

Speculation served no purpose. Malcolm squeezed it out of his thoughts. He must think only of the words building within, begging to be set loose.

Brother John had finished embracing the Brothers. He

was towering over Malcolm again, the .45 pointed and ready.

"Okay, preacher," John's eyes narrowed, "we've stalled long enough. Tell your good people about Abba."

Malcolm looked at the staring muzzle. It had no hold over him, not any longer. Perhaps he should be afraid for Miriam and Malcolm Jr. and little Beth. But he was not. They were in the hands of the Lord, and so was he.

Purposefully, he looked away from the gun and directly at Brother Nathanael. "God loves you and offers a wonderful plan for your life, if only you'll accept Him."

"Abba. You mean 'Abba loves you,'" John corrected, seemingly unaware of what Malcolm was doing.

"*God* loves you," Malcolm repeated deliberately. His voice rang across the congregation. "For God so loved the world, that he gave his only begotten Son, that whosoever believeth in him should not perish, but have everlasting life."

"You fool!" John's eyes bulged with outrage. "I warned you, preacher. I warned you. You're making me do this. You're making me kill your family! Sister Courage—"

"Is this the love which Abba gives?" Malcolm shouted over John. "Does he murder women and children? Is that love?"

"Sister Cour—"

"The Bible says, 'But the fruit of the Spirit is love, joy, peace, patience, kindness, goodness, fruitfulness, gentleness, self-control . . .'"

"Sister!" John's anger made itself heard over Malcolm's tirade. "Bring that woman and kids up here!"

"Not just love, but joy, peace, patience," Malcolm hammered, his eyes locked with Nathanael's. Nathanael's blue eyes widened. Something was happening behind those orbs and Malcolm was not about to let go.

"Have you seen any of these things in your Brotherhood? Any evidence of them?" Malcolm's question was rhetorical—he did not give Nathanael time to consider an answer. "You know you haven't. And, you do know that's what's in scripture."

"Yes," Nathanael nodded. He seemed almost detached, moonstruck. "I've seen it. Galatians, chapter five."

"And the Bible says the Spirit is of God. Not Abba, but the one, true, living, almighty God!" The words leaped forcefully from Malcolm's throat. Nathanael's eyes darted at each of them.

A grip tightened on Malcolm's shoulder. It was so sudden and punishing, Malcolm was driven to look away from Nathanael and into the eyes of Brother John.

Brother John's face was etched in the same demonic cast Malcolm had seen there when the man gunned down Harold Thomas. His teeth were clenched, and the veins in his neck stood out.

"You double-crossed me, preacher," his hot breath caught Malcolm full in his face, "and your little girl is going to pay the price!"

With the hand that held the pistol, John gestured toward Miriam and the children. They were being herded to the platform by the fragile girl with the rifle.

"They're going to pay the price," John twisted the statement with spleen.

"No," Malcolm coldly rebutted, "those who murder her, those who deny the real God, will pay the price for eternity."

From Beth came a small whimper. "Daddy, I'm scared."

Miriam reached out and touched her daughter with tender reassurance. "Daddy won't let them hurt you, Beth. He won't. Will you, Malcolm?"

Pushing Miriam aside, John grabbed Beth's wrist and savagely whipped her around so that she was face-to-face with her father. Beth's eyes widened. Tears burst forth from terror.

"What kind of a father are you?" John taunted. "Look at

her. Doesn't your daughter mean anything to you?"

Malcolm tried to put his arms around Beth, to draw her close. John slapped his arms away.

"Doesn't she mean anything at all to you?"

"Yes, oh, yes," Malcolm cried, "but, as a father who loves her, I would rather see her dead than have her bow down to your Abba."

"Abba is—"

"Abba is *not* God," Malcolm finished the sentence for Brother John and wrenched away from his grasp. He prayed Beth would understand. His eyes frantically sought out Brother Nathanael.

"Are you going to stand there and let him kill my daughter because 'Abba is Love'? Well, let me tell you about *real* love." He quoted, "God demonstrates His own love toward us, in that while we were yet sinners, Christ died for us."

"Daddy? He's hurting me. Please, make him stop. Please."

I'm trying, he thought. *I'm trying, honey!* To Nathanael he continued, "Christ died for our sins . . . He was buried . . ." The words tumbled out in a rush. Each might be his last. The next sound that interrupted him might be the shot that killed Beth.

But he could not quit. The words kept coming. "He was raised on the third day, according to the Scriptures . . ."

"Don't you see?" Malcolm implored, "the love you're looking for comes only from Christ, not some man who pretends to be God, but from *God,* Himself, the Triune God of the Holy Bible."

"What are you waiting for, Sister?" John railed. "Kill her. And if the preacher still doesn't shut his mouth, kill the boy and then the wife. Kill them. Kill them!"

"Malcolm!" Miriam threw herself protectively between Beth and the girl with the rifle. "Malcolm, he means it!"

Malcolm heard the unmistakable scrape of a sliding rifle

bolt.

"Daddy!"

His heart sank.

"No, Sister, no!" It was the voice of Nathanael. He took a step toward Malcolm. "Let him finish."

"I'm giving orders here," John's protest was immediate and icy.

Nathanael dipped his own rifle in John's direction. "No one says you aren't. Just let him finish, that's all."

John's jaw worked in frustrated anger. He stared at Nathanael, unable to comprehend the mutiny. He swung the pistol in his hand until it aimed at Nathanael's chest. "I'm gonna' kill you, Brother!"

"What's the matter, Brother John?" Malcolm asked softly, piercing the tension in the only way he knew how. "Are you afraid of the truth I'm speaking?"

John froze. He looked at Nathanael, then the gun in his hand, and finally at Malcolm. Consternation was written on his face, and then it was erased by a surprised laugh.

"Oh, I see what you're trying to do, preacher," he smirked. "You're trying to get us to turn on ourselves. You're trying to make me look like a fool.

"Well, it won't work. I'm not afraid of you, because Abba is with me, and Abba is God. So, you just go on like Nathanael, here, wants. Babble your lies. But, you see, I know about Jesus. Abba has explained all about him. He was just a man, a created man. You think you can fool me? I know the Bible, preacher, as well as you. Abba taught it to me, and he should know. He had it written about himself.

"You say Jesus is Lord? Where in the Bible does it say that?"

"John 1:1," Malcolm said. "In the beginning was the Word, and the Word was with God, and the Word was God."

"You got something better than that, don't you? Go on,

preacher," Brother John urged scornfully. "The floor is yours. The Brotherhood yields to the holy man from Jee-sus Land."

Sadly, Malcolm said, "May He forgive you. You hear the gospel and you mock. The Word, Jesus, came to earth to die for our sins—your sins. He made Himself a sacrifice for us. He loved us—loved you—that much. And, He loved us enough to give us victory over death by rising from the dead to show us eternal life. Because of Him and what He did, I can love you in spite of what you're doing to me and my family."

"If I was you, preacher, I'd step back," John ridiculed. "Because, if you're speaking the right of it, Jesus is gonna' zap me with a lightning bolt."

"No. He won't do that. He loves you, John, even in your rebellion." Malcolm knew he had said all he could. The rest was up to God.

"Hallelujah! Jesus saves!" John hooted. "Well, he'd better get to saving, preacher, because you're dead."

The cruel humor suddenly vanished. John's face turned bitterly hard. His eyes met Malcolm's and fastened on them. Without turning, he said, "Sister Courage, I've changed my mind. Brother Nathanael, the honor is yours. I want you to kill the girl."

The first terrible second dragged by, and another.

"I'm waiting, Brother Nathanael," John said peevishly, his eyes still holding Malcolm's.

Malcolm's own heart drummed against his ribs. He wanted to look at Nathanael, at Beth, but he could not. He glared into the unflinching pupils of the cultist. He couldn't afford to show weakness now.

Abruptly, Brother John broke the eye contact and wheeled on Nathanael.

"What's the matter with you, Brother? When I give an order, I—"

Nathanael was gaping at the rifle he held. His hands

were shaking. His face was pale. He looked at Malcolm and began to raise the rifle.

Malcolm had no chance to comprehend why the rifle never drew down on its target, for at that moment there was a scream from the balcony.

Malcolm glanced up to see a woman running along the rail. Despite the bright television lights, he could make out that she was a Sister. She was armed.

Two Brothers were stumbling after her, trying to catch her. She was bewildered, hysterical.

"What the—?" A gasp of surprise escaped Brother John's lips. He shouted up at her, "Sister, get back to your post! Get back to the control room!"

She tripped, caught herself on the rail and noticed John on the platform.

"Brother John . . . Brother John," she screeched. "They've killed him. They destroyed our Temple. Abba is dead!"

"Somebody get her out of here!" Brother John roared.

Two Brothers were closing in on her from each side. She eyed them as an animal trapped.

"You don't understand. It's finished. Abba is dead!" Before anyone could stop her, she put her gun in her mouth and pulled the trigger.

2:09 p.m.

Burch Zimmerman had just arrived on the street in front of the Denton Building when the downtown area was rocked by the explosion. Windows in the stores all along the avenue had been shaken in their moldings and more than one cracked.

First reactions were that it had come from the church, but it soon became apparent that the explosion had occurred several blocks away.

"Probably a jet breaking the sound barrier," one of the uniformed officers had offered.

"Naw, that wasn't no jet," another one disagreed. "That was a blast. Maybe the refinery out on Old Road."

Burch had been wondering if the church and the blast were somehow connected when Sergeant Shaw was heard on the transceiver. He had been so emotional, Burch had had a hard time understanding him.

"Zim, Zim! *Good night,* Zim, I just saw it on TV. That old hotel on Seventeenth just blew to smithereens. And some of our boys was in there!" Shaw had slobbered.

Burch had hunted for Max Vigeveno. He had wanted to send the lieutenant over to the scene of the explosion to check it out, but the schlepp was nowhere to be seen. Burch had had to send Faulkner instead, and Faulkner still had not gotten back to him.

Burch was standing in the entrance of the Denton Building, watching the terrorists on the portico of the church, and thinking maybe the planned SWAT attack was premature—no telling how those freaks had booby-trapped the church—when Lieutenant Gomez approached. Gomez was so blatantly out of shape his rumpled white shirt gapped over his belly. Sweat rolled down his pudgy cheeks with each step.

In back of Gomez was a tall, lean man in a well-cut pin-striped suit. Burch knew the man was an attorney before Gomez introduced him.

"Sorry, no civilians are allowed," Burch grumbled.

"This guy thinks he might be able to help," Gomez said shyly.

The attorney offered Burch a limp handshake and introduced himself. He said he had been following the Brotherhood for some months. He had been retained by some of the parents of a few of the young people in the cult. His job was to get the youngsters out, if he could, and have them deprogrammed.

"Yeah," Burch picked his teeth with the end of a match. "But, excuse me—I don't want to offend—how does that help us?"

"I was hoping you could help me." From his inside coat pocket, the attorney produced three wallet-sized photographs. "Have you seen any of these youngsters today, Captain?"

Burch took the three pictures and shuffled through them, studying each one carefully. The first was a clean-cut college boy. The second looked to be a high school girl with braces on her teeth. The third was another young man in the uniform of the United States Army.

"Of course, their appearances are probably changed some," the attorney offered.

"These kids are in the Brotherhood, huh?" Burch asked

as he shuffled through the pictures again.

"We think so, yes," the attorney said. "I tried to watch the situation on television today, to see if I could recognize any of them. But it's difficult to make a positive identification on the tube."

"Yes," Burch agreed, remembering his ex-wife's insistence that Sandy was in the church.

He gave the photographs one last perusal and handed them back. "Sorry. None of them look familiar."

"Yeah. Well, it was worth a shot." The attorney put the pictures away, his disappointment showing.

Burch took out his package of cigarettes and proffered one to the lawyer. "Smoke?"

"No, thank you."

Gomez quickly jumped in. "Don't mind if I do, Captain."

Giving Gomez a "you-weren't-invited" glance, Burch watched irritably as the fat policeman helped himself anyway.

Burch tugged his own cigarette from the package and put it back in his shirt pocket. From another pocket, he produced a book of paper matches and struck one. As he lit up, Gomez edged closer, expecting Burch to light his cigarette for him.

Instead, Burch fanned out the match. Gomez would have to use his own match. It was bad enough that he had glommed one of Burch's precious smokes, Burch wasn't about to lend him the means of smoking it.

"I need a match," Gomez said foolishly.

"Too bad. I'm fresh out," Burch responded pointedly.

"Oh," Gomez looked at his unlighted cigarette tip. Guess I'll have to light it from yours then."

Burch took a drag. "Sorry, Gomez, but that'd be bad luck." Burch didn't give a hang about luck, but he was determined to keep the fat cop from enjoying that pilfered smoke.

"Aw, yeah, luck." Gomez took on the look of a baffled

St. Bernard. Unabashed, he carefully tucked the offending yenem in his hatband for safekeeping.

Through all this, the attorney stood first on one foot and then on the other, as if he was embarrassed by Burch's put-down of Gomez's greed.

"So," Burch said to him, blowing smoke out of the side of his mouth, "you're an expert on this Brotherhood."

"I guess I know them as well as anyone does on the outside," the attorney acknowledged. It was not a boast.

Burch decided the man might possibly be a source of some more information, information he needed before the final decision to send his men into the breech.

"Tell me," he said easily, drawing the attorney out, "how many kids you rescued from them?"

The attorney looked Burch straight in the eye. "Captain, I'm good at what I do. I've had a great deal of success with other cults, but not this one. Very few have ever been taken out of it alive. In fact, only two that I know of, and one of them—Harold Thomas—is in that church across the street.

"I think that's what this whole thing is all about. The Brotherhood doesn't like one of its former members speaking out publicly about cult secrets."

"Yeah, well, if you're so interested in the Brotherhood, how come you didn't attend Stansfield's service this morning?"

The lawyer thoughtfully stroked his pencil-thin mustache. "You know, that's the funny thing. I had planned to go, but just as I was going to leave my apartment, my mother called from Dallas. She's never called on Sunday morning before, but today she did. She talked for more than forty-five minutes about nothing. I decided I would be too late, then, so I started to watch it on TV. Funny thing. My mother calling like that. If she hadn't, I'd be in there with the rest of the hostages right now."

"Praise God who helps without fee," Burch commented.

"I beg your pardon?"

"Nothing. Just an old Yiddish prayer." Another drag on the cigarette. "What if I should tell you I'm thinking of sending some of my men in there to free those hostages?"

"I'd say somebody will die. The kids in there have been programmed to kill, and they'll do it."

The cigarette suddenly tasted flat to Burch. "What if I should ask, then, about talking them out?"

"You mean negotiation? No way it would work. Their leader, Abba, has too strong a hold over them."

"That's what I thought." Burch abandoned his smoldering cigarette to the concrete. "Suppose I should tell you we have an ace. Suppose I should tell you that this leader was said to be at his headquarters, and those headquarters were just blown to bits?"

The attorney was grim. "That was the explosion we heard?"

"Just now," Burch nodded.

"And Abba?"

"We don't know. Maybe he's over there in First Church with his henchmen, it's hard to say. But suppose he was in the hotel when the walls came tumbling down."

The attorney gave a long whistle.

"The minds of the kids in the church—would that change them? Would they give up?"

The attorney stroked his mustache more pensively, "I don't think I'd let them know it, if I were you. I've heard of a strange murder-suicide pact as a contingency in the event of Abba's death."

"Like Jonestown, you mean?"

"More binding. If they received so much as a hint that their leader had been killed, the hostages would be immediately shot like so many cattle."

"This Abba, he would have that strong a hold over them, even if he was dead?"

"Yes. They'd do anything for him, and have."

"So what's the answer?" Burch asked.

"I'm just glad I'm not in your shoes, Captain," the attorney said softly.

"Me, too." Burch scratched his chin. That settled it. The old way was the best way. Guns blazing going in. The doubts about that decision had been vanquished.

And something else, too. He realized how much he needed action, to be just a cop again, to forget about the ghosts of his dead daughter and dead marriage.

"Escort this good citizen to the Press area, Gomez." It almost sounded like the old Burch, the Burch Zimmerman who had existed once before Sandy died.

There was more verve in his manner as he shouted after the retreating lawyer, "Thank you. If we arrest any of the kids alive, I promise you you'll be the first citizen to lay eyes. Maybe we'll both get lucky. Maybe, your clients will be among them."

The attorney signaled his appreciation as Burch turned and walked to the nearest uniformed man. "Spread the word," Burch told him. "When we open up, shoot to kill."

Hunkering down behind the lead squad car, Burch checked his revolver and was about to reach for another cigarette when Kelly's call came over his transceiver. SWAT was in position.

This was it. Burch took a deep breath, exhaled slowly, then pressed the talk button. "Everyone ready. We'll go in fifteen, fourteen, thirteen . . ."

Marking the cadence, he picked up the bullhorn which had been placed beside the car for his use. He pondered giving the suspects one last warning and concluded against it. Those yenzas didn't deserve it.

Simultaneously to both the transceiver and the bullhorn, he shouted, "Go!"

Only God could stop the killing now.

2:13 p.m.

Brother John stood unmoving, staring at the place where the Sister had put the gun in her mouth and died. His face was impassive. The only hint that turbulent emotions might be churning within was the way he kept opening and closing his fist.

Malcolm stood motionless with him, unable to comprehend another terrible image in a day filled with terrible images. The violence had become a narcotic, anesthetizing him against all but the smallest stirrings of regret and sorrow that a young woman had taken her life without knowing the saving grace of the Lord Jesus Christ.

A long, low wail built in Brother John's throat. The anguish of it was not human. A shiver ran up Malcolm's spine.

"You!" John's accusation came in a drawn out, grinding rasp which seemed a voice from another world. "You, preacher! You did this to her. You murdered her!"

He turned on Malcolm, outrage ravishing his sallow face, his eyes fevered with hatred. Unwillingly, Malcolm gave ground.

Brother John advanced. "All you had to say was, 'Abba is Lord.' But, no, you wouldn't do that, and a Sister is dead because of you."

"Didn't you hear her, son?" Malcolm fought to maintain his composure. "Abba is dead. She killed herself, because she knew. Your Abba is dead."

"Liar!"

Malcolm's eyes darted about, searching for something, anything to use in defense. There was nothing.

Brother John took another step forward. "In the name of holy Abba, I judge you, preacher. I sentence you. The blood of the Sister is on your filthy, lying head."

He raised his pistol. His hand was shaking. He brought his other hand up to steady his aim. A wicked ecstasy consumed him.

Malcolm braced for the bullet. It never came.

Brother John's mouth flew open in shock. His eyes rolled up. With great effort, he took another step. A ragged stain spread across the front of his jacket. His mouth moved as he tried to speak. Then, suddenly, he pitched forward, still clutching his pistol.

It took a moment for Malcolm to realize that Brother John had been shot. He looked around wildly. He had heard nothing. Where had it come from?

Nathanael and another Brother were also down. The girl guarding Miriam screamed and started toward John. A heavy slug plowed into the pulpit just behind where she had been.

A steady barrage of gunfire had begun outside in the street. The sound of it brought Malcolm back to his senses.

A Brother burst through the narthex doors at the back of the sanctuary. "Up here! The cops are coming in this way!"

Some of the Brothers and Sisters ran toward the doors. The gunfire increased. The people in the pews were scattering in every direction.

Malcolm's only thought was of Miriam and the children. They were standing unprotected in the midst of the insane maelstrom.

Somehow, he reached them, and somehow he got them to the shelter of the pulpit. He pushed them down behind it and covered them with his own body.

As he did so, his hand brushed against the rifle Brother John had left leaning there. Malcolm seized it. He put his back to Miriam and the children, facing out from the back of the pulpit, determined to use the unfamiliar weapon if he had to.

It was then he saw the four men materialize from the baptistry. They wore blue coveralls and baseball caps. They, too, carried rifles. Thank God, they were police.

Two of them, a tall blond man and a dark-skinned Mexican, were shouting. They could not be heard over the heavy gunfire at the front of the church and the screaming in the auditorium.

In unison, they raised their weapons and fired a salvo toward the ceiling. The bullets riddled the plaster.

A stunned hush fell over the scene.

In the lull, the tall blond yelled, "Police! Drop your weapons. You're under arrest. I said, drop 'em!"

A new shot. A bullet whistled past the blond and splintered the edge of a bench in the choir loft.

The four policemen dove for cover while their rifles spewed smoke and fire into the auditorium.

Then, silence.

Gradually, there came a few muted whimpers, and the shuffle of tiny movements.

The police straightened, watchfully. The blond took a walkie-talkie from his hip pocket.

"This is Kelly," Malcolm heard him say. "We got 'em. You can come on in, Captain."

Malcolm raised up, thinking, *Praise God, it's finished. Praise God.*

He did not hear the dark-skinned officer warn, "Better sit tight for a minute, preacher."

The sudden release of tension, the joy that it was, indeed,

done with, filled him. He could see the entire auditorium now from behind the pulpit in which he had preached so many sermons.

The Brothers and Sisters who were still standing had thrown down their weapons. Their hands were in the air. In the center aisle, two Brothers and one Sister were sprawled in grotesque poses.

Through the narthex doors came a wedge of more police. One of the Brotherhood removed his combat jacket and tried to lose himself among the shocked survivors in the pews. Two of the officers saw him. They descended upon him and handcuffed him.

Malcolm blinked back tears of rejoicing and gratitude. God had not failed. Christ was still on His throne.

Then, out of the corner of his eye, he caught a movement. The girl who had gone to the aid of Brother John had her back to the police. They were advancing up the aisle toward the platform. They could not see her pry the pistol from John's hands. The motion was shielded from their view by her body.

The police on the platform did not seem to notice her either. They were still intent on covering the auditorium with their rifles.

The girl stood up, her back still to the police.

"Look out!" Malcolm shouted. "She's got a gun!"

2:18 p.m.

Burch Zimmerman was leading his men down the center aisle of the church, and already he was congratulating himself. The gunfire had been brutal, but they had come through it. As far as he knew, not one of his men had sustained so much as a scratch.

The punks on the portico and in the narthex had surrendered the minute they saw that the cops meant business. They had dropped their weapons like lambs. And the punks here in the sanctuary had surrendered, too.

Programmed killers? Look at them. Kids. That's all they were, overgrown kids who had been playing cops and robbers. They didn't want to die anymore than Burch, himself, wanted to die.

He marched past the pews. The frightened faces of the hostages watched him as he went, not fully realizing yet that they were rescued, that they could leave this place and go on with their lives.

He moved on, pausing only momentarily at the body of a young man in the aisle, to make sure he was dead. The boy's lifeblood was collecting in a small pool on the tiled floor. There was no pulse.

"Call some ambulances," Burch said to one of the officers with him.

Ahead on the platform, Burch saw the SWAT commanders and the other two members of their SWAT teams. He saw three more bodies, evidence that the sharpshooters across the street in the Denton Building had not missed. And, he saw the girl.

She was a fragile girl, so thin her green combat jacket dwarfed her. Even from the back, he could tell she had seen more trouble than any girl her age should have seen.

She was bending over one of the bodies on the platform, maybe her boyfriend. *Too bad little girl,* Burch thought, *but that schlepp deserved what he got.*

The girl pushed herself to her feet.

Burch heard a shouted warning. He saw her turning toward him, the .45 automatic coming into view from behind her jacket.

He raised his revolver. "Honey, put it down," he barked.

But she did not put it down. She was turning straight to him. How she must hate, to do something so crazy, so . . .

No, it couldn't be! Recognition jolted through his frame. She was thinner, much thinner. She looked older, older than her years. But he'd know those eyes, that face anywhere.

It was. It was Sandy. Sandy come back from the grave. His Sandy.

Gerry had been right. Sandy was here. Sandy was in the church. Sandy was with the cult. He had found her. After all these years of knowing she was dead, and she was alive. She was alive after all!

She did not recognize him. She raised the .45 higher and began to squeeze at the trigger.

"Sandy! It's me, Daddy. Look at me. Don't shoot, it's Daddy!"

The gun leaped with the recoil. The last shot of Cult Sunday had been fired.

11:27 p.m.

Wally Nichols pushed his chair back from the switcher and knuckled his bloodshot eyes. He had just finished feeding the last of the wrap-up footage to the network in New York.

"It's all yours, Bob," he said to the KBEX night man.

Bob nodded an acknowledgment, but did not glance up. He was already preparing to take the 11:30 station break.

George Peloubet came from the film room, looking every bit as weary as Wally felt.

"Glad that's over," Peloubet said.

"Yeah," Wally yawned and stretched. "Hey, Peloubet, you never did tell me."

"Tell you what?"

"The answer to that riddle. How *do* you make eights add up to an even thousand?"

Peloubet smiled. "That's not a riddle, that's a brain twister. And, I'm too tired to give you the answer tonight."

"You know what?" Wally said. "I'm too tired to care."

"You won't be able to catch a city bus this time of night," Peloubet changed the subject. "Want a lift?"

"Sure. Thanks. I'll catch up with you in the locker room. Got to finish my paperwork first."

"Don't be too thorough," Peloubet cautioned with an

exhausted grin. "We've both seen enough of this place for one day."

He moved on toward the locker room.

Wally pulled himself from the chair, leaned over the shelf in front of the switcher, signed his name to the last page of his log and threw it in the "Out" basket. It would be picked up there in the morning and routed back to the Traffic Department, where it would be checked and filed in case the FCC had any questions about what KBEX had telecast that day.

He stretched again and took the Thermos and the model railroading magazine from the shelf behind him. He regarded the cover of the hobby journal. Somehow, model trains didn't seem so important anymore.

He rolled the magazine up and stuck it under his arm. He was hungry and needed a shower. And, after that, a good night's sleep.

Maybe he wouldn't work the morning shift next Sunday. Maybe he'd take Grace to church next Sunday. Yeah, maybe he would.

"'Night, Bob," he said.

"Super job, Wally. Have a good one."

As he headed to meet Peloubet, the music for the opening credits of the late show came blaring over the control room speaker.

"It's already forgotten," Wally mused. "People died and who cares? It was a good show, while it lasted, but it's over. Who cares?"

Malcolm Stansfield could not forget, no matter how hard he tried. He lay in bed with Miriam beside him, the bits and pieces of Cult Sunday flashing before him.

Sixteen had died at the church. Stan Brown had passed away at City Memorial in the early evening. And Peggy Brown was a widow and her mother was with her, and day-after-tomorrow, Malcolm would have to preach the funeral.

Sixteen at the church. And, that was not all. It would be days before all the bodies had been pulled from the rubble of the old hotel. Some said the death toll would mount to more than two hundred then.

Two hundred. And for what?

And gentle old George Perkins. His funeral would be day-after-tomorrow, too. What could he say to comfort his widow and all those children, Malcolm wondered.

And Joseph Holmes. He was a casualty, as well. Not a statistic in the column of death, but a casualty, nonetheless.

Malcolm had visited the old man in the hospital shortly after Stan Brown died. Joseph showed no response as Malcolm addressed him soothingly and prayed with Kate, who staunchly hovered at her husband's side.

"Do you know what he told me a little while ago?" Kate asked. "Joseph said it was all his fault. He had put too much store in that stained-glass window. God destroyed it, he said, because He wanted him to learn there was more to a church than a window and a building."

Yes, Joseph Holmes was a casualty. Guilt was killing him. Malcolm prayed that he would be able to get through to Joseph, to help ease his burden before it was too late.

And there were other walking casualties. No one who had been at First Church that day would ever be the same. Malcolm had held Beth while she cried herself to sleep in his arms. And Malcolm Jr. had wanted the light in his room left on. From the time he was a baby, he had always been able to sleep without a night-light before.

And the Press. Pounding the survivors with questions. And one question above all others: "Why do you think it happened, Reverend Stansfield?"

These were the bits and pieces which crowded in on Malcolm's thoughts as he lay in bed. These were the fragments which kept his fatigued body from slumber.

Absently, he put his fingers to his swollen, battered jaw and winced.

"You all right?" Miriam asked from her side of the bed.

He didn't answer.

"Want to talk about it?" It was the wifely inquiry of a woman who understood her husband.

He grunted and stared at the ceiling.

She snuggled up to him, her head resting against his shoulder. After awhile she said, "I don't understand how God could let it happen."

"God didn't let it happen," he said. "We did. The whole Cult Sunday idea was wrong from the beginning. It's not the way to fight the cults."

"How do you do it, then, Malcolm?"

He thought for a moment. "By the slow and steady teaching of sound doctrine. By making certain our children see and feel the real love of Christ from the time they're babes. That should be the goal of every parent—and every church."

"Train up a child in the way he should go: and when he is old, he will not depart from it," she quoted from Proverbs.

"It's the training that's hard," he said. "We can't just teach them to memorize Scriptures. We have to teach them the meanings of those memorized verses in context. We have to show how to put on 'the full armour of God.' "

"It sounds so easy," she said wistfully.

"But it's not. The armor of God is forged by the love of Christ. The simplest thing in the world to have, and because it's simple, so many find it difficult to accept. They keep thinking they should have to do more. Why can't they just accept Christ's love?" He lapsed into his own deep thoughts.

"I keep thinking about the way that girl looked when she pointed the gun at the policeman, and he was her own father."

"I know," Malcolm said, putting his arm around Miriam.

"If you hadn't—"

"I know," he sighed, remembering how the girl had leveled the pistol and would have fired at Captain Zimmerman, despite the fact that he was her own flesh and blood.

In that final, fatal instant, Malcolm had made a desperate lunge. He had crashed into her arm just as she pulled the trigger. The bullet went harmlessly wide of its mark, and by the grace of God, had missed all the other people it could have hit.

Just before Malcolm had come to bed, he had received a phone call from Burch Zimmerman.

"I wouldn't believe it, if I hadn't seen it with my own eyes," Zimmerman had reported. "The deprogrammer has been working with her, and already she's starting to come out. There's a long way to go, but at least our Sandy is back again."

The captain went on to explain how he had asked Sandy about her locket, found buried with the skeleton. She had given it to one of her close friends among the cult Sisters, who later had mysteriously disappeared. A cult Priest had only told Sandy that her friend was serving Abba in another part of the country.

But one of the captured Brothers, under intense questioning from Zimmerman at the police station that evening, had disclosed the real fate of Sandy's friend. She had borne one of Abba's children, and when the baby had been taken from her to be raised in the Slave's nursery, Sandy's friend had tried to steal her baby back and flee the Brotherhood. Her efforts brought about her gruesome end in the shallow California grave. It was her skeleton, with the locket, that Burch had mistaken for Sandy.

"It's a good thing that Abba was blown to bits in his own temple," Burch Zimmerman's voice had become hard on the phone. "It's a good thing he can't do to other kids what he did to my daughter."

Malcolm remembered Burch Zimmerman's words, and rolled over to kiss Miriam.

"Let's say a prayer, hon," he said.

Downtown, at the Greyhound bus terminal, a man of medium height boarded a bus to Los Angeles. His face was pink and raw where he had shaved off his beard, but his eyes still had a quality about them which set him apart.

He sidled down the aisle between other embarking passengers and their baggage, searching for a vacant seat. Then, he saw her. A girl in faded jeans. Not more than sixteen. Alone. She had a knapsack on her lap and was crying.

A runaway. She had to be. He knew all about runaways.

Gripping the little black satchel he carried, he worked his way toward her and sat down beside her.

"You look like you could use a friend," he smiled, fixing her with those eyes that changed moods a hundred times a minute.

She looked away from him and out the window.

"Now, don't be that way," he said, putting a fatherly hand on her shoulder. "I might be able to help you."

By degrees, her tear-streaked face came around. She needed a friend. She could not resist those eyes.

The engine roared to life and the bus lurched forward. Over the rumble of the diesel, the man said something and smiled brightly.

Only the girl heard him as he said softly, "Those close to me, call me Abba . . ."

"For many deceivers are entered into the world, who confess not that Jesus Christ is come in the flesh. This is a deceiver and an antichrist."
II John 7

An Afterword

Could "Cult Sunday" happen in America? Yes. As shocking as it might seem, most of it has happened already.

Of course, none of it has occurred exactly as depicted in this novel. All of the characters are figments of this writer's imagination. However, the major events portrayed in the story have, indeed, taken place at different intervals in different locales within the United States.

For example, a church service was actually interrupted by demonstrators in a U.S. city within the last decade. It had nothing to do with a cult, and there were no casualties. Nevertheless, it is a fact of history, and history, we are told, has a way of repeating itself.

The Temple of the Brotherhood as I have described it, is fictional also, but most of its practices and its beliefs are taken from cults which do, in fact, exist at this moment.

Several actual cult leaders are called "Father" (the English translation of Abba) by their followers. Of particular note in this group is Sun Myung Moon, head of the Unification Church—the

Moonies.

Former members of the Moonies report that they were taught that Moon "is God." Jesus, they are taught, was simply "a sinless man who failed in his mission" as Saviour of the world.

Moon is adored and worshiped. He has the best of everything. The incident of the oranges, which Harold Thomas related to Malcolm Stansfield in this novel, was adapted from an actual incident detailed by an ex-member of the Moon cult about Moon.

The use of brainwashing within the cults is widespread. Often, it is more subtle than pictured here. But the techniques of isolation of a new or prospective cult member, the deprivation of sleep, the continuous playing of audiotapes and mental and physical torture have all been documented by eyewitnesses who have emerged from the ranks of these neo-religious organizations.

The giving up of all of one's material possessions to the cult is also practiced widely. There have been many recorded instances of cultists donating all their money, their belongings, their automobiles, even the clothes on their backs for "the good of the order," while under the influences of brainwashing.

While some of the cult leaders are, no doubt, sincere, the potential for corruption is huge. More often than not, cult leaders live in luxury, in literal mansions, while the majority of their followers are made to exist in poverty and squalor.

Of course, most frightening of all is the threat of violence to themselves and society which exists in more than a few of the cults. The People's Temple and their tragedy in Jonestown, Guyana, were spectacularly recounted in the media.

Not so well reported has been the fact that some

Muslim sects and other Middle Eastern religions practice "Conversion by the Sword," as does the Brotherhood of this book. Recently, these religions have begun to enjoy increasing popularity in the western hemisphere.

Nor does a cult have to be Middle Eastern in origin to preach violence and physical harm to anyone who stands in their way. Ron Hubbard, founder of the Church of Scientology, has written, "An Enemy [anyone who speaks out against Scientology] may be considered fair game [and] may be deprived of property or injured by any means by any Scientologist without any discipline of the Scientologist. [They] May be tricked, sued, or lied to, or destroyed." (Quoted from *Scientology: The Now Religion* by George Malko, Delacorte Press, New York, N.Y.)

The interpretation of the phrase ". . . or destroyed," is left up to the individual reader.

The point is, while the Temple of the Brotherhood is fictional, it does have some very real counterparts in the America of today. And these cults continue to flourish and prosper. How and why?

It becomes apparent to even the most casual student of the cult phenomenon that what the cults pretend to offer to the young—and the not-so-young—who fall prey to them, is a sense of "love" and "belonging," which is sadly missing from many of the so-called mainline Christian churches.

We live in a selfish society, where the selfless love of Jesus Christ is often spoken of but not frequently evidenced. To the individual who seeks something more from life than a plastic materialism, the cults can seem to offer an attractive alternative. But the attractiveness is shallow and leaves in its wake broken homes, broken families, grieving relatives and broken individuals.

What can we do to battle the cults? I, for one, do not believe the answer lies in stricter laws. For the same laws which could inhibit the cults, could also be turned against the legitimate organized religions which helped build this nation.

No, as with any social evil, the answer is not better laws, but better-informed people.

Part of the answer certainly lies in learning all we can about the false teachings of the cults and exposing them to others. Not in the flamboyant fashion attempted by Malcolm Stansfield and his church, but in quiet, logical exposition.

But that is only part of the answer. For evangelical Christians, the real answer is found in the words of Paul: "Put on the whole armour of God, that ye may be able to stand against the wiles of the devil. For we wrestle not against flesh and blood, but against principalities, against powers, against the rulers of the darkness of this world, against the spiritual wickedness in high places.

"Wherefore take unto you the whole armour of God, that ye may be able to withstand in the evil day, and having done all, to stand.

"Stand therefore, having your loins girt about with truth, and having on the breastplate of righteousness; And your feet shod with the preparation of the gospel of peace: Above all, taking the shield of faith, wherewith ye shall be able to quench all the fiery darts of the wicked.

"And take the helmet of salvation, and the sword of the Spirit, which is the word of God: Praying always . . . and watching thereunto with all perseverance and supplication for all saints" (Ephesians 6:11-18).

If we take the armor for ourselves, and as Malcolm Stansfield says, give it also to our children by teaching them the context of the Scriptures and the sound doctrines of our faith, we will be victorious.

And, then, as Jesus said, "This is my commandment, That ye love one another, as I have loved you."

In our churches, in our businesses, in our relationships with other people, and most importantly, in the home, the love of John 15:12 quoted above must be evident to all who know us, and especially to our families.

We must do these things, because the cults are there, preaching and recruiting. They are in the streets, on school grounds, at college campuses, waiting for our confused, our troubled and our unloved.

One of the books which I used for reference in preparation of this work demonstrates how easy it is for an individual—even an individual from a loving, Christian home—to be drawn into a cult. The book is *Escape,* by Rachel Martin as told to Bonnie Palmer Young (Accent Books, Denver).

The story Rachel Martin tells is in many ways far more terrifying than any author of fiction could create. I would recommend you read it.

Which brings me to the acknowledgment of a great debt I owe to Rachel Martin Dugger, her husband and her parents. For, it was over a luncheon with them and through the experiences they so generously shared, that the idea of *Cult Sunday* was born.

I also owe a debt of gratitude to Brooke Dolphe who took time to give me the benefit of his knowledge of police procedures gleaned from his background as a former police officer.

Likewise, my gratitude to Sergeant Dale King of the Colorado State Highway Patrol, who also provided me with much valuable insight into the way the authorities might respond to the situation at the First Church of Grunnell. Doing this on his day off was above and beyond the call of duty.

Thanks, too, as always to my expert and patient editors Violet T. Pearson and Dan Benson, and to Dr. Robert Mosier, President of Accent Books; to my wife and children, to my mother and father, all of whom continually encouraged me during the writing of this novel—particularly through the difficult days of a rather lengthy illness which interrupted the preparation of the manuscript—and to Ron Nichols who gerry-rigged a wheelchair so I could sit at my typewriter as I convalesced.

And, finally, thank you's to Wilton (Bud) Steffen, Edith Quinlan, and a dozen others who deserve mention for the invaluable aid they rendered.

To all of them and to you, I want to recall that great passage quoted so many times in the telling of this story . . .

"Greater is he that is in you, than he that is in the world."

(I John 4:4)

William D. Rodgers
Littleton, Colorado